©Noboru K

6

GOBLIN SLAYER

"Sure am!"
"No, you're not."

"…And who're you, his wife?"
©Noboru Kannatuki

“Goblin Slayer, siiir…”
“What’s wrong?”
“Sounds like they were talking about promoting her.”
“She didn’t pass?”
“I guess not.”

©Noboru Kannatuki
"I don't know."
"Oh, you…"

They were certainly enthusiastic. And serious. They were good girls.

But that was no guarantee that they would survive.

"What do you think of our Obsidian and Porcelain adventurers?"

"Hmm."

Contents

GOBLIN SLAYER

VOLUME 6

KUMO KAGYU

Illustration by
NOBORU KANNATUKI

NEW YORK

KUMO KAGYU

Translation by Kevin Steinbach ✣ Cover art by Noboru Kannatuki

GOBLIN SLAYER vol. 6

Original Japanese edition published in 2017 by SB Creative Corp.
This English edition is published by arrangement with SB Creative Corp., Tokyo, in care of Tuttle-Mori Agency, Inc., Tokyo.

Yen On
1290 Avenue of the Americas
New York, NY 10104

Visit us at yenpress.com ✣ facebook.com/yenpress ✣ twitter.com/yenpress
yenpress.tumblr.com ✣ instagram.com/yenpress

First Yen On Edition: January 2019

Yen On is an imprint of Yen Press, LLC.
The Yen On name and logo are trademarks of Yen Press, LLC.

The publisher is not responsible for websites (or their content) that are not owned by the publisher.

Library of Congress Cataloging-in-Publication Data
Names: Kagyū, Kumo, author. | Kannatuki, Noboru, illustrator.
Title: Goblin slayer / Kumo Kagyu ; illustration by Noboru Kannatuki.
Other titles: Goburin sureiyā. English
Description: New York, NY : Yen On, 2016–
Identifiers: LCCN 2016033529 | ISBN 9780316501590 (v. 1 : pbk.) | ISBN 9780316553223 (v. 2 : pbk.) | ISBN 9780316553230 (v. 3 : pbk.) | ISBN 9780316411882 (v. 4 : pbk.) | ISBN 9781975326487 (v. 5 : pbk.) | ISBN 9781975327842 (v. 6 : pbk.)
Subjects: LCSH: Goblins—Fiction. | GSAFD: Fantasy fiction.
Classification: LCC PL872.5.A367 G6313 2016 | DDC 895.63/6—dc23
LC record available at https://lccn.loc.gov/2016033529

ISBNs: 978-1-9753-2784-2 (paperback)
978-1-9753-2785-9 (ebook)

10 9 8 7 6 5 4 3 2 1

LSC-C

Printed in the United States of America

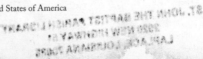

GOBLIN SLAYER

Volume 6

"I am to goblins what goblins are to us."

GOBLIN SLAYER

A strange adventurer active on the frontier. He is famous for reaching Silver (3rd) rank hunting only goblins.

"Protect, heal, save."
—The Three Holy Tenets of the Earth Mother

PRIESTESS

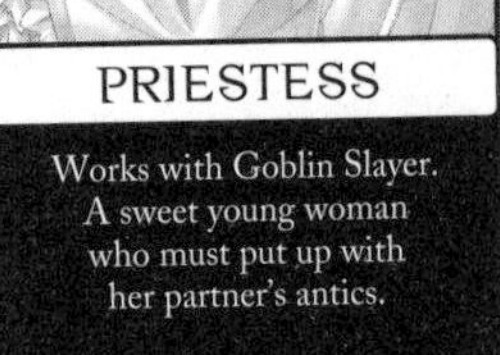

Works with Goblin Slayer. A sweet young woman who must put up with her partner's antics.

"Ignorance is bliss, for learning is the highest joy." —Elven proverb

HIGH ELF ARCHER

An elf girl who adventures with Goblin Slayer. A ranger and a skilled archer.

The only things that matter to her are the weather, the animals, the crops…and him.

COW GIRL

A girl who works on the farm where Goblin Slayer lives. The two are old friends.

"How can you go adventuring without pen and paper?"

GUILD GIRL

A girl who works at the Adventurers Guild. Goblin Slayer's preference for goblin slaying always helps her out.

"Before they're polished, jewels and precious metals all look like rocks. No dwarf would judge a thing by its appearance alone."

DWARF SHAMAN

A dwarf spell caster who adventures with Goblin Slayer.

"A naga does not run."

LIZARD PRIEST

A lizardman priest who adventures with Goblin Slayer.

"Train yourself: kill with the blade. If blood flows, let it be the enemy's."—First of the "Secrets of Steel."

HEAVY WARRIOR

A Silver-ranked adventurer associated with the Guild in the frontier town. Along with Female Knight and his other companions, his party is one of the best on the frontier.

"Only a tangled skein awaits those who carelessly spin tales about love or the universe's mysteries...not to mention a woman's beauty."

WITCH

A Silver-ranked adventurer at the frontier town's Adventurers Guild.

"I won't make friends tomorrow with an enemy I respect. I'll do it today."

SPEARMAN

A Silver-ranked adventurer at the frontier town's Adventurers Guild.

"Love does not consist in gazing at each other, but in looking outward in the same direction."—A poet

SWORD MAIDEN

Archbishop of the Supreme God in the water town. Also a Gold-ranked adventurer who once fought with the Demon Lord.

O adventurer, O journey of mine
Does a dragon or a golem await me
Or perhaps a ghostly knight?
And there must be legendary armament somewhere
But with just a torch and a spear
And a staff, life is easy.

To east or west, I cross a bridge
Perhaps to die on the other side
But I seek only love
A princess I would cherish, but I don't ask much
Only a night's pleasure
O adventurer, O journey of mine!

CHAPTER 1

An Ordinary Spring Day

The season had arrived when a pleasant wind blew from the east.

The cold had been driven out, leaving only a refreshing chill in the air, and the sunshine was gentle and warm.

The field of daisies about a half-day's walk from the frontier town was equally pleasurable.

It was a rolling plain, full of rich grass dotted with shrubs—nothing else. The road stretched on past it, and given the distance from village to village, town to town, it was nice to know there was a decent camping site available.

Just one thing—or rather, one person—moved through that field.

It was a strange adventurer. He wore grimy leather armor and a cheap-looking helmet; at his hip was a sword of a strange length, and a small, round shield was tied to his left arm. Even a novice would have better equipment than what he carried.

He walked the road in silence; when he came to the field, his bold, nonchalant stride carried him violently through the shrubbery. His steps were as sure, as determined, as if he was following a sign. Right, left, through the grass—it could not have taken him more than five minutes, if that.

Then he stopped.

There still didn't seem to be anything there.

But in the bushes, he heard a crinkling under the heel of his boot.

He knelt down and picked up the source of the noise. Ashes, of something utterly consumed by fire. He squeezed them between his fingers until they were nothing more than sooty marks on his gloves.

Something had burned here. Was it a tree? Human bones? That much remained unclear.

Impossible.

He shook his head as if sternly dismissing the possibility.

It's been ten years already.

No human bones, no human ashes would still be recognizable after a decade lying exposed to the elements. And even if anything had lasted this long—whose remains would they be?

"..."

The wind gusted over the field. It was a warm and gentle wind announcing the changing of the seasons, the arrival of spring.

The grass rustled, tiny ripples running through it all along the hill. He heard the faint sound of running water. When he turned his head, he could see the lake, right where he remembered it.

Seized by a whim, he glanced up. The sky was staggeringly clear and blue; it seemed to spread out across the entire world. The faintly visible clouds were so thin it seemed like the colors had run.

"...And so what?"

He clapped his hands together brusquely, wiping off the soot.

He knew these were not the remains of his older sister.

He knew what had become of her and what had become of her blood and flesh and bones.

He knew, too, that there used to be a village here.

And finally, he knew that plans had been made to build a training ground for adventurers on this spot.

"...Guess I'll head back."

There were only three other people who knew that he had lived in the village that once stood here.

It never occurred to Goblin Slayer to ask how the two people on the farm felt about this.

§

"Hee-hee-hee!"

Priestess smiled, in high spirits. The Adventurers Guild was busy all year round, but that liveliness redoubled in spring. Monsters awakened from hibernation and began to threaten villages, while adventurers who had been living off their savings during winter came out to work again. Nor was there any shortage of young men and women inspired by the fine weather to go forth and seek their fortunes.

"Next! Customer number fifteen, please come to reception window three!"

"Quest! I got a quest here! Cess-eaters in the sewers! Anyone have a few minutes to come and help?"

"Got your weapons and gear? Potions? Memorized all your spells? Got your five-foot pole? Great, let's go!"

"Scuse me very much, but a bear done gone and wandered into our village. Yeah, a grizzly."

Staff members rushed back and forth, adventurers shouted to one another, and quest givers explained what they needed. It wasn't exactly a festive atmosphere, but there was no denying the buzz in the air.

Surrounded by this swirl of activity, Priestess couldn't keep herself from beaming happily, her smile like a flower in bloom. She was seated squarely on the long bench that had become their de facto waiting area, holding her sounding staff and not remotely trying to hide how happy she felt.

Beside her, High Elf Archer was resting her chin in her hands and idly watching the crowd go by. She turned her gaze to Priestess.

"Someone's in a good mood."

"It's because I'm starting my second year of adventuring now. I think it wouldn't be strange for some of them to start calling me their senior!"

"Ahh, has it been that long already?"

"It sure has! Plus, I think I'll be promoted from ninth rank to eighth any time now." She puffed out her small chest triumphantly. Priestess was the youngest member of their party. High Elf Archer knew what that was like, being the youngest, and so her ears twitched sympathetically.

I guess I could get away with acting a bit like an older sister here.

"Maybe so, but don't let it distract you. The back row has a crucial role to play, all right?" High Elf Archer shook her index finger gracefully as she chided Priestess.

"Yes, ma'am. I know." Priestess nodded obediently.

High Elf Archer ran a hand through Priestess's golden hair, working out the tangles. The younger girl giggled, and her eyes lit up happily. She really was like a sweet younger sister—although High Elf Archer had the sense that if she said such a thing aloud, Dwarf Shaman would never let her hear the end of it. Instead, she deliberately let her eyes wander around the bustling Guild Hall.

"It sure is busy, isn't it?"

The place was full of people dying to be adventurers. Although…

Maybe dying *isn't quite the best word.*

That didn't sound very auspicious to High Elf Archer. How about people *hoping* to be adventurers? Yes, that was better. *Hope* was a good word.

Those hoping to become adventurers were lined up at the reception desk, a huge queue of them. There were wizards and warriors, monks and scouts, as well as people of every imaginable race, gender, and age. The two things they all shared were the passion burning in their eyes—and the equipment they wore.

From gear so new and unblemished it looked like there might still be a price tag attached, to old armor practically rusting through, the quality might have been low, but each and every piece was polished to a sparkle.

"Hmm," High Elf Archer muttered, flicking her long ears. "I think they could learn a thing or two from Orcbolg."

"Mr. Goblin Slayer isn't fond of shiny things, is he?"

He can be rather difficult.

With that murmur, Priestess's cheeks suddenly turned red, and she shifted uncomfortably.

"Something wrong?" High Elf Archer asked, but Priestess squeaked out, "No," and looked away.

The elf cocked her head in befuddlement, but it didn't take her long to put the pieces together. Perhaps it only made sense.

An advanced adventurer, accompanied by two unmistakably beautiful women. One of them a high elf, no less.

The periodic glances of the waiting candidates hadn't been lost on her.

"Whoa... What a couple of cuties..."

"Man, when I'm an adventurer, I'm definitely gonna be able to meet some girls like them, too."

"An elf! Man, I wish I knew one..."

High Elf Archer gave a little snort. Did they think they could have a conversation that an elf wouldn't hear? She wished they would be less interested in her race and show a little more admiration for the fact that she was a Silver-ranked adventurer.

"Last year, I was in that line..."

Unlike High Elf Archer, who had puffed out her flat chest in hopes of emphasizing the level tag hanging around her neck, Priestess had put a hand to her heart. She had a level tag, too—one that showed she had advanced from Porcelain to Obsidian, the tenth to the ninth rank.

"There weren't so many people then."

She had been just like them, listening in amazement to the conversations around her.

A training ground that had been long in the works was finally to be unveiled. It was nominally in response to the attack by the goblin lord, but planning had gone slowly, and now that battle was a year distant.

The two girls standing there knew why things had suddenly started to move so quickly.

"Did you read the letter?" Priestess asked.

"You better believe I did!" High Elf Archer pulled the folded sheet out of a pocket. The crease was crisp; she must have read it many times.

"You carry it around with you?"

"Don't you? It's a letter from a friend."

"Mine's in my room. I've entrusted it to the Earth Mother."

Precisely because it's from a friend, Priestess added internally, smiling shyly.

A friend. Namely Noble Fencer, a female adventurer with whom they had assaulted a goblin fortress in the north some months prior. The memory of her was still fresh in Priestess's mind: Noble Fencer had lost her friends and been grossly abused herself, yet she had refused to break. And during that experience of coming face to face with death, something had apparently changed within her. After their adventure, Noble Fighter went back to the home she had effectively fled and told them everything.

Since that time, they had exchanged several letters.

"She said she's starting a fund to support new adventurers," said High Elf Archer. "That girl certainly wastes no time."

"Yes indeed," responded Priestess.

Noble Fighter's letters informed them that she would be part of the fight not as an adventurer herself but as a supporter.

The neat, precise handwriting in the letters they received was so like her, it was impossible not to appreciate it. She wrote that she had been able to reconcile with her family and that she wanted to see Priestess, High Elf Archer, and the others again sometime.

"Still just as pigheaded as ever, isn't she?"

"Ha-ha…"

Despite High Elf Archer's teasing remark, the care with which she folded the letter revealed how she really felt. She didn't need to say it, for Priestess felt the same way.

Priestess and Noble Fencer had both experienced the brutality of goblins firsthand. For each of them, barely a roll of the dice separated perfectly timed salvation from destruction. And thus, Noble Fencer's obstinacy was the greatest possible encouragement for Priestess.

It meant she wasn't broken yet. That neither of them was.

"…A few lessons before you start out really makes such a difference," Priestess mused.

"I dunno, I just think it wouldn't matter all that much."

Not that I'm trying to deny her tenacity. Priestess frowned in response, and High Elf Archer gave her a placating little wave before adding, "I mean, some people are gonna do stupid things no matter how many lessons you give them, y'know?"

"But without instruction, how will they know what they're doing wrong?"

For instance… there really were so many instances in which novices could go wrong.

They could become so absorbed in chatting that they forgot to keep space between the front and back rows.

Or they might assume that they didn't have to watch their rear just because they were in a tunnel.

And above all, they might take goblins too lightly.

On reflection, she could see how many lessons she had learned on that first adventure.

"Sure, I won't argue with that," High Elf Archer said. "It's just..." She waved her hand again, perhaps not certain how to take Priestess's gloomy expression. "Some people just don't care to *listen*. Like... dwarves, for example."

"Oh, I'm listening all right, Long-Ears," grumbled a voice from behind the bench.

High Elf Archer gave a smile and a triumphant little snort. "I was hoping you were. It wouldn't have been any fun otherwise." She looked back over her shoulder at the bald-pated dwarven shaman grasping the back of the bench and glaring down at her. The slight flush in his cheeks suggested he had started in on the wine even though it was still morning—although that was perfectly normal for a dwarf.

At the smell of his breath, High Elf Archer made a show of coughing daintily.

"Anyway, you're one to talk," Dwarf Shaman said. "There's no one in the world who listens less than an elf."

"I'm sorry? Which of us has the bigger ears?"

"Heh! Sarcasm doesn't get through to an anvil, I see."

"Who's an anvil...?"

"Put a hand on your chest and answer your own question."

"Why, you—!"

It was the usual noisy banter. Priestess used to get flustered by this, but now she took it in stride; lately, she even found it comforting to listen to. She wasn't sure if arguing really brought people closer together, but she did know that she was in a good party.

On top of that, many faces in the Adventurers Guild had become familiar to her. Each time she saw one of the people she had come to know in the previous year, she gave them a little bow.

"Heh-heh-heh. It's quite, lively, isn't it?"

"Don't act too interested. We wanna look good for the newbies."

There was Witch with her alluring smile, accompanied by Spearman, who spoke to her as he made a face. Heavy Warrior was walking down the hallway, engaged in a verbal spat with Female Knight…

"Didn't I tell you? I said a little friendly exchange would bring us together…"

"That's some poor excuse for a drunken brawl. You're supposed to be lawful good!"

…while Scout Boy, Rhea Druid Girl, and Half-Elf Light Warrior followed behind them, patently refusing to get involved.

"Hullo!"

"Good morning, everyone."

"Good luck on your quests today!"

Then came a casual greeting from Rookie Warrior, who was quickly chided by Apprentice Cleric.

"Hey, it's the Gobber's bunch!"

"Oh, for goodness' sake! You could stand to be a little more polite! How am I supposed to show my face with you talking to people like that?"

It was all just the same as ever.

"Ah, good. Friendly as usual, I see." A massive form loomed over them. It was Lizard Priest. His body was covered in scales and he wore an unusual outfit. Seeing the jabbering elf and dwarf, he rolled his eyes happily. He seemed content to put off his customary intervention and let them argue.

Lizard Priest turned to Priestess and pressed his hands together in his usual eccentric greeting.

"The warm weather seems to have brought out everyone's energy. Something with which I fully sympathize."

"Winter was hard for you, wasn't it?" Priestess gave a small deep-throated chuckle, even as Lizard Priest nodded and responded somberly.

"Indeed. Even the fearsome nagas cannot prevail over an ice age. Nature, the very way of this world, can be a terrible thing."

As his appearance suggested, Lizard Priest was vulnerable to cold. This might have been because he came from the jungles to the south or perhaps because so much of his reptilian ancestry remained in him. Whatever the case, their earlier adventure to the snowy mountain had been quite an ordeal for him.

"But I've heard there are ice dragons who have blizzard breath," Priestess said. "What about them?"

"They are no relations of mine, you understand," Lizard Priest replied. Was he serious or joking? There was a subtle lightness to his solemn tone.

Then Lizard Priest craned his long neck, looking around a Guild Hall awash in novice adventurers.

"What of milord Goblin Slayer? Where is he?"

"Oh, um, he said he would be a little late today. Apparently, he went out somewhere yesterday."

"Oh-ho. Well, that is most unusual."

"It certainly is."

Priestess added quietly that she thought he would come soon, however.

Goblin Slayer.

It was impossible to imagine that weird adventurer going anywhere on vacation. The girl who looked after the farm he lived at reported that even on his days off, he busied himself with maintaining his weapons and gear. Recently, Guild Girl and Cow Girl had both invited him to a festival, yet he managed to spend most of it patrolling the town. Left to his own devices, he would silently disappear to kill goblins. They couldn't take their eyes off him.

Goodness gracious. An affectionate sigh escaped Priestess's lips. "He's really hopeless, isn't he?"

At that moment, a murmur began to run through the hall. An adventurer had pushed open the swinging door.

He walked with a bold, nonchalant, yet almost violent stride. He wore a cheap-looking steel helmet and grimy leather armor. A sword of a strange length hung at his waist, and tied to his left arm was a small, round shield. Even a novice, it seemed, would have better equipment.

But the little tag that hung around his neck was silver. The third rank.

"Goblin Slayer, sir!" Priestess called out, provoking a chorus of chuckles among the newcomers. Someone who slays goblins? The weakest of all monsters?

There were a few among them, of course, who didn't laugh. Over the course of five years, Goblin Slayer had been the salvation of a great number of villages. And some of those who had set out to become adventurers today were from those villages. They knew very well about the adventurer who single-handedly faced goblins. Some others had perhaps heard of him in song. Bards tended to mangle the facts, but his reputation still came through.

Even so, the laughter could be forgiven. Most of the would-be adventurers in the Guild Hall had yet to experience goblin slaying; those with experience had usually just driven off one or two that had wandered too close to their village. Perhaps a few of them had even been down in a cave someplace, but one thing never changed: the fact that goblins were the weakest monster.

Goblin Slayer ignored all of them, the quiet and the chortling alike. "Yes," he responded to Priestess, nodding. The helmet moved slowly, taking in High Elf Archer, Dwarf Shaman, Lizard Priest, and then Priestess, one by one.

"You're all here already."

"You're late, Orcbolg!" High Elf Archer said in her clear and dignified voice. She broke off the argument she had been having with Dwarf Shaman, pointing one elegant finger directly at the newcomer. Her eyebrows arched, and her long ears pressed back; they gave a great twitch. Everything about her conspired to communicate how intently she had been waiting.

She gave a little snort and crossed her arms importantly. "So. What're we doing today?"

"Goblin slaying."

"Well! Isn't that a surprise," Dwarf Shaman said, chuckling and stroking his long white beard. "When you leave it to Beard-cutter, you know what kind of adventure you're gonna get."

"Hrm..."

"If you have some preference, I'll listen."

Priestess went slightly red at Goblin Slayer's remark. She had the distinct impression that some of his roughest edges had been polished over the last year. And what about her? Had she changed? Had she grown? It wasn't such an easy thing to judge.

"Personally, anything that contributes to the greater good is acceptable," Lizard Priest said, his tail sweeping noisily across the floor. "I should think goblin slaying meets that criterion quite nicely. No doubt there will be many of the little devils abroad as the season turns."

High Elf Archer made a long, low groaning sound then threw up her hands in resignation. "Fine. I get it. Great. Goblins it is. Count me in, for your sake!"

"Thanks," Goblin Slayer murmured, and then he turned smartly on his heel and strode directly over to the reception desk where all the adventurers were waiting. The collective gawk of the novices did not seem to bother him one bit.

Those adventurers who knew him had quite the opposite reaction, calling out jovially, "Yo, Goblin Slayer! Gonna slay some more goblins?"

"Yes," he said with a nod.

"You never get tired of that, do ya?"

"Us guys are takin' a bit of a trip. Checkin' out some old ruins."

"Is that so?"

"You just be careful, okay?"

"Yes."

This would all be quite difficult to grasp for the newcomers, who didn't understand the dynamic at play. The novices looked at one another and whispered as quietly as they could.

High Elf Archer, waiting back by the bench for Goblin Slayer, frowned. Priestess leaned in to speak into the elf's long ear.

"What are they saying?" she whispered.

"You don't wanna know."

Fair enough. Priestess didn't have to be able to hear them to take a good guess at their conversations. She puffed out her cheeks in annoyance and pursed her lips, but it didn't do any particular good. The fact that Lizard Priest and Dwarf Shaman didn't seem bothered by it somehow rankled her as well.

§

"Next, please!"

As Goblin Slayer's companions waited, the adventurers in line were attended one by one. Finally, Guild Girl looked up from dutifully calling the next person in line to see a grimy steel helmet.

The pasted-on smile she had been wearing until that moment blossomed into a genuinely happy face.

"Goblin Slayer!"

"Goblin quests. Do you have any?"

"We certainly do! I've got them right here for you…er, by which I mean there were too many to fit on the board." She hid her mouth behind a sheaf of paper as she teasingly stuck out her tongue, then Guild Girl pulled some quest papers from a shelf. Her practiced motion and the neatly organized paperwork spoke to what a fine and experienced employee she was. She pulled out several pieces of paper with her slim, neatly manicured hands and set them down in front of Goblin Slayer.

Five pages altogether.

"None of these incidents seem to be on a very large scale, but—"

"But there are a lot of them."

"Exactly. I guess that's how you know spring has come. The goblins become more active just like everybody else."

"It happens every year."

"We have all these quests, and this is after several of the novices took some."

"Did they look capable?"

Guild Girl responded to Goblin Slayer's blunt question with an arch of one well-formed eyebrow and complete silence. Maybe it meant she just didn't know.

For all but the most careful parties, coming home alive was down to a roll of the dice. The dice rolled by the gods in heaven determined fate and chance, and sometimes even the gods were disappointed by the outcome.

Guild Girl glanced over Goblin Slayer's shoulder at the line of newly minted adventurers behind him. Should she entrust some of these quests to them?

She thought for a moment then looked up beseechingly at Goblin Slayer.

"Could I ask you to do something for me?"

"I don't mind," Goblin Slayer replied immediately. "Show me the quests the others accepted."

"Thank you so much. I'm sorry to always bother you with these things."

Adventuring required candidates to take responsibility for themselves, and the Adventurers Guild was no charity. Unlike other professional organizations, it had no mentoring system; but neither did it have the authority to force adventurers to do anything. It simply verified the identity of adventurers who joined it, helped connect them with work, and would disavow them if they caused too much trouble.

Working in this organization was by no means an easy job.

For one thing, it wasn't possible to look out for each and every newcomer who came through their doors. What were they supposed to do about seemingly piddling work like goblin slaying? The look of distress that came over Guild Girl's face was entirely understandable.

"Once the training facility is completed, maybe you won't have to do this so often."

Goblin Slayer didn't say anything but flipped silently through the quests.

Their content was all too familiar to him. *There's a goblin nest near our village. Get rid of it, please.*

In some places, livestock and crops were being destroyed. In others, they weren't. People had already been kidnapped in some cases but not in others.

Goblin Slayer moved the quests involving abducted women to the top of the pile. Those to which adventurers had already been dispatched went to the bottom. Cases with only slight damage were in the middle.

About ten quests in total. But Goblin Slayer said coolly, "I'll tackle them in this order."

"Right, understood. Be careful! Oh—any potions, or…?"

"Yes, please." He glanced back briefly at his companions. He would need five—no, six, to be safe.

"Healing potions, antidotes, and Stamina potions. Six each."

"Sure thing!"

He pulled eighteen gold coins from his item pouch and set them on the counter while Guild Girl brought out the items.

Eighteen potions for a little goblin slaying! The news rippled through the onlooking novices, their whispers rising like a wave. Was this caution, or was it cowardice? Either way, it quickly became the subject of ridicule. Some people were laughing openly—but a few might have been jealous. After all, once they had purchased the necessary equipment, many of them had scant luxury to indulge in the likes of potions. Perhaps if the entire party pooled their resources, they might manage to buy a single vial.

And here, this man was buying eighteen potions! One of each for every member of his party, plus extras to be safe! He was so calm about it. Was he trying to show off? It was enough to raise their hackles.

"Ahh, here. That should be eighteen. Please count them to be sure."

"I will."

"Be careful, now!"

Goblin Slayer, for his part, ignored the chatter and the stares.

§

The first thing Goblin Slayer did when he left the smiling Guild Girl and got back to his party was to take out some twine. He sat down heavily on the bench and then lined up all eighteen potions. Six each of three different colors. First, he tied some string to the healing potions.

Next came the antidotes. Here, he added an extra knot to the string. For the Stamina potions, he added two extra knots, a total of three.

Now it was possible to differentiate the type of potion by the number of knots.

I've never seen anyone do that before, High Elf Archer reflected. She leaned in to watch with her ears bouncing and her eyes shining.

"Uh, Orcbolg? What are you doing?"

"Recently we have needed to access our potions quickly," he said. His hands kept moving mechanically; the motion was as natural as the gentle scent of an evergreen forest. "I'm ensuring that we can tell which is which by feel."

"Oh, let me help!" Priestess said eagerly.

"Please do." Goblin Slayer scooted over to make room for her.

Priestess sat down on her tiny behind and began the delicate work of tying the strings. As soon as a set of three bottles was ready, High Elf Archer grabbed them with a "Gotcha."

"Listen here, Long-Ears," Dwarf Shaman said gruffly. "You could stand to show a little more restraint."

"Oh, you think so?" She shook her ears, her face innocent. "This from a dwarf—the embodiment of greed."

In a single fluid motion, she reached into her money pouch and withdrew three gold coins, setting them on the bench and tapping them with her finger.

"Hrm," the dwarf said, belatedly taking out three coins of his own and setting them down.

"I don't particularly need those," Goblin Slayer said without lifting his eyes (or more precisely, his helmet) from his work.

"Now, that won't do," Dwarf Shaman said with a shake of his head. "Never let money or gear come between friends."

"I see."

"Putting that aside, you do have some intriguing ideas, don't you?" Dwarf Shaman said.

"This is simple but effective."

"Ah—I'll pay you when I'm done," Priestess added.

"...Okay."

"Let us see here...," Lizard Priest said, taking out some money. But at the same moment he set it on the bench, something rather odd happened.

"Uh... Excuse me," a hesitant voice addressed the party.

Lizard Priest looked over to see a warrior—clearly a novice, judging by her brand-new equipment. She was a young woman of distinctly small stature. The way her ears came to a gentle point marked her out as one of the grass people, a rhea.

Her equipment looked like she had just bought it. She wore leggings

over her slim legs, but from the ankles down she was barefoot, as was the way of her people.

The rhea girl looked nervous enough; behind her stood the rest of her party, practically trembling. She sized up Goblin Slayer's party and then, for some inexplicable reason, seemed to decide Lizard Priest would be the easiest to talk to.

"Um, what...? What are you doing?"

"Hmm." Lizard Priest narrowed his eyes in what he probably intended as a show of friendliness. The rhea girl shook a little harder. "We are preparing potions," he said. He picked up one of the bottles with a scaly hand. Liquid splashed audibly inside. A healing potion. "They are being marked so we do not confuse one for another if we must use one in a hurry."

"Marked..."

"There are no guarantees that there will be time to look at which potion is which when we need it."

The idea seemed to sink in with the girl; she nodded admiringly.

"I will warn you," Goblin Slayer said, not so much as looking up at the young adventurer, "if you try to mark everything in your pouch, you'll never remember what's what."

"Oh—uh, o-obviously. I'd never do that... Ha-ha." The girl's face froze. It was probably exactly what she had been planning to do. High Elf Archer laughed, clear as a bell, causing the girl to blush and look at the ground.

"Only mark things you may need in a hurry. And—"

Goblin Slayer finished the last batch of potions. He tucked them carefully in his bag, making sure they were well protected.

"—be careful of goblins. Start by slaying rats or something."

"Oh, uh, right! S-sure thing!"

The rhea girl bowed her head several times and then hurried back to her group. They immediately formed a circle and started whispering together; it looked like they had already started to get along. They were even coordinated enough to split up into two groups, one to affix string to their items and another to look for a quest.

"Great sheep who walked the chalk path, guide these to be some small part of your battle which is ever spoken of." Lizard Priest made a mysterious gesture, praying for the adventurers' success, brave deeds, and glorious deaths.

True, some adventurers preferred to gossip and ridicule, but others strived to absorb the knowledge they would need to survive. One was not better than the other; one was not right and the other wrong. Being attentive to advice was no guarantee of success, nor did refusing to heed the words of others inevitably assure failure.

And yet, still—indeed.

"I do hope they survive."

"...Who can say?" The words seemed to be squeezed out of Goblin Slayer.

Every person's time would come when it came, even against giant rats. And if they survived, the quests would only grow more fearsome as they rose through one rank and then the next, and then the next.

If adventuring were a safe occupation, it wouldn't be called adventuring.

Goblin Slayer finished putting away the potions he had prepared, then he slowly rose from his seat.

"Oh, Goblin Slayer, sir, your money." Priestess sprang up after him, hastily fishing through her pouch for some coins.

"...Right." Goblin Slayer traded her for the sheaf of quest papers in his hand, saying, "I accepted these jobs."

"Wow..." From the thickness of the bundle, Priestess guessed that he must have taken on all the remaining goblin quests. She fought back the smile trying to work its way to her lips, forcing herself to focus on the words on the page.

'Start by slaying rats or something,' indeed!

There wouldn't be any goblin-slaying quests left even if those kids wanted one. Priestess had no idea whether this was intentional on his part. *For goodness' sake!*

"Well?"

In this context, that meant, *I'm going. What about the rest of you?*

She had come to accept that this was one habit of Goblin Slayer's that seemed unlikely ever to change. Priestess gave a melodramatic sigh and shook her head. "*Well*, yourself. You know I'm going—that's why I'm here."

"Hrk..."

"You would just go by yourself if we let you," Priestess added. "And we won't let you."

"There's such a thing as not caring enough about what other people think, Orcbolg," High Elf Archer said, sniffing in annoyance. "Doesn't it bother you, everyone gabbing about you like that?"

"Not to speak of," Goblin Slayer said shortly. He gave a gentle shake of his helmeted head. "I don't really understand what they expect of me."

"That's my boy, Beard-cutter. Goblins it is!"

"No question of that," Lizard Priest said, giving Goblin Slayer a jolly pat on the back with his great tail. Dwarf Shaman let out a huge, carrying laugh.

Now it was obvious how alone High Elf Archer was in her opinion. "Fine, who cares?" she said, turning around and beginning to pout.

"There, there," Priestess said comfortingly, and then she turned her attention to a quick check of her equipment.

Gear, check. Items, check. Provisions, check. Not forgetting the Adventurer's Toolkit. And a change of clothes.

"All right. I think I'm ready to go."

"Let's go, then."

A human warrior, an elf ranger, a dwarf spell caster, a human cleric, and a lizardman monk.

The five adventurers, differing in race, class, and gender, put the Guild behind them.

An adventuring party are also traveling companions.

As the words flitted through Priestess's mind, she slackened her pace just a little. Even just walking through the brush, she felt a strange affinity for these people.

"Hey! Keep outta my way if you don't wanna get hurt!!"

"Eek?!"

A boy came charging past them, practically shoving Priestess aside. His cape fluttered open, revealing a large staff in his hand—he must have been a wizard.

Priestess, reeling from the encounter, felt Goblin Slayer's hand catch her.

"Th-thanks. Sorry."

"It's all right."

Priestess straightened her cap. Goblin Slayer started walking away as if the scene held no more interest for him. Dwarf Shaman, however, was less temperate, shaking his fist and shouting at the boy, "Hey, watch where you're going, why don't you!"

"Piss off! It's her fault for dawdling in the middle of the road! Next time I'll let my Fireball do the talking!" The boy didn't stop racing toward the Guild even as he shouted back. The way he carved a line directly toward his destination did sort of resemble a Fireball.

"Grr… Kids these days," Dwarf Shaman growled.

"Finally feeling your age, Gramps?" High Elf Archer asked.

"Says the one person here older than me!" The shaman narrowed his eyes and glared at the archer. More precisely, he glared directly at her flat chest, clad in hunter's garb. "Don't you think you should wear something more age-appropriate, Anvil?"

"Wh-why—J-just you— Barrel!" High Elf Archer's face went red and her ears laid flat against her head.

The familiar sniping back and forth brought a smile to Priestess's face. But…

She glanced behind her toward the Adventurers Guild. The massive building was still clearly visible despite the crowd outside.

"Well, with enough newcomers, there's bound to be a few rash individuals." Lizard Priest leaned down to look at Priestess. "Is anything the matter?"

"Oh, uh, no," Priestess said, waving a hand to dismiss the notion. "Nothing." Then she faced forward again.

Keep walking. Follow your companions. Stay with your party.

She hurried along behind the others, but she couldn't quite get the image of the red-haired spell caster out of her mind.

Maybe I'm just imagining things, but…he looked really familiar.

§

"ORAGARARA?!"

"Seven goblins ahead of us! Actually—six now!" A clear voice echoed through the cavern, underlined by a goblin scream. High Elf

Archer had loosed an arrow even as they rushed down the narrow, dank passageway.

The party members each vaulted the goblin corpse, over the arrow sprouting from its eye, and kept going.

"Good," Goblin Slayer muttered. As he led them along, he flipped the blade in his right hand into a reverse grip then flung it forward in a single motion.

"GRAB?!"

"GRROB! GRARB!!"

The sword caught a goblin in the throat, causing the creature to begin choking on his own blood. Beside him, one of his companions holding a rusty sword cackled: What a foolish adventurer. Throwing away their own weapon!

The goblin's sword glinted in the light from Goblin Slayer's torch. The monster gave a shout and jumped forward.

"GRAARBROOR!!"

"Hmph."

Goblin Slayer blocked the goblin's sword with his shield. He quickly transferred the torch to his right hand and clubbed the monster with it.

"GRAB?!"

A cry rang out. The pain of a shattered nose being shoved back into the brain, the agony of a face scorched with fire. The goblin died in the grip of suffering far less acute than what he had inflicted throughout his hideous life.

"Two, three."

Kick the new corpse aside, take up its blade, move on.

Four left. Or rather—

"KREEEEYYAAAHHH!!"

From beside Goblin Slayer came Lizard Priest's bellow and his prayer. Even as he shouted, he swung a Swordclaw with immense strength, shattering the goblins before him. No goblin could survive a slash directly across the windpipe.

"GROAROROB?!"

"Four. Three left."

Goblin Slayer left Lizard Priest to finish off that one; he had already found the other enemies. Far in the darkness at the end of the tunnel, something dully reflected the light of his torch. Without hesitation, Goblin Slayer raised his shield in front of his face.

A series of flat *twang*s reverberated, and some objects flew through the dark air. Almost simultaneously, Goblin Slayer felt a shock run through his left arm as though it had been struck. He clicked his tongue.

"GRORB!"

"GRAROROBR!"

He didn't have to look to know what it was: an arrow had lodged itself in his shield. Of the other two bolts, one had flown over the heads of the party, while Lizard Priest had deflected the third. It was too obvious that there were goblin archers hiding in the dark.

Enemies armed with crossbows were to be feared, but luckily, these creatures carried only regular bows.

"Tsk..." Goblin Slayer clicked his tongue at having noticed so late. Then he casually took the arrow, shaft and all, and pulled it out. He didn't seem concerned that extracting the hooked end meant doing damage to his own equipment. Instead, he was focused on the dark, ominous liquid that drenched the arrowhead.

"Poison!" he announced then threw the arrow away.

An answer came shooting back: "Leave it to me!" High Elf Archer was already drawing back her bow. The sound of the string was almost musical as she loosed her shot, piercing a goblin archer through the throat. Challenging an elf to a contest of archery was sheer folly. That made five.

"Six!"

Goblin Slayer was already rushing down the tunnel, making contact with the enemy. He easily lodged a sword in the neck of a howling goblin. He kicked the corpse away, freeing the blade, then raised his shield to defend as he backed away from the other advancing foes.

"Hrroooooh!!" Lizard Priest leaped in with his sword, slicing at the creatures until seven goblins lay dead on the ground.

For a brief moment, the only sound in the dim, smelly tunnel was the heightened breathing of the five party members.

"I-is that a-all of—of them?" Priestess asked, struggling to get her breath under control.

"Most likely," Goblin Slayer said, tossing away his torch. It had burned down to a nub, perhaps in part due to his rough treatment of it.

Three of the party members were perfectly capable of seeing in the dark, but that didn't mean they could go without a source of light.

"Oh, Goblin Slayer, sir, here..." When Priestess saw him quickly pulling a new torch out of his pouch, she was swift to ready some flint.

"Thanks."

"Not at all," Priestess replied with a hint of a smile. She made some sparks with the flint, letting out a soft sigh of relief when the torch caught.

She took the opportunity for a fresh look around. The stone cavern offered tight quarters, and the stench of blood and gore joined with the reek of rot that was so characteristic of goblin nests.

"Ugh..."

She had grown used to it, yes, but that didn't mean she enjoyed it. High Elf Archer wrinkled her nose and grimaced. Even so, she kept her bow in one hand, and her long ears listened to everything around them.

"I know we went quite a ways down, but are we still not at the surface yet?"

"What are we going to do? The numbers just keep increasing..."

Their voices carried a distinct note of fatigue. Priestess offered a water skin to High Elf Archer, who accepted it gratefully and took a long swig.

They had entered a cave on the banks of a river near the village. They were already working their way out, yet they had no real feeling that they were making any progress.

The answer to High Elf Archer's question was already drawing nearer.

"GROORORB!"

"GRAARB! GROB! GRORRB!!"

Hideous voices echoed in the earth. The cave was like an anthill; it was an abyss, a labyrinth, a maze. The seemingly inexhaustible supply of goblins would have been enough on its own to break the spirits of any novice adventurers.

The party had gone practically without rest for several hours now. The six or seven kills they had recently counted off were only the number of goblins in this most recent group they had stumbled across. How many goblins had they exterminated in total? Dozens. Many dozens.

"...There's more coming." Priestess's naturally pale skin turned even paler as the blood drained from her face; she bit her lip. Her hands, wrapped around her sounding staff, shook slightly, just enough that it could almost be mistaken as an excess of strength.

"Can you fight?" Goblin Slayer asked calmly.

"Y...yes," Priestess responded, nodding as firmly as she could. Even if she had answered *No, I can't*, nothing would have changed... Still, it was comforting to her that he had been considerate enough to ask.

She sucked in a breath and let it out again. Her fingers almost didn't feel like they belonged to her as she loosened them and readjusted her grip.

"It is well that we were the ones who took on this quest," Lizard Priest remarked, eyeing Priestess as he shook the blood from his Swordclaw.

The disorderly, undisciplined footsteps of the goblins came closer. The sound echoed from the dark, narrow side tunnels, as if to envelop the adventurers.

"And how many of the enemy face we this time?"

"No more than thirty would be my guess," High Elf Archer said, twitching her ears. "But no fewer than ten."

"Let us consider it twenty, then," Lizard Priest said. "Goblin slaying is seen as a newcomer's pursuit, but numbers would surely prevail in this instance."

And yet, they had only five people. Lizard Priest made a grumbling sound deep in his throat, craning his neck to see down the tunnel. He slapped his tail against the ground. To summon a Dragontooth Warrior or not? To consume a spell or not? It was a matter of considerable concern.

"Hrm. Well, this could be a bit of a handful," Dwarf Shaman growled, setting down the load on his back. It was a young woman, dirty, covered in scrapes, not even conscious. He leaned her against the wall as he said, "We have to make sure she stays safe, too, after all."

This was, in fact, how things usually went. But for all its commonness, it was something that easily destroyed people's lives.

This, essentially, was what had happened: Some goblins had taken up residence near the village. The young people had been cautious, but some young woman—gathering medicinal herbs or tending sheep—had been kidnapped. And the village desperately wanted the goblins slain.

Go to any of the four corners of the world, and you would hear the same story ad nauseam. Goblins were a problem always and everywhere.

As it happened, in the case of the little riverside settlement Goblin Slayer had headed to first, the victim had been a boatman's daughter. It was hard to say if she was lucky or not: Using a long pole to guide the boat back and forth across the river every day, she had become far physically tougher than many a hapless man. Hence, she had the strength to endure the brutality and abuse of the goblins. She had even retained her sanity. How she would live her life after this, after what she had been through, the adventurers didn't know. Their duty was to get her out alive.

"If they multiply any further, they could begin raiding the surface all too easily." Goblin Slayer's judgment was decisive: "We're going to kill all the goblins."

What other response could there be?

Yes, all this was perfectly ordinary.

At least, it was for Goblin Slayer.

"What's your opinion of the situation?"

"If we meet them in a narrow tunnel, it will largely neutralize the number disadvantage," Lizard Priest said thoughtfully. "But…" He scratched a claw along the wall of the tunnel. The earth was soft. It was packed tightly enough that a collapse was unlikely, but it would be easy enough to dig through. "If the little devils were to burst out of the walls around us, we might find ourselves hard-pressed. I believe a change of locale is in order."

"That settles it, then," Goblin Slayer said, checking over his weapon. "We have spells remaining, yes?"

"Oh, yes." Priestess was the first to answer. "It looked like this was going to be a long fight, so I've saved all three of my miracles."

"As for me, I only just used a Swordclaw." That meant three left. Goblin Slayer nodded. It would be enough.

"M'self, I've got four shots," Dwarf Shaman said, counting on his fingers. He opened his bag and looked into it, frowning. "But as I recall, you said there were about ten hot spots in all, didn't you?"

"Kinda crazy, huh?"

Ignoring High Elf Archer's little jab, Goblin Slayer shook his head. "We can take time to rest."

"Not the problem."

Cleric or mage, miracles or spells, rewriting the very logic of the world was a taxing endeavor. Each could only do it so many times per day. If you weren't a Platinum-ranked magic user, perhaps that was the best you could hope for. Hence, it was a basic tenet of adventuring to give your magic users ample rest. Those who ignored this law could be putting themselves in mortal peril (although everyone died when their time came, regardless of how refreshed a spell caster was).

Lizard Priest, standing next to Goblin Slayer, understood what the dwarf was getting at. "It's a matter of catalysts, isn't it?"

"'Sright. I offer what I can, but magical items are pretty—you know."

"Very well." Goblin Slayer retrieved a gore-covered blade and wiped it down quickly with a goblin's loincloth. If he could use it to kill one or two more enemies, that would be enough. His own foes would bring weapons to him, after all. There was nothing to worry about.

"Use Tunnel, then. That doesn't require a catalyst."

"True enough. But why use—ahh, is that what you're thinking?" Dwarf Shaman gave his beard half a stroke, but he hardly had to think to understand what Goblin Slayer wanted. His face folded into a smile.

"For better or for worse, Beard-cutter, I think you're rubbing off on me. Hey, Scaly, gimme a hand—er, a shoulder."

"Ha-ha. Yes, it makes sense. Here. Will my back be enough?"

Dwarf Shaman sighed deeply then scrambled up Lizard Priest's proffered back. He pulled a black jar and a brush out of his bag and began drawing a pattern on the ceiling in a fluid hand.

High Elf Archer had not yet managed to put the pieces together.

She gave her ears a suspicious shake and grunted as she watched Dwarf Shaman draw.

It was incomprehensible. "Does this make sense to you?" she asked Priestess, but the other girl replied, "Not really," and looked a little embarrassed.

"Hey, Orcbolg, what's the story?" she asked. "Tell us what's going on!"

In the face of this pointed demand, Goblin Slayer's response was as mechanical and gruff as ever. "I will warn you," he said.

"About what?"

"This is an emergency escape route."

"What is?"

"We rescued the hostage. There's no more problem."

That was all he said, then he tossed something to High Elf Archer. Even in the dim light, she could see what it was; she caught it out of the air.

"I will show you the way to use…well."

High Elf Archer continued to look perplexed, but Priestess said, "Oh," as if a bit disappointed. "I thought it might come to that," she added.

In the archer's hand was an underwater breathing ring.

§

It was a perfectly ordinary thing for the goblins, too: adventurers. The obnoxious creatures were always barging into the goblins' homes right when they were trying to relax.

Five of them this time. And what luck: two were women. Both young, and one an elf.

For some reason, they didn't smell quite right, but one look was enough to arouse the goblins' lust.

"GRAORB!"

"ORGA!"

In their dank hole, the goblins laughed their dark laughs and relished their dark desires.

How very lucky we are! Two women. We can have all the fun we want and grow our family to boot.

In the wars among those who had words, men were the most valuable captives and hostages. That, of course, was because they were the best laborers. In a proper war, prisoners could be put to proper work.

For the goblins, however, things were different. Men were dangerous; they were quick to anger and violent, making the goblins justly frightened of them. They could cut off a man's limbs and throw him in a cell, but after that, it was simply a question of whether to eat him or make sport of him. A lot of work for very little reward.

In that regard, women—females—were quite a different proposition. Impregnating them was enough to keep them from fleeing. You could have your way with them as you pleased; a woman without hands and feet was still useful.

And above all, they were fun. That counted for a lot. And they could make more goblins. All this value rolled into just one human.

If you got tired of them, or if they died on you, then you could eat them. Vastly more versatile creatures than men.

"GROB! GROAR!"

"GROORB!"

The goblins jabbered together as they hacked their way through the soft earth with a panoply of crude tools and a great deal of ill will.

Give the smaller girl two or three good pokes and she would surely grow obedient. The elf looked like a bit of a firebrand. Start by breaking a leg, maybe…

No, no. Shatter her fingers so she can't use her bow again. That would be best.

The fat one, the dwarf. He looked like he could be food for days. Nice, rich belly meat.

Pull the scales off the lizardman. Put a string through them and they make good armor. His bones and claws and fangs would be perfect for spears as well.

And then there was the armored one. Everything he carried, his sword and his shield and all his equipment, seemed tailor-made for goblins.

What fools these adventurers were!

Not for an instant did it cross any of the goblins' minds that they might be defeated.

Goblins had no strength, except in their numbers. They understood that instinctively; it was what made them goblins. If they had been given the slightest degree of wit, there was no question that they would long ago have been driven to extinction.

At last, the feeling of the earthen wall began to change. They listened closely; they could hear faint voices.

This was the place.

The goblins looked at one another and nodded. Ugly smiles split their faces.

All of them had weapons in their hands—the same items used to dig through the earth. Most were made of bones or stones or branches, although here and there was a shovel they had managed to steal.

Strategy played no role at this point. While their companions were being killed, they would strike a lucky blow and slaughter their foes.

Those idiotic adventurers seemed to be planning something, but the goblins would never let them get away with it. The creatures had conveniently forgotten what they had done to the boat captain's daughter. They thought only of the rage they felt for their twenty murdered companions.

They'll pay for marching in here and turning our house upside down!

Kill! Rape! Steal!

"GOROROB!!"

"GRAB! ORGRAAROB!!"

With a chorus of shouts, the goblin horde burst through the wall and leaped into space. A wave of goblins rushed toward the adventurers.

"Fools."

At that instant, a scroll was unleashed, and an actual wave came crashing toward the goblins and swallowed them up.

§

A tremendous rumble came from underground, and a white pillar spewed into the field.

No—the whiff of salt that came along with the scent of early spring made it clear that this was seawater, summoned from the unthinkable depths of the ocean.

The spout of water rose up through the tunnel toward the surface—and, of course, carried the adventurers along with it.

"Ahhhh?! I hate this!! I hate it, I hate it, I hate it!!"

"Ha! Ha! Ha! Ha! Ha! Goodness gracious me, this is truly something!"

High Elf Archer's shrill scream could hardly have been further removed from Lizard Priest's jovial laughter. Her ears were straight back, and her eyes were squeezed shut; the customary dignity of a High Elf had completely abandoned her. In fact, one could say it had been squeezed right out of her…

"I suppose it is understandable."

"How can you be so calm?!"

"My people teach that we are distant relatives of the birds," Lizard Priest replied.

Having said that—breathing was one thing, but coming down after being flung up in the air? Damage was assured. If the Earth Mother was indeed merciful, it might not be critical.

"We—we're falling! I'm falling! Hurry, please…!" Priestess begged from the bottom of her heart, even as she tried desperately to keep her skirt from being blown up by the wind.

If only we had a miracle that would make the earth nice and soft—it's no fair!

This somewhat inappropriate thought passed through her head, but she was met with only the rushing wind, carrying the tears away from her eyes.

"Right, then! Leave it t'me!"

Good thing I knew this might be coming.

Dwarf Shaman, seemingly unruffled and with the captive girl still on his back, began a complicated incantation even as he hung in midair.

"Come out, you gnomes, and let it go! Here it comes, look out below! Turn those buckets upside-down—empty all upon the ground!"

And the adventurers, who had so recently looked like they were going to slam straight into the unforgiving earth, floated toward the surface as gently as feathers. Priestess heaved a sigh, relieved to have avoided becoming a bloody smear on the ground.

©Noboru Kannatuki

"It's—it's okay now, isn't it?" she asked hesitantly.

"It most certainly isn't!" High Elf Archer exclaimed. "It's absolutely not okay! I don't know if I'll ever open my eyes again!" Her ears were trembling violently, and she was shaking her head.

"It's true Falling Control is good for going up or coming down," Dwarf Shaman said. (Although it was originally intended to help when tumbling from high places or trapped in a pit.) "But, Beard-cutter, how did you get by before you met us?"

"I secured my body soundly, and then once I was underwater, I walked."

"Rubbish!" the dwarf barked.

"In this case, there was no time."

Dwarf Shaman's suspicious stare didn't seem to bother Goblin Slayer. Gravity shortly guided the party gently to the ground.

The explosion of seawater had turned the entire vicinity to mud, and the smell of salt in the air was very strange. It would be years before the salt was completely worked out of the ground and this field was good for cultivating again.

"Oh, for… I knew I should've brought a change of clothes," Priestess sighed, being careful not to let her feet get caught in the muck. She rolled up the hem of her dress, which was thoroughly soaked, and squeezed it out. It left her pale legs exposed right up to her thighs, but there were a great many things that took priority over embarrassment.

"Oh, but…don't look over here, okay?"

"I won't."

Goblin Slayer, of course, had never so much as glanced in her direction, and it would be lying to say that didn't annoy her just a little.

"Of course you won't," she muttered, and then with a grunt, she pulled off her overclothes. There was nothing else to do—the seawater would cause her mail to rust otherwise.

"Oh, ah, g-grr…no! No! This is off-limits. Not allowed. I absolutely will not let him do this again…" High Elf Archer had practically withdrawn into herself. Priestess stole a glance at the elf. As Priestess recalled, High Elf Archer had no metal equipment.

So she should be fine, right?

Priestess hadn't yet been granted a miracle of calming, and anyway, it wouldn't do to rely overmuch on supernatural aid. With enough time, High Elf Archer would calm down on her own. That would be best.

With something like detachment, Priestess decided to let High Elf Archer dry out in the sun. The spring sun was out; surely it would do her some good in short order.

"All right, then…" When Priestess looked back toward Goblin Slayer, he had returned to his own work. Which, as his name implied, was killing goblins.

As the effect of Tunnel wore off, earth gradually began to fill the hole back in. The seawater would shortly run into the mouth of the cave, and the goblins would be flooded out.

Exactly what the adventurers wanted.

Goblin Slayer tightened his grip on his sword, which he had never let go even amid the violent spray. He bounded through the mud, advancing implacably.

Several goblins who had been blown out of the cave along with them were lying on the ground.

"Hmph."

"ORGAR?!"

That was one. Without a moment's hesitation, Goblin Slayer put his blade through its brain. The creature gave a scream and a twitch. Goblin Slayer twisted the sword, and when he was sure the goblin was still, he pulled his weapon back out.

"Oh-ho. Still alive, eh?" Lizard Priest said.

"The luck of the *dice*," Goblin Slayer remarked.

It happens from time to time, he added to himself, and then he silently continued about his work.

When he found one, he stabbed it with his sword. He checked to be sure it was dead, and if it wasn't, he waited until it was.

His blade soon became dull, so he threw it away. There was a mountain of weapons here anyway. He grabbed a club from a random goblin, and in lieu of gratitude, he smashed its skull in.

Most of the goblins were dead. But one or two were still alive. That was just the nature of probability. Goblin Slayer, however, had no intention of overlooking them.

"When she gets her wits back, wipe down her equipment and we'll move on to the next thing."

"You got it." Dwarf Shaman popped the cork from a bottle of fire wine. "Gods above. This has to be about as bad a day as these goblins have ever had."

Here, Long-Ears. He forced a bit of the alcohol down High Elf Archer's throat, just to bring her to her senses, which she returned to with another scream. Her ears sprang up, her face went red, and she immediately set to verbally assaulting the dwarf.

Goblin Slayer completely ignored his companions' blathering, but he muttered, "That's not necessarily true."

CHAPTER 2

The Red-Haired Wizard Boy

"I don't know. I really think it's too much for one person…"

"Oh yeah? I know the stories. Like how the Second Hero battled the Demon Lord single-handedly, all those years ago!"

"True, but they were Platinum-ranked. I think you'd be better off starting a party or finding one to join."

"No adventurer alive can gain my confidence."

"………Hmmm, this is a tough one, all right."

Guild Girl sat behind the reception desk of the now-empty Guild building idly twirling her braids.

The sun had long since set, and there were no adventurers to be seen. Anyone who hadn't gone adventuring was either asleep or off enjoying themselves. She was the only remaining staff still there.

Under normal circumstances, she could—and probably should—have simply chased away the adventurer boy who stood there seeking a quest with his implacable gaze.

"…I guess there's nothing else to do," she said.

Why am I like this?

Guild Girl got up from her seat with a deep sigh.

"I'll put on some tea." She gave him a wink and turned for the supply room in the back. "After all, I'm waiting, too."

©Noboru Kannatuki

§

Night had fallen by the time Goblin Slayer and the others passed back through the gate of the frontier town.

Light had vanished from the now-empty street; the moons and stars above gave the only illumination.

"...Oh, uh, ah, w-we're here...?"

"That we are, Long-Ears, that we are."

"Mistress Cleric, it seems we are at our wits' end."

"Hnn... Ughhh..."

They were all profoundly fatigued. High Elf Archer's ears were drooping; it was all she could do to keep her heavy eyelids from closing.

As for Priestess, she had practically dozed off during a ride on Lizard Priest's back.

The three men, covered in blood and sweat and mud from days of battle, looked at one another and nodded.

"Perhaps I can entrust her to you, milord Goblin Slayer?"

"Yes. And her to you?"

"I'm on it. C'mon, Long-Ears, pull yourself together, now."

"Mmph... Sooo sleepy... I'mma just...take a nap..."

"Wait until we get you back to your room first. The middle of the street's not for sleeping."

Dwarf Shaman put all of his small body into supporting the lolling elf.

They were heading for the second floor of the Guild Hall, which doubled as an inn. Rare was the adventurer with a home to call their own. Most stayed at some inn or otherwise rented a room at the Guild.

"See you tomorrow, then," Lizard Priest said with one of his strange palms-together gestures.

"Right." Goblin Slayer nodded.

The giant lizard shuffled off after his companions, the petite girl still clinging to his back.

"...Oh. Good...good...ni...ght," she said faintly, almost a whisper. Goblin Slayer gave a shake of his helmet.

"Hrm."

Companions.

The word came suddenly and naturally to his mind. He didn't dislike the sound of it.

These were people he had not known a year ago. People he could hardly believe he had known a whole year.

What would the old him have done in a situation like this?

What about his gear? His strategies? His time? His resources? What would those be like if the four of them weren't here?

Without them—with that one small thing being different—Goblin Slayer's range of options would be severely constricted. Fearsomely so.

To think it would be so different.

It was with those thoughts running through his head that he pushed open the door of the Guild.

"Erk…"

Something didn't feel right.

Light.

The staff should all be gone by now, yet he had come here to make his report.

Goblins?

Half-reflexively, Goblin Slayer's hand went to the hatchet he had crammed into his scabbard. He dropped into a deep stance and walked into the building almost silently. The door swung shut behind him.

It was almost comical, but he didn't see it that way. Who was to say that goblins might not appear in town?

Goblin Slayer's glance happened to fall on the bench in the waiting area, drawn there because he thought he saw movement from a silhouette curled up on the seat.

No— It wasn't his imagination.

Something was squirming there; it almost looked like a human covered in a blanket.

Goblin Slayer took a step forward, provoking a squeak from the floor.

"Hr… Hrn?"

Then the blanket was pushed aside, and the silhouette slowly sat up.

It rubbed its eyes and gave a small yawn. It was a boy with red hair.

As he sat up, he knocked over his staff, which had been leaning against the bench; it clattered to the floor.

"…H-hey, lady… Just five more— Huh?"

He blinked the sleep from his eyes and took in the figure before him. Now his eyes were open wide; he could see Goblin Slayer standing there in the dark.

What he saw was a man covered in mud and blood, wearing a cheap-looking helmet and grimy weather armor, with a rusty hatchet in his hand.

"Ah." The boy's mouth twitched, then twisted, and then he screamed, "Eeeeeyaahhh!"

"Hrm…"

Huh. So it wasn't a goblin.

That was the only thought the echoing yell elicited from Goblin Slayer.

"Eek?!" At the same time, Guild Girl gave a cute little yelp, and there was the sound of a chair falling over. Goblin Slayer looked up to see her come flying out into the room.

"Oh, uh, ah! G-Goblin Slayer, sir?! I'm not asleep, I promise, I wasn't asleep!"

She hurriedly straightened her hair, smoothed the creases out of her dress, and blushed furiously before giving a small cough. Her smile, however, wasn't the pasted-on expression she so often wore, but a genuine, spontaneous grin.

"Ahem. Good work today."

Goblin Slayer relaxed his fingers one by one and finally let go of the hatchet.

§

Without a sound, Goblin Slayer took the proffered cup of tea and drank it down in a single swig.

He probably couldn't even taste it, drinking it like that—but Guild Girl smiled.

She went through the familiar routine: get some paper ready, shave down the tip of a quill pen, open a pot of ink, get ready to record.

"So how did it go? Were there a lot of them again this time?"

"Yes," Goblin Slayer said with a firm nod. "There were goblins."

"How many?" Guild Girl asked, her pen scratching on the paper. "Oh, and break them down by quest, please."

"Thirty-four for the first quest."

He suddenly fell silent. Guild Girl stopped writing and looked up, and Goblin Slayer added quietly, "and ten or less missing."

"Missing?"

"We went in, rescued the hostage, and flooded the nest. I confirmed thirty-four bodies. There can't be more than ten left."

"Ah..."

Guild Girl snickered, her cheeks softening into a smile. It wasn't resignation, exactly—this was simply something that couldn't be helped. If anything, she was secretly pleased to see that he was his usual self.

"And what about the second quest?"

"There were goblins," he reported. "Twenty and three of them..."

And so it went, the nonchalant talk of goblin slaying. Flooding them, burning them, burying them, or simply charging in and slaughtering them. Weapons thrown and thrust, stolen, exchanged; forced to work with whatever equipment they'd had ready beforehand.

"......"

The young man had his back turned to them, but he seemed to be hanging on every word.

He must have been about fifteen or so. He had hair so red it seemed to be on fire—but it was neatly trimmed, and his cape appeared brand-new as well. His staff did not bear a jewel indicating graduation, so presumably, he was one of those mages who had left the Academy before finishing their studies.

Affecting disinterest, he dug through his belongings as if he had just thought of something. His rummaging produced a small notebook and a charcoal pencil. Was he going to take notes? What a very good student he must have been.

But Goblin Slayer, seemingly without even looking at the boy, commanded, "Don't."

"?!"

Wizard Boy nearly jumped out of his seat. He wasn't quite cowed, though; he cast a petulant glance at Goblin Slayer and grumbled, "Aw, what? I know everyone thinks goblins are no big deal, but taking some notes isn't going to hurt anything, is—?"

"It could."

Goblin Slayer met the boy's almost canine whining with a blunt, cold, quiet response.

"What if your notes fell into the hands of goblins?"

The boy's temple throbbed, and his frown was evident even in the dim lamplight.

"Are you suggesting I might lose to some goblins?!"

"There's a distinct possibility."

"How dare you—?!"

The boy jumped out of his seat without a second thought. Goblin Slayer turned toward him with palpable exasperation.

Maybe now's the right time?

Guild Girl gave a forced smile and indicated the young man's cup.

"Do you need a little more tea?"

"Oh, uh, no, I…" Caught at the zenith of his anger, the boy scratched his cheek guiltily. "I guess I… I do."

"Here you are, then." There was the sound of flowing liquid as Guild Girl poured more of the steaming tea into the boy's cup. The young wizard watched her intently. Yes, she could see it now: he was fifteen or thereabouts, and he looked it.

Well, I guess he is *becoming an adventurer.*

Was it dreams or hopes? Money or fame? Some such reasons were suitable, others greedy and pretentious.

Guild Girl poured more tea into Goblin Slayer's empty cup.

"Thanks."

"Not at all! ♪ No need to thank me."

Wizard Boy blinked at her beaming expression. It was the same look she had worn earlier, when she first greeted this strange, armored adventurer. He couldn't quite express it, but it was obviously different from the smile she had given him when he was first registering.

He swallowed heavily then hesitantly opened his mouth.

"So you're…the one they call…Goblin Slayer?"

"Some call me that." He nodded. Wizard Boy leaned a little closer. Behind his glasses, his green eyes sparkled, growing ever wider, reflecting Goblin Slayer's visage.

Nervousness, tension, excitement, anticipation, and anxiety were all evident on Wizard Boy's face and in his voice as he said, "Then teach me how to kill goblins!"

"No," Goblin Slayer replied flatly.

"Why not?!"

"If you don't plan to do anything until you've been taught, then my teaching you won't change anything."

"Huh?!"

With that, Goblin Slayer picked up the fresh cup of tea, downing it in one swig. *Gulp.*

He set the cup down with a *clink* and turned back to Guild Girl. He didn't even look at the flummoxed young man as he took the papers Guild Girl handed him. The reports were all ready; Goblin Slayer only needed to sign them.

He took a quill and put down his name. Then he gave Guild Girl a look of perplexity. Why was she here so late? It took him two or three seconds to work out the answer.

"Sorry. Thanks for the help."

"Don't mention it. You always work so hard for us. Oh, your reward..."

"Divide it up equally. Give me only my share."

"Sure thing!"

Guild Girl turned with a movement so sprightly that she seemed neither sleepy nor tired. She opened the safe, took out a bag full of coins, and measured them out with a scale. Goblin Slayer watched the braids bounce against her back and mumbled, "Ah. There was that party that was recently registered." He thought a moment then added, "It had a rhea girl in it."

"Oh, them?" A small chuckle escaped her lips. She was glad he couldn't see her face. "They're fine. Well, they sustained a giant rat bite or two. But they had antidotes."

"I see."

"Are you relieved?"

"Yes."

Guild Girl turned back with a happy look on her face and placed a small tray with a leather pouch full of coins in front of Goblin Slayer.

He took it without bothering to count the contents. The bag made a heavy clicking sound from the gold coins within.

Goblin slaying did not pay well; even less when the reward was split five ways. But what if one multiplied that number by ten? It was enough to equal the full reward for two goblin-slaying quests. Twice as much money as the members of any one frontier village had managed to save with all their sweat and care.

As he tucked the pouch among his other items, Goblin Slayer gestured with his chin. "Who's he?"

"He just registered as an adventurer."

"Why is he here?"

"Well, he..." Guild Girl looked around then stretched out over the counter, leaning close to the steel helmet as though she were going to share a secret. The fabric of her uniform stretched, distorting the area around her chest ever so slightly. "He says he wants to kill goblins and nothing else..."

"Does he have a party?"

The braids bounced from side to side as Guild Girl shook her head.

"It doesn't look like it."

"Foolishness."

Guild Girl gave him a look as if she wasn't quite sure what to say. *Are you of all people in a position to say that?* it seemed to ask. She rubbed her temples.

"So what do we do, Mr. Goblin Slayer?"

"Hrm..."

The pleading look, the beseeching voice.

The Guild Hall was silent. There was only the soft sound of breathing and the occasional scratching of armor. The lamp wick burned assiduously. From above came the faint sound of creaking floorboards. Had the earlier scream woken someone up, or was somebody simply keeping watch? Whatever the case, anything that would intrude on an adventurer's rest time had to be either very urgent or very stupid.

"You." The young man, who had been fixated on the floor, looked up with a start when Goblin Slayer spoke to him. "Do you have a room?"

"Er, uh..." He didn't quite seem to know how to answer. He opened and closed his mouth, again and again, and pushed his glasses up his nose.

Goblin Slayer waited for a response.

"...I don't see what that has to do with anything," the boy finally said.

"I see."

That was his entire response to the boy's sour pronouncement, after which he turned to Guild Girl. She crossed her index fingers to form an X and shook her head. It was clear enough what she meant.

"No rooms available?"

"..."

"It's spring. He won't catch a cold outside, but..."

Goblin Slayer stood up. The boy found himself watching the adventurer as he set off at his bold pace. Goblin Slayer, however, didn't spare the young mage a glance as he pushed open the swinging door.

"Come with me."

One short command. With that, Goblin Slayer left for the darkened town, leaving the young man behind.

He glanced hurriedly from the door to Guild Girl, then he rushed for the exit.

"H-hey, wait for me! What does he think he's doing, just dragging me along like this...?!"

He suddenly stopped. He spun around and gave a slight nod to Guild Girl.

"...Thanks. For the tea."

Then he dashed out. The door made a creaking sound as it swung, letting in the fresh breeze.

"...Phew." Guild Girl sighed once more and stood up. She collected the paperwork and made sure the safe was securely shut and locked. Yes, the staff at the first floor bar was here, and the keeper of the rooms above, but she was the last of the desk employees.

This gave a new meaning to the word *overtime*, but she felt no impulse to complain. She picked up her overcoat (a light one she had brought, since it was now spring) and put her belongings in her bag.

"I guess you really have rubbed off on me."

She giggled and blew out the lamp almost as if she were giving it a kiss.

§

It almost seemed like there was a sea outside the door. The breeze rippled through the grass, and the stars and two moons shone in the sky.

"Hmph."

Goblin Slayer spared a glance up at the green moon then quickly set off walking. The boy hurried to follow after him.

"H-hey, what the heck? Where are you taking me...?" His voice sounded a little strained—perhaps from nervousness or fear.

"Come with me, and you'll see." Goblin Slayer walked purposefully along the road, not so much as looking at the scenery. Notwithstanding the starlight and the relatively good quality of the path, it was impressive the way he never slowed down.

The young man, less than pleased, kicked some small stones that happened to be nearby, letting out a sound of annoyance.

At last, they could see it.

If the field was a sea, then this was a lighthouse, a bright point in the distance gradually growing closer.

Various shapes began to resolve themselves out of the darkness. A small gate. A fence, probably made out of wood. Several buildings visible as looming shadows. The young man, his eyes now adjusted to the night dark, thought he heard the faint lowing of cows.

"Is this...a farm?"

"What else could it be?"

"Hey, I just thought... I mean, the way you were talking, I assumed we were going to an inn or something."

"We are not." Goblin Slayer opened the gate as he spoke. There was a thump from the old wooden bar.

"Oh! You're back!" Despite the depth of the night, the voice that greeted them might as well have been a breaking sun.

"Whoa?!" The boy shook with surprise, his head whipping around as he tried to identify the source of the voice.

It was a young woman, her voluptuous body wrapped in work clothes. She had come jogging up from somewhere.

Cow Girl gave Goblin Slayer's shoulder a friendly pat, then she exhaled.

"Welcome back," she said.

"Yes," Goblin Slayer said with a nod. "I'm back."

The words evoked a "Good" and a bright nod from Cow Girl. "You were out for a while this time," she said. "How was it? You're not hurt?"

"There were goblins. But no other problems besides that." Then he inclined his helmet just a bit. "You're still awake?"

"Heh-heh. I've turned into quite the night owl these last few days," she said with a hint of pride. Her chest jiggled, and the young mage found himself swallowing heavily.

"Whoa, they're *huge*..."

"Hmm?"

He had been careless, letting the words slip out of his mouth. Cow Girl caught his mutter, and now she leaned forward to get a good look at him.

"Well, now, who's this?"

"Ee—yipes!" The boy stumbled backward and fell on his behind. He felt heat rush to his face. His mouth worked open and shut.

"I—I'm an a-ad-adventurer!"

The face of an older woman so close to his own. The sweet odor of sweat mingled with a just-detectable aroma from the grass.

"He's new," Goblin Slayer said shortly, on behalf of the boy, who couldn't even seem to say his own name. "It seems he doesn't have a place to stay."

"Oh, is that right?" Cow Girl said. "I see, I see." She nodded several times, as if happy about something. "Well, I don't mind."

"Thanks," Goblin Slayer said with a nod. "That helps."

"Seriously, don't worry about it. It's so you, somehow."

"I would like to speak to your uncle as well. Is he awake?"

"Probably."

"I see."

Goblin Slayer dodged around Cow Girl and strode into the house. He truly did seem to be at home.

That left the young man. He looked from Cow Girl to the farm gate and back several times.

"...And who're you, his wife?"

"Sure am!"

"No, you're not," a voice interjected from behind Cow Girl.

She stuck out her tongue as if disappointed to have been overheard. The young man gave her a suspicious glance.

"Well, what's going on, then?"

"Can't you tell?" Cow Girl laughed. "He wants to let you sleep here."

"I don't get any of this!"

"Aw, don't worry about it. Here, come inside."

"Stop that. Hey, let go of me!"

"Come on, now, no need to get rough!"

A novice mage versus a veteran farmer: in a contest of strength, the winner was clear.

§

"No."

All the more so an older and even more experienced farmer.

A powerful, well-muscled man seated at the table in the dining room of the main house turned down his boarder's request with a single word.

Before him was Goblin Slayer, flanked on one side by a red-haired boy and on the other by the farmer's niece.

It was Cow Girl, her lips pursed, who was the first to argue. "Oh, come on, Uncle. It's just one night. Why not let him stay?"

"Now, you listen..." The man's sunbaked features pinched as he looked at his fearless niece. How could she still act so childish? *No*, he corrected himself, *her childhood was stolen from her.* He heaved a great sigh. "A newly registered adventurer is no different from any other ruffian who comes wandering along."

"Hey!" This agitated the boy. He slammed his fist down on the table, causing the utensils to jump, and leaned in as he said, "The hell's with you, old man?! Are you saying I'm just some riffraff?!"

"Be quiet."

It was only two words, spoken softly and evenly, yet they contained overwhelming force. They would have been enough to cow even a man who had been through the hell of a battlefield and back.

This was a man who observed the earth every day, thought of nothing but his family and working his farm. His words carried the sober authority of someone who had done this month after month, year after year.

"Er..." The boy swallowed. The owner of the farm eyed him as if he were a crow or a fox.

"Outbursts like that are exactly why I don't, and can't, trust you."

The goal of the adventurer system and the Guild was precisely this: adventurers were by nature a rough lot, and the Guild gave them a measure of credibility, while at the same time preventing them from committing any crimes. It served to protect public order.

Yes, their stated goal was the elimination of monsters, but keeping the various homeless wanderers in one place was a good idea. True, it also served to help limit gossip...

But if adventurers could stay clear of the law, earn some money, and perhaps even gain a reputation, who would complain? Unlike other occupations, as dangerous as adventuring might be, at least effort was directly related to reward.

So what about novices, newcomers, and Porcelains, the very bottom of the ranking system? We hardly need to speak of it; or rather, they were hardly spoken to.

It was natural enough, as such adventurers had yet to gain anyone's trust. Being adventurers, they weren't exactly lawless criminals. But anyone ought to know that manners make all the difference. How was one supposed to trust such an obviously hot-blooded youngster?

And there was something else on the farm owner's mind.

"I have a young woman living here with me. What will I do if anything happens to her?"

"Uncle, I keep telling you, you worry too much..."

"You keep quiet, too," he commanded, and Cow Girl snapped her mouth shut to keep any more words from coming out. *Aww, but—! Oh, come on—!* No little jibes would move the owner of the farm.

"In that case," Goblin Slayer cut in. With a languorous gesture, he indicated the small building outside, now cloaked in darkness. It was the old outbuilding the farmer allowed him to stay in. "What about the shed I'm renting?"

"If anything happens to her," the man said, indicating his niece, "can you take responsibility?"

No, Goblin Slayer replied with a gentle shake of his helmeted head. Then he said calmly, "That is why I will stand guard the entire night."

The farmer made a sort of groan through gritted teeth.

What in the world was he supposed to say to this?

What had this man—this sad, unchecked young boy—seen and done? The farm owner could not claim to be ignorant.

Cow Girl gently laid a hand on the fist the farmer didn't know he'd been clenching and whispered to him.

"Uncle..."

"......I understand. Very well, then."

At last, he had bent. It had been inevitable. What was he to do, throw the boy out among the night dew? Force an obviously exhausted child to go without sleep?

The farmer was not a cruel enough man to make that choice.

He took his hand away from his niece's and placed both his hands against his forehead as if in prayer.

"To repay me, get a proper sleep. All of you."

"Sorry."

"Don't apologize. An adventurer's health is his most important asset, isn't it?"

"Yes. Thank you very much." Goblin Slayer nodded earnestly. He fully understood that neither his apology nor his gratitude would bring the man any happiness. But he did not want to become someone so divorced from decency that he didn't offer them anyway.

"Ah. One other thing." That was exactly why Goblin Slayer fished through his items, withdrawing a pouch of gold coins and setting it on the tabletop. It made a heavy clanking sound as the coins inside settled. "This is for this month."

"Uh-huh..."

Money was a simple index. It was far more reliable than the goodness of any one person. But was it admirable to express oneself with money? That was a thorny question.

The farmer, still not sure what to say, sighed and took the bag of coins. Goblin Slayer watched him.

"All right," announced Goblin Slayer, rising from his chair. "Let's go."

"Huh? Oh, y-yeah." The boy discovered he had no choice but to follow obediently along.

Cow Girl stood up, too, and tugged on Goblin Slayer's arm.

"Hey," she said, "what are you gonna do about tomorrow?"

"It depends on the quests, but we only just returned. I expect everyone will want to rest."

"I'm not asking about everyone, I'm asking about you."

Sheesh. Cow Girl was used to this by now; she scratched her cheek and didn't try any harder to get an answer out of him.

"Well, never mind," she murmured and gave a little smile, releasing his arm. She didn't bother to lift her hand as she gave a tiny little wave. "I'll have breakfast ready for you. Sleep tight!"

"I will," Goblin Slayer nodded. "Good night."

Then he opened the door, and he and the boy left the house.

Goblin Slayer's shed was at the back of the farm. It was well weathered, but he had made all the necessary repairs.

"So what the heck is with them anyway?" the boy asked sullenly.

"What do you mean?"

The newcomer looked around the shed. A dusty lamp cast a red glow over a room that was almost criminally untidy. Shelves overflowed with junk he couldn't identify; the air was full of dust and a faint smell of medicine. It was like the office of one of the instructors at the Academy, the boy thought distantly. And he hated it.

Adding to his dissatisfaction was the pile of straw he was offered to sleep on in lieu of a bed. When he asked just how he was supposed to sleep on something like that, Goblin Slayer said, "Lay your cape over it."

The boy muttered that that would get his cape all covered in straw, but he did as he was told.

"So she's not your wife. She's not part of your family at all, is she?"

"...That's true."

The boy lay down on the straw and found it surprisingly soft.

To his surprise, Goblin Slayer simply plopped himself down in front of the door.

"I can't venture to guess what she thinks, though," continued Goblin Slayer.

"What are you even talking about?"

"They are my acquaintances from long ago. A landlord and his niece. Objectively, that's our relationship."

Then Goblin Slayer fell silent. The boy stared at him from atop the pile of straw, but there was no way to know what expression, if any, was under that metal helmet.

The boy gave up wondering and gazed at the ceiling instead, then he turned over again and looked at the shelves with all their various and sundry items. The skull of some unidentifiable creature, bottles full of medicinal liquids, and three unusual throwing knives. What did he use all this stuff for? It was beyond the boy's ability to imagine.

After a while, he turned over again and saw Goblin Slayer, who hadn't so much as shifted since he sat down. The boy let out a breath.

"...Aren't you gonna sleep?"

The answer came with a terrible quietness.

"I can sleep even with one eye open."

"Sheesh. You're the one who asked me to stay here, and even you're suspicious of me."

"No." Goblin Slayer's helmet moved ever so slightly. The boy realized he was shaking his head. "It's in case any goblins come."

"Say what?"

"I sleep away from the main house. It would be problematic if I couldn't respond immediately."

"...The heck's up with that?"

"If you want to kill goblins, this is the least you must do."

The boy fell silent. A little while later, he rolled over onto his back. The lamp hanging from the ceiling cast a faint light, creaking quietly in the breeze. He closed his eyes, but a hint of the red glow filtered in through his eyelids. And to think, the light wasn't even that bright.

Glaring directly up at the little flame, the boy pursed his lips. "We don't need this."

"I see," Goblin Slayer said. "Put it out, then."

"..."

"Sleep. Tomorrow, I'll take you back to the Guild."

With that, the strange adventurer in his strange armor fell silent.

What in the world is he thinking? The boy looked dubiously at the dirty helmet, his mind whirling. The adventurer had been so forceful that the boy had allowed himself to be swept along to this point, but everything about this seemed bizarre. Who would invite a novice adventurer they had never met to stay in their room? Even going so far as to argue with their wife or family or whatever about it?

If he had been some brainless noble with lots of money—for that matter, if he had been a young woman—then it might have been more understandable. But what did they have to gain by offering him shelter?

Or was this one of those people he had heard about? The ones who waylaid new adventurers and beat them up for their equipment?

But he's Silver-ranked...

It seemed very unlikely that the Guild would risk its reputation conspiring in business like that. He had even heard that before the Guild had been established, adventurers were sometimes simply outright murdered when they came into town.

Look at this guy's armor, though. That helmet. It's so dirty and scary.

He turned over on the straw pile as if to get away from the helmet whose gaze seemed fixed on him in the dimness.

Could a guy who looks like that just turn out to be...nice?

"...Impossible." The world didn't work that way. The boy nodded to himself then gently put a hand on the knife he had hidden under his clothes.

Dammit! If he thinks I'll just roll over and die...

The boy fancied himself someone who never let his guard down. Whatever this adventurer might be planning, he would be damned if he would let himself be murdered in his sleep.

Thus convinced, the boy failed to notice as he slowly drifted off.

§

"...Hng... Huh?"

When consciousness returned, the boy heard a *pound, pound, pound,* a flat, irregular noise.

The first thing he felt as he sat up was the prickly straw. The room that floated in his blurry vision was certainly not his dorm at the Academy.

For starters, they don't have straw beds there.

He scrabbled around for his glasses, which he had set next to his pillow—or rather, beside the straw by his head—and put them on.

Sunlight filtered into the junk-filled shed, motes of dust dancing in the beam.

"Ahh... Right..."

Oh yeah.

He had been sleeping here on account of that "Goblin Slayer" or whoever.

The weird adventurer who had been sleeping by the door was already gone. Even though, judging by the angle of the sunlight, it was still only just past dawn.

"Sheesh. That guy doesn't make a lick of sense. Aw, crap... I knew it'd get covered in straw."

He clicked his tongue. He stood and picked up the cape he'd been using for a blanket.

He glanced around and then—not without a moment's hesitation—gave the garment a great shake to get the straw off. When he put it back on, he could still feel prickles here and there, but he simply frowned and left the shed.

"...Yikes. It's real cold out here."

Spring was beginning, but the last breath of winter still washed over the early mornings. The boy raised the collar of his cape and shivered.

A thin white mist floated over the ground, as though milk had been spilled over the entire farm. He almost felt like he was out in the fog.

Having arrived in the middle of the night, he had no sense of the farm's geography, but he picked a likely direction and started walking.

As he expected, before long, he came across a cozy well with a roof over it. A crossbeam was set over the top of the well, strung with a rope attached to a bucket on one end and a counterweight on the other. A simple well sweep.

The boy lowered the bucket into the well, letting the stone counterweight pull it down deep. Then he relaxed the hand with the rope, and the stone began to sink again, bringing the bucket back up.

He took off his glasses and plunged his face into the cold water.

"Hrrrrrrr… Fwah!"

He soaked in the shockingly frigid water then brought his face up and shook his head, scattering droplets everywhere. Then he used a dipper to wash his mouth, spitting into the grass at his feet and, finally, wiping his face vigorously with the hem of his cape.

It wasn't much in the way of making himself presentable in the morning, but for a moment's work, it would do.

"…Hmm?"

The sound came again from beyond the white mist. *Pound, pound.*

It didn't sound like cooking. Nor was it quite the noise of construction work, or even of someone chopping wood.

In order to follow the wizard's path, a strong sense of curiosity was a must. The boy decided to follow the sound—but at that moment, he realized he was empty-handed.

"Oh, crap!"

He rushed back to the shed and grabbed his staff, still leaning next to his bed.

The dull sound continued unchanged; it seemed it wasn't far away.

Before long, he arrived at a shadow moving in the mist. The morning sun was growing stronger, and he didn't need to use a spell to see clearly what was in front of him.

"Oh…"

It was Goblin Slayer.

He was still wearing his grimy armor and his cheap-looking helmet; his hips were set down in a low stance. He seemed to be confronting part of the wooden fence that surrounded the farm. A round target was affixed to it at an abnormally low position.

The knife sticking out of the target had presumably been thrown by

Goblin Slayer. The boy figured out what had been causing the sound more easily than he had solved riddles at the Academy.

"...What're you doing?"

"Practicing." Goblin Slayer strode toward the target and casually retrieved the weapon.

To the boy, it didn't look like the knife was especially suited for throwing; it was a perfectly unremarkable dagger.

Wait—it wasn't just a knife. Now that he looked more closely at the target, he could see it had been scored by a sword, a spear, an ax, and...was that a hatchet?

With all that practice, Goblin Slayer could probably just as easily fling a stone he found in the grass.

Throwing.

The word whipped around in his mind.

I thought warriors were supposed to swing weapons not fling them.

"How can you fight if you throw all your weapons away? Dumbass."

"I simply steal more." Goblin Slayer ran a finger over the blade of the knife, inspecting it. "From the goblins," he added.

The boy grunted at that answer. "...It'd be better just to have high-quality weapons from the get-go."

"Is that so?"

"You're supposed to be able to take care of a few goblins with a single spell."

"Is that so?"

"Look, I thought you were supposed to be taking today off. Isn't that what you told that chick?"

"I once took a lengthy break. I found my reactions had dulled afterward."

He calmly tossed some weapons to the ground as he spoke. Then, steadying his breath, he turned his back on the target.

"You never know if the next thing you do will kill your enemy."

As soon as he had spoken, he spun. He grabbed one of the weapons at his feet and, with no time to aim, threw it.

The dagger flew through the air, spinning once, and landed in the center of the target with a dry *thump.*

"Hmph."

He picked up the weapons one by one and threw them.

Silently, without a word, he threw them then collected them and started again.

This is boring. The boy sat down in the grass and yawned. He rubbed his eyes, trying to work out the last grains the sandman had left there.

"What good does it do you to learn how to hit an immobile target?"

"I don't know."

"And you've got it so low, too."

"It's the height of a goblin's throat."

The boy fell silent. From the distance came a warm voice calling, "Breakfast!"

He noticed now that the fog had burned off; he could see all the way to the farmhouse, where Cow Girl was leaning out of a window and waving.

Goblin Slayer stopped and looked in her direction, somehow brightly, and nodded.

"All right," he said. Then the helmet turned toward the boy. "Let's go."

Ugh. Not expecting much from this meal.

The boy nodded grudgingly then heaved himself to his feet and followed after Goblin Slayer.

If the food sucks, I'm knocking over that table.

§

There was stew for breakfast.

The boy ended up asking for three extra helpings.

§

"Ergggg…"

"You overate."

They had left the farm on the outskirts and were heading for the Guild, but the boy walked along the path unsteadily. He clung to his staff as he made every effort to move. This must be what it was like, he thought, after an especially draining and dispiriting adventure.

Perhaps this was what adventurers felt like after trekking through an endless field only to see the castle finally come into view.

When they finally passed through the swinging doors and into the noisy waiting area, the boy collapsed onto a seat.

Once again, there were plenty of adventurers visiting the Guild. Some had come to register just today, while others were looking for another day's work.

"Hrggg..."

"How could you be so excited about finding an elevator in some old ruins that you went and got yourself a hangover? How stupid are you?"

"I thought some spirits might restore my spirit..."

"*How* stupid are you?"

Hungover adventurers were not an uncommon sight, some of them slumped on the benches even now. People didn't pay much attention to the young boy who had just come in; maybe they thought he was one of the drunkards.

"I'm going, then," Goblin Slayer said, looking down at the groaning young man, who had lain down so he now took up an entire bench. "You should start in the sewers. Kill those giant— What is it again? —Giant rats."

"*I*...am gonna...k-kill goblins...!"

"I see."

With that, Goblin Slayer turned away from the young man. Who was he to interfere with the boy's wishes? Goblin Slayer strode boldly away, heading for his usual spot: a bench in the far corner of the Guild waiting area.

Five—no, six years ago, when he had first become an adventurer, he had been the only one there.

But now things were different.

His companions were there, as were those who had some business with him, and even others who just wanted to say hello.

Today was more of the same. There was Lizard Priest, swishing his tail. High Elf Archer and Dwarf Shaman sat on either side of Priestess. And yet…

"Goblin Slayer, siiir…"

Somehow it felt different from usual. At the center of the circle of faces, Priestess's hands clutched her knees, and her voice was weak.

"What's wrong?"

"Sounds like they were talking about promoting her," High Elf Archer answered in Priestess's stead.

"Ah," Goblin Slayer nodded. "It was about that time."

Adventurers were divided into ten ranks, from Porcelain to Platinum. Notwithstanding Platinum rank, which was special, the divisions were made based on what were popularly called "experience points." In other words, the rewards one had earned, combined with how much good one had done for those around them, along with one's personality.

It had been a year earlier that Priestess had been promoted to Obsidian for defeating the whatever-it-was-called in the underground ruins. Then there was the giant eyeball they had encountered at the water town, and the leader of the goblin army that had attacked their own town.

Having further survived the battle with the goblin paladin in the North, she should have had more than enough in the way of rewards and social contributions. And her interpersonal comportment was beyond reproach.

Yes, it was more than appropriate that the possibility of promotion should have been raised.

But if she was looking so down, that meant…

"She didn't pass?"

"I guess not."

"*And you even had a letter of recommendation, huh?*" High Elf Archer whispered to Priestess, who simply responded, "Yes."

She looked as pathetic as a puppy left out in the rain and sounded as if she might start weeping at any moment.

"I guess—they think—they say I haven't contributed enough yet."

"I suppose it's understandable," Lizard Priest said. "The rest of us are Silver-ranked, after all."

Dwarf Shaman let out a dissatisfied snort and tugged at his beard. "What, do they think she's piggybacking on us? Who would believe that?" It was an inappropriate but not unheard-of thing for a group of experienced adventurers to do.

"Hrm," Goblin Slayer grunted quietly.

Priestess's first party no longer existed. The people with whom she should have grown and matured from Porcelain up through the ranks were already gone.

Goblin Slayer glanced over at Guild Girl, but she was busy with other adventurers, rushing back and forth like a frenzied mouse. She noticed him looking at her and put her hands together in a gesture of apology. That meant there was little that could be done. After all, it was not she who ran the Guild. Her superiors were involved, as were paperwork, inspectors, and bureaucratic red tape. That was simply the way the world worked. Personal effort was indispensable, but it was not always enough.

"U-um, please d-don't worry about it," Priestess said bravely as if to comfort Goblin Slayer and her other companions, who had fallen into reflection. "I'm sure that if I work hard enough, I can get them to promote me eventually..."

"That's the spirit," Dwarf Shaman said. "You've got plenty of skills, and you're more than doing your part to help out. They just need to understand that."

"Mm," Lizard Priest hissed from where he leaned against the wall with his arms crossed thoughtfully. His tail moved with a rustle. "Among my people, we speak of the importance of conveying the technique of battle to the next generation."

"That's it!" High Elf Archer said, attempting to snap her fingers. She got only a soft clicking sound. Then she pursed her lips again: Dwarf Shaman was trying to suppress a laugh at her failed attempt. "...What?"

"Oh, nothing. I just wondered what you were talking about," he replied, totally unperturbed by High Elf Archer's piercing glare.

"I'm not gonna forget this," the elf said as the dwarf stood laughing and stroking his beard. "But anyway, if rank is the problem, why not find some Porcelains and Obsidians to adventure with?"

"That's just the thing," the dwarf said. "This is the Guild, after all. Show them you're mentoring someone, you know?"

"Um..." Priestess looked around at them, confused. Her eyes watered a little. She ran her tongue gently over dry lips then held up her pointer finger as if to make sure she was following them. "You mean...go adventuring without all of you?"

"Yes," Goblin Slayer said brusquely.

"It would not be such a bad idea," added Lizard Priest.

"Well, that settles it," High Elf Archer said, her ears twitching brightly. She was practically immortal; logistical niceties didn't tend to worry her. "Just pick a random Porcelain—well, maybe *random* isn't the right word, but—"

Her party seemed just about to get things underway when a taunting voice sounded:

"Heh! I know you're back-row, but there's no way someone as weepy and blubbering as you could ever get promoted!"

That sent High Elf Archer's ears straight back, and she began looking for their antagonist. The owner of the voice rose unsteadily from one of the benches.

It was the red-haired boy—dressed in a robe, holding a staff, wearing glasses. That wizard.

Priestess spent only a second with her mouth open in shock, then the corners of her eyes tightened angrily.

"I—I'm not *weepy*!"

"I dunno 'bout that. I hear all you clerics like a good cry." He gave a dismissive sniff and didn't even open his eyes all the way as he looked at Priestess. Maybe he thought all this diligent ridicule made him look cool.

He didn't seem to realize that it just made him seem like a slimy villain.

"Whenever you're in trouble, it's *O gods, please, save me! Boo-hoo-hoo!*, right?"

"Hey—!" Priestess hardly knew what to say to this unexpected display of meanness, but her pale face grew visibly red. She was uncharacteristically—but very much understandably—agitated. "That's not how it is at all! I have all kinds of—"

All kinds of what? Was there any way she could finish that sentence proudly, confidently?

She followed instructions and used miracles, praying for everyone's safety. Praying to the gods. But could she herself do anything? If so, what?

Priestess found she could no longer speak. She looked at the ground, clenching a shaking fist.

The young man stuck out his chest triumphantly. But he took a hesitant step back, then two, as Lizard Priest approached him aggressively. "To judge others invites judgment upon oneself," the lizardman said. "For if you insult one cleric, you have insulted them all."

Lizard Priest made a broad gesture with his head. The boy looked around, and only then did he realize: from the newest to the most experienced, every adventurer in the room was looking at him and Priestess, who was blushing furiously.

"I think you may find this world a difficult one to survive in without some help from the gods," Lizard Priest continued. Who could blame the boy for the slight groan that escaped him then? He had been shouting in front of all these people, with no thought for the future.

"Hey, you! How about you look me in the eye and say that?"

"Come off it, moron. We've got giant rats to hunt. It'll be good practice for us."

"Let go! Lemme go! I'm gonna teach that guy a lesson! Let! Me! Go!"

Apprentice Cleric flailed about, waving her staff, as Rookie Warrior dragged her away.

The apprentice's reaction was somewhat extreme, but all around the room, responses were similar. Perhaps some favored Priestess because she was a girl, others because hers was a familiar face against one they didn't know. But most of the reproachful glances leveled at the boy were motivated by more than that.

Some adventurers derided clerics, who didn't stand in the front row, as nothing but healing machines. But there were plenty of adventurers who had been saved by those same clerics. Everyone got injured at one time or another. Writhing in pain, poisoned, cursed, abandoned: none of these were pleasant.

If you had a cleric in your party, then you were in good stead, and of course, anyone who offered alms could be treated at a temple. How could anyone look down on those who worked for them, prayed for them, made miracles happen for them?

"H-hey, I'm—" But no adventurer would simply back down like that. "I'm an adventurer, too!"

The boy announced himself boldly, although he knew he was at a disadvantage here. His passion caused a few of the onlooking eyes to widen with admiration.

The business of adventuring was, ultimately, one in which everyone must take responsibility for themselves. So if there was a person who really had the strength to stand completely on their own, with no divine aid, then they could quite well make fun of clerics and get away with it.

"Goblins? Hah! They're nothing! So what does that make a Goblin Slayer?"

He jabbed his staff in Goblin Slayer's direction as if he might cast a spell on the adventurer, a classic pose of wizard contempt.

"*Don't take notes*! *I won't teach you my goblin-slaying secrets*! *Try some rats instead*! It's bullshit, all of it!"

All the emotions he had held back until that moment came pouring out of him.

"I damn well *will* kill goblins!"

In the face of all this aggressive shouting, Goblin Slayer only tilted his head the slightest bit, quizzically. Beside him, High Elf Archer's ears twitched and she crossed her arms as she looked at Goblin Slayer. "Who's this, Orcbolg? Your little brother?"

"No," Goblin Slayer said firmly. "I only had an older sister."

"Oh?" The archer let out a sigh and shrugged with the sort of grace attainable only by elves. "I guess I just hear that sort of talk so much these days that it doesn't surprise me anymore."

"Is that so?"

"So who exactly is this kid?"

"A newcomer," Goblin Slayer said. "A wizard, it would seem."

Goblin Slayer wasn't looking at the outthrust staff, but at Priestess. She was still peering at the ground, her shoulders stiff, completely silent. She was fifteen—no, sixteen now. She had been an adventurer for an entire year, but she was still young. What could he say to her, when the work of that year had been denied as if she had done nothing important?

"Well, that makes it easy, doesn't it?" a bright, eager voice broke in. Everyone turned to look at the new speaker. "I heard everything. And as a Lawful Good knight, I can't let it go!"

Female Knight stood there, snorting triumphantly. Her wide smile made it all too clear that she had butted in mostly for the fun of it. Behind her, Heavy Warrior muttered, "I couldn't stop her," and held up an apologetic hand.

"The hell? …Who're you? This doesn't involve you."

"Heh-heh! One day I'll be a famous paladin, but I don't blame you for not recognizing me now." The boy's disbelief didn't seem to faze Female Knight, who puffed out her chest importantly. "But hear me now, young man. I have an excellent idea!"

Female Knight was not the most refined person in the room, but she gave an elegant snap of her fingers, the noise audible throughout the Guild Hall. She didn't seem to notice the look of displeasure that came over High Elf Archer's face. Instead, she pointed directly at the young man. "If you're so confident, then go slay some goblins."

"Th-that's exactly what I wanna do!"

"You all heard him," Female Knight said, her eyes shining dangerously. "However!" She wielded her pointer finger like the tip of a sword. "Your leader will be that cleric girl!"

"Whaaa?!" Priestess, fixed by that finger, came back to herself with a yelp. She could hardly figure out what was happening, as she looked back and forth between the outstretched pointer finger and the wizard boy. "I-I-I'm supposed to give—orders? To— To *this* boy?"

"Whaddaya mean, 'this boy'? And hey, it's no fair to add conditions!"

"Don't be naive, young man. Knights know better than to show their hand. Better to curse yourself for having been taken in!"

"U-um, I haven't said I'll accept yet…"

"Nor do you need to!"

Priestess's attempts at objection were adorable. Heavy Warrior looked up at the ceiling without a word. No lightning bolts came crashing down. Apparently, the Supreme God was admitting that Female Knight was indeed Lawful Good. *They'll let anyone be an agent of Order these days…*

"Hrm," muttered Goblin Slayer, who had kept his distance from the commotion. "What do you think?"

"I presume the boy's failure to be reflective springs from a lack of experience," Lizard Priest responded with a somber nod. He rolled his eyes once. "I do not know how many spells he can use, nor how many times he can use them, but I do like his spirit."

"We don't know about his spells," Goblin Slayer agreed, and after a moment he added, "I assume he can use one, or maybe two."

"What do you think, master spell caster?"

"For better or for worse, he's unpolished," Dwarf Shaman responded without a moment's hesitation, merrily stroking his beard.

Deeply engaged in his argument, the boy had no idea he was being evaluated from the sidelines like this.

"He's rough-hewn," the dwarf went on. "Just dug up. Still got bits of earth clinging to him. We won't know what's in there until he's been polished up a bit."

"Shall we do a bit of polishing?"

"I'm for it."

"Then it's decided."

A calloused hand landed on Goblin Slayer's shoulder. It belonged to a giant—Heavy Warrior.

"You're not usually the type to praise another adventurer, Goblin Slayer."

"I wasn't trying to praise him…" It was impossible to tell whether he was being ironic or simply honest. Because he couldn't tell, Goblin Slayer tilted his head. "Did I?"

"You did."

"I see… And I think it's unusual for you to worry about anyone else."

"Hey, it wasn't me that was worried. Blame her." Heavy Warrior jerked his chin in Female Knight's direction, taking in Priestess and the boy along with it.

At a glance, perhaps it seemed they were simply arguing. But in the end, Goblin Slayer had been unable to say anything to her.

Why Priestess was part of his party now, and what had happened to her first group: these were things only she and he knew.

And yet, it was Lizard Priest who had interceded against the young man, and Female Knight who had changed the subject.

He had not been able to do either of those things.

"…Sorry for the trouble. It's a help."

"Don't fret," Heavy Warrior replied with deliberate bluntness. He looked away, scratching his cheek. "I owe you more than this. I'll pay you back a little at a time."

This caused Goblin Slayer to lapse into thought. He had no memory of a debt. But this seemed important to Heavy Warrior.

"…Is that so?"

"Yeah, it is."

"I see," Goblin Slayer said shortly. Inside his helmet, he followed Heavy Warrior with his gaze. "I believe I owe you a debt as well."

"Repay it a bit at a time, then."

"I see."

"…So. What's on your mind?"

"I am thinking about how to kill goblins."

Heavy Warrior seemed caught between a frown and the slightest of smiles. "Mighta guessed," he muttered. It was the natural reaction of any adventurer familiar with this man.

This Goblin Slayer.

People called him strange or weird for talking endlessly about goblins, but they called him that out of affection, for they knew him well.

"However," Goblin Slayer said quietly as he looked around the Guild.

There were Female Knight and the new boy, still arguing, while High Elf Archer had given up trying to snap her fingers and had settled for complaining instead.

There were Lizard Priest and Dwarf Shaman, watching the room and laughing as they made plans.

There were various adventurers, some he recognized, others he didn't, standing at the fringes of the group and occasionally offering jabs or jeers.

An inspector at the reception desk was chortling, while Guild Girl herself couldn't restrain a small smile.

There was Spearman, having just accepted an assignment, exclaiming "Yahoo!" and bounding off, only to be chided by Witch.

And in the midst of it all, looking thoroughly confused, was Priestess.

She was saying, "I can do it, too," and snapping her fingers for the edification of High Elf Archer. The cleric seemed a little panicked, a little flummoxed, and more than a little awkward, but she also seemed to be enjoying herself—to be truly happy.

It was how things always looked here. The people, the faces, might change, but the scene would go on.

"However," Goblin Slayer said once more. "It would be best if all goes well."

"You got that right," Heavy Warrior said with a smile, and he clapped Goblin Slayer heartily on the shoulder.

CHAPTER 3
Magical Resources

First, we should elucidate the mistake they made.

They had all their gear. The party was well balanced.

They were vigilant and resolute, and they let nothing disrupt their formation.

Yet, they were all destroyed. Why?

The god Truth, seated in the high heaven, would no doubt smile and say:

"Just because I was set on bringing down a party today."

§

The quest they had taken on was to clean up monsters around the area where the training facility was to be built.

The battle with the Non-Prayers was endless, reaching back to the Age of the Gods. Most of the fortresses and castles built during that time were now nothing more than ruins.

The five of them had challenged just such an ancient place.

They were a mix of ninth-rank Obsidians and tenth-rank Porcelains, but all of them were novice adventurers. They had met with success on a number of adventures, and they approached these ruins as they had their other quests.

They attacked the goblins who nested there.

Forming their battle lines, they readied their spells, and burst through the door. Their swords flashed, lightning bolts and fireballs flew, corpses were trampled upon and treasure chests were opened. A textbook hack and slash.

"Heh! I told you, goblins just aren't quite satisfying," a lizardman said, sheathing his serrated shark-tooth sword and letting out a breath. His carefully cultivated muscles bulged under his scales, obviously the body of a warrior. "As long as you keep them in front of you, there's no way you can lose."

"Oh?" came a laugh from a young human girl. "I really had fun." She looked healthy and trim, but suitably feminine; she was dressed in armor that could hardly be considered anything other than underwear. The massive battle-ax at her feet indicated there was more to her than met the eye. A warrior-priest and servant of the Valkyrie, she seemed to be triumphantly displaying her body.

Another party member glanced at her and sighed. He was a human wizard well into middle age. He put a hand to his receding hairline and focused his eyes as craggy as a cliff directly on the young woman.

"I'm glad you're enjoying yourself, but please don't go diving in among the enemy like that. It makes it impossible to aim my spells."

"Aw, is our dear general upset?" Warrior-Priest seemed unmoved by the mage's reproachful look; her smile didn't shrink at all. "What's the big deal? You get to save your spells, and I get to do what I do best."

"That's not the—well, never mind. I'll save the lecture for later. More importantly, what's our status?"

"Wait."

The response came not from Warrior-Priest but from a man in a black outfit, who crouched in front of a treasure chest the goblins had left behind and spoke in low, dark tones.

"The cheeky little creatures have left us a trap," he said. He was covered from head to toe, and given the skill with which he worked at the lock on the chest, it was easy to tell he was a thief.

His skill was superhuman—indeed, he wasn't human. Black ears peeked out from his bandanna. He was a dark elf who had become a Pray-er.

"Can you open it?" the leader asked.

“Don’t patronize me,” the dark elf snorted. “Compared with my fellows’ work, this is child’s play.”

“Well, I hope it contains more than a child’s pittance.”

There was a soft click and the chest opened. A well-endowed cleric leaned in for a look.

Hanging from her neck was a golden wheel on a chain, the symbol of the Trade God, who protected travelers and merchants.

The acolyte frowned unhappily and put a hand to her cheek, her expression dispirited.

The entire contents of the chest consisted of old coins. It would be a chore to get them out of there.

“If only you all didn’t have so many weapons and items and provisions, this money wouldn’t be so much trouble,” she said.

“Hey, only a fool mocks provisions.” A large, scaly hand settled on her shoulder. “How can we fight on empty stomachs?”

“Yes, I understand that very well,” she said, placing her hand over the lizardman’s with an intimate smile. “That’s exactly why we need to earn more than we do.”

“Gawd, you two lovebirds…” Warrior-Priest pointedly made a disgusted face and said, “Come on, let’s go on to the next one. There are still three doors left in this burial chamber.”

“So there are,” the mage said. “Come on, check the doors. Start on the north side.”

“No traps,” the dark elf replied, quickly pressing his ear to the door and feeling it with his fingers. He didn’t have to listen hard to hear the harsh breath on the other side. “Our next prey is right through here.”

Eyes all around the party sparkled at that.

Battle, monsters, treasure, victory. Everything they wanted from an adventure. There was no better job in the world.

They took their familiar positions for battle. Lizardman and Warrior-Priest were in the front row, General and Acolyte were in the middle, and Thief stood in the back with a dagger at the ready, watching for sneak attacks.

“Here we go!” With a great shout, Lizardman burst through the ancient, rotten door. It crashed inward and the party piled into the room.

A massive shadow loomed in the middle of the dim burial chamber. Some unidentified monster.

As it slowly sat up, though, club in hand, General realized what it was. His eyes went wide, and the usually reserved man cried a warning at the top of his lungs:

"Trollllll!"

A troll. The monster was a troll. Stupid, but strong. Slow, but incredibly powerful. It had no scales, no rocky hide. But any wounds it received, save those inflicted with fire, quickly healed.

How can there be a troll here...?!

For an instant, General couldn't think straight. It crossed his mind that goblins sometimes hired bodyguards. Was that what this was?

Can we beat it?

A troll was nothing compared with an ogre, which could use magic, but it was no trifling threat, either.

No—we can win. We will win!

General forcefully pushed aside the fear and astonishment that assailed him and began giving orders as if this were any other battle.

"Front row, intercept him. Acolyte, buff them. Thief, use an ambush. I'll get some fire ready."

"You don't want me guarding the rear, then?"

"If we don't bring to bear everything we've got, we're going to pay for it!"

"Understood." Thief melted into the shadows of the burial chamber, while Warrior-Priest burst out, "I'm going iiiin!" and the battle began.

"Bring us victory!"

"OLRLLLLRT?!"

The blow from the battle-ax, boosted by Holy Smite, caught the monster on the shin, and the troll staggered like a tree in a hurricane.

"Heh! Don't like that, do you?"

"Yaaaaaah!" Lizardman didn't miss the opportunity to bring his blade into the fight. Carved from the fangs of a sea monster, it literally bit into the troll's grey skin. But then—

"H-huh?! This thing is tough!" Numbness ran up Lizardman's

arm, the same feeling he got when he slammed a wooden sword into a boulder.

"Why is it you're always ahead of me?" Acolyte complained.

"It's your fault for being so slow," Lizardman shouted as he fell back, the troll's club smashing the ground where he had been standing just a moment ago.

"TOOOORLLL!!"

The burial chamber, which had stood for a thousand years, now found itself hard-pressed; the room trembled, and pebbles rained down from the ceiling.

"Hrh… This thing's all brawn!" Acolyte said. With a mixture of chagrin and distaste, she brought her hands together and closed her eyes. It shaved away a certain part of one's soul to pray like this, but it allowed one to beg for a miracle directly from the gods in heaven.

"O my god of the wind that comes and goes, may fortune smile on our road!"

There was a *whoosh* as the sacred wind of the miracle Blessing gusted through the chamber. The lizardman's blade was sharpened by its pure breeze and the power of the gods.

"Now, that's more like it! *O my forebear Yinlong, behold my deeds in battle!*"

"If you're going to exclaim to anyone, it ought to be the Trade God!"

A single blow from Lizardman's enhanced muscles caught the troll's club square on.

"OLLLT?!"

"Aw, yeah!"

The two weapons met with a *crack*, the momentum bouncing them back off each other. At the instant the troll stumbled, a burst of light struck at his ankles: a sneak attack by the dark elf.

There was an unpleasant crackling as the blow cut his ligaments. In any other case, the strike would have ended the fight.

"TOORRRRROO!!"

"Yikes! Look out, look out, look out! I think we just ticked him off!"

They, however, were dealing with a troll.

Warrior-Priest dropped and rolled with a shout, narrowly dodging the descending club.

The monster's skin bubbled, wounds closing themselves up. It was a vision of utmost fear to the warrior. How much damage had their attacks actually done? And this was when they had a holy miracle on their side—a miracle that wouldn't last forever.

"Where's that magic?!" Acolyte demanded, sweat pouring down her forehead.

"I'm working on it!" General shouted back then jacked into his own consciousness.

He pulled out the words of true power that were carved into his mind, used them to override and refigure the world itself.

"Carbunculus... Crescunt... Iacta!!"

Thus he was the first of them to die.

The Fireball he cast flew in a random direction, scorching stone and vanishing in a shower of sparks. Do you suppose General recognized, at the moment of his death, the source of the blunt sound that accompanied the blow to the back of his head?

The goblin's stone ax scattered that brilliant brain all over the floor of the burial chamber.

"GROORB!!"

"GORR!"

"A rear attack?!"

Who was it who sent up the shout?

Now they saw the goblins pouring through the doorway behind. It was too late to curse the gods. Closing the door would have meant cutting off their own escape route. What other outcome, then, could there have been?

"GORBBBO!!"

"OOOTLLTL!!"

Lizardman, seeing how quickly the battlefield situation had changed, beat back the troll's club and shouted, "The two of us will handle this. Fall back!"

Instead of an answer, he saw a dark shape slipping around the burial chamber. The dark elf had gotten behind the troll and somersaulted in, seemingly in an attempt to protect Acolyte.

"You get back, too! In that armor, you're just asking to die!"

"No way! I can't, I can't, I can't!" Warrior-Priest yammered. She was working her weapon as hard as she could, but the situation did not look good.

The group of three who had been fighting the monster now had to contend with just two party members. And all while watching their backs.

The goblins had let the troll distract the adventurers then ambushed them from the other burial chambers. How clever and cruel.

Sometimes you crit, and sometimes it's a natural one.

"...Hng—"

Acolyte desperately looked away from General, his brains still leaking onto the floor; she bit her lip hard enough to draw blood. In that moment, the real tragedy was the loss of magical resources. She had to think of the battlefield she was on. If she wanted to survive, if she wanted to claim victory, then she had to put the death of her comrade out of her mind at this moment.

Acolyte repeated these things over and over to herself as she brought her hands together and began trying to pray again.

"GRORORB...!"

After all, she herself was not yet out of danger. There were several goblins coming up behind her—indeed, nearly a dozen. And goblins were not famous for their mercy toward prisoners.

Goblins divided the world into three categories: toys for themselves, loot to steal, and enemies. Just as adventurers would slaughter any goblins they found, goblins would surely let no adventurer go alive.

"Ah— Ahh!" Acolyte stumbled forward as she dodged a rusty dagger.

"Keep giving support!" the dark elf said as he came in to cover her. He deflected the goblin weapon in a hail of sparks then administered a second blow that cut the monster's throat. There was a wheezing sound and a spray of blood; the dark elf gave the creature a ruthless kick.

"We aren't gonna last long over here!"

"Right! Miracle, coming right up—!"

Acolyte grasped the holy mark that had fallen down between her bouncing breasts, sweat running down her bloodless cheeks as she intoned her miracle once more. *"O my god of the wind that comes and goes, may fortune smile on our road!"*

Money makes the world go round, as do travelers. The Trade God oversaw them both. He sent a fresh wind blowing into the burial chamber, chasing away the moldy stench that had prevailed in the room.

"H-hrraaahhh! Graaahhh!" Lizardman bellowed.

"TOOTLOR!!"

The troll raised its club. The two of them met head on.

Warrior-Priest, her hair in complete disarray, prepared to bring her battle-ax down on the troll's foot.

"T-take this! Both together now!"

"Let's do it!"

The holy ax and the Blessed serrated blade tore without mercy through flesh and muscle.

"TOORL?!"

There was a spray of blood and an ear-splitting screech from the troll, and the shouts of the two warriors rang throughout the chamber.

None of this changed the fact that the situation was very, very dire.

All the injuries they had inflicted on the troll were relatively minor. And a three-on-one fight had been reduced to two-on-one—or perhaps more accurately, five-on-one had become four-on-eleven.

Without a mage, the party had no way to strike a decisive blow. Yet, at the same time, their escape route was cut off and they couldn't retreat. Could they hope to do anything that might turn the situation around?

"Damn… Damn! Dammit!!"

Great, wet tears formed in Warrior-Priest's eyes and began to stream down her face. She and Lizardman fought like lions, but eventually they would reach their limit.

There was no fear. Only regret.

If they'd had their dark elf scout watching their rear, maybe they wouldn't have been taken unawares. And yet, if they had done that, they would have had no good way of attacking the troll. The outcome, she suspected, would have been the same.

Warrior-Priest well understood that there are no *ifs* in battle. But somehow that only made the regret sting all the more. Where had they gone wrong? Why had it turned out this way? She hated all the questions she couldn't answer.

"Grr…!"

The second to fall in battle that day was the dark elf thief. He stopped one goblin, killed a second, buried a third—but then a goblin dagger grazed his cheek. The fact that he recognized the seemingly unidentifiable liquid slathered on the blade as poison was perhaps testament to his being a dark elf.

With a free hand, he reached back to grab a bottle from his belt. An antidote.

"GRORB!"

"GROB! GRRRORB!!"

The goblins, naturally, were not about to give him the time to drink it. Relying on their numbers, they threw themselves at him relentlessly. The dark elf's movements began to slow visibly, and then…

"Grgh—hagh!"

He was overwhelmed, dragged to the ground, and there the goblins sliced him up until there was no life left in him.

"Ahhh!" Lizardman clearly heard Acolyte's involuntary scream. Unfortunately.

"Hey, are you all right?!"

It was a careless lapse. Yet, who could blame him? The lizardman's passion for battle was fueled by that beautiful acolyte.

The next instant, he registered the club rising, and coming down, and no way to avoid it.

A troll is born with strength enough to shame a tree; their regenerative powers, too, are natural. As weapons go, the club is quite crude—but plenty powerful.

This creature was strong, an enemy to be feared. Was that not enough? They had been good companions, and this was a good enemy. It was a good life.

Would the troll do him the service of eating his heart?

That was his only disappointment. But even if not, his remains would one day rot away and return to the great cycle.

What else could he say, then, at the end?

"—Brilliant!"

The lizardman warrior's skull ended up inside his chest armor, and he died. It almost looked as if the body had been beheaded, but it collapsed without so much as a spurt of blood. His weapon fell out of his hand and clattered to the ground.

"N—"

Acolyte saw it all. She stood dumbly with her eyes wide, and then against every effort of her will, a strangled scream rose out of her. "Nooooooo! It's not true! It can't be…!" She was about to dash over to where her fallen companion lay.

"Don't do it, idiot! It's too late now!"

That is to say, she was about to run over to the troll.

The scream had been more than enough to get the monster's attention, and that of the goblins as well. The hideous smiles on their faces made plain what they were imagining in their polluted little minds.

"Y-you sons of—!"

Warrior-Priest gave just a slight stutter before she went diving in among them.

If she had had any thought of running away, she might have been able to. If she had been willing to abandon Acolyte, she could have gone home alive.

Instead, it was all going to go to waste: Everything, from the moment she had been born until this very instant. All the training. All the friends. Her dreams. Her future.

She knew that full well. And yet, in her mind, the choice of doing nothing didn't exist.

"Outta the way!"

"Ah!"

She shoved Acolyte aside. The last expression the young woman saw on Warrior-Priest's face was that of a girl who had run out of strength.

Then with a crushing sound, Warrior-Priest vanished, what was left of her splattering on Acolyte's cheeks. From underneath the club that now rested firmly on the floor, only a few strands of hair and a single twitching limb could be seen.

Up rose the club, a few threads of blood clinging to it, and all that was left was a quivering mass of flesh.

"Ah—ahh—ahh—ah—"

Acolyte's legs trembled, and her strength left her. She could hardly stand up anymore. She felt something warm and damp running down her leg.

"GRRROR…!"

"GROB! GROB!"

One by one, step by step, the goblins came closer with an agonizing slowness. Their dirty yellow eyes burned with cruel desire; their disgusting gazes ran up and down Acolyte's body. Acolyte, who had fallen on her behind, could only flail both hands in the direction of the approaching monsters.

"N-noo! Stop—stop it, please…!"

She struggled and fought.

One of the goblins gave an annoyed wave of his hand to their bodyguard, the troll.

"GROB!"

"TOOOORLL!"

Whoosh. A single swing of the club. It was as easy as snapping a twig.

There was a dry crack as Acolyte's leg broke, pointing off in an unnatural direction.

"Eeeyyaaaarrrrrghhh!!?!?"

Her pitiful shout echoed throughout the burial chamber.

It was only moments before Acolyte vanished behind a wall of goblins.

Sad to say, for her and her friends, the adventure ended here.

§

We repeat ourselves, but it bears reiteration. We should elucidate the mistake they made.

They had all their gear. The party was well balanced.

They were vigilant and resolute, and they let nothing disrupt their formation.

Yet, they were all destroyed. Why?

The god Truth, seated in the high heaven, would no doubt smile and say:

"Just because I was set on bringing down a party today."

§

O adventurer, O journey of mine
Does a dragon or a golem await me
Or perhaps a ghostly knight?
And there must be legendary gear somewhere
With just a torch and a spear
And a staff, life is easy.

To east or west, I cross a bridge
Perhaps to die on the other side
But I seek only love
A princess I would cherish, but I don't ask much
Just a night's pleasure
O adventurer, O journey of mine!

The six party members headed for the intended site of the training facility, accompanied by Priestess humming a little song. Once, supposedly, there had been a small village here, but the field was now covered in tents, with people milling about busily.

Some of those present bore the marks of old wounds on their bodies; they must have been retired adventurers. Were they happy that there was still work for them to do even after they had quit adventuring? Or were they frustrated that they had to keep working even after they had retired?

Priestess, unable to decide, looked from one person to the next. Then she saw a woman coming their way, and she blinked.

It was an elf. An especially beautiful one, her sensuous body draped in revealing clothes. The hint of perfume that lingered as she passed by immediately marked her out as a prostitute.

"Whoa..." the boy breathed. Apparently, Priestess wasn't the only one whose attention the elf had caught.

A sidelong glance at High Elf Archer showed that her face was red; she was turned away and trying to pretend nothing was happening.

Priestess was relieved to discover that Goblin Slayer didn't appear to have any particular reaction; she tried to suppress the flush in her own cheeks.

"Y-you know, I had heard rumors, but…"

"Ha-ha-ha-ha. Men are simple creatures, aren't they?" Lizard Priest said with a great guffaw, slapping his tail against the earth. "When there's a way to spend money, they will spend it like water. And then they'll work to earn more to spend."

"Yeah," High Elf Archer said, glancing at Dwarf Shaman beside her. Almost as if by magic, he had pulled out a skewer of meat from somewhere and was digging in lustily. "I see what you mean…"

"It's that insufferable nobility of yours that keeps you from enjoying the pleasures of a good bit of street food," Dwarf Shaman said, munching away. He finished the entire skewer with the gusto of a starving man then casually cracked the wooden stick in two. He licked the grease off his fingers then let out a pointed sigh and eyed High Elf Archer's thin frame. "I know you elves like to keep the weight off, but you could use a *little* meat on your bones, if you know what I mean…"

"…Hmph! I resent that! I'll have you know that elves—"

And off they went, bantering as ever. The rest of the party regarded this as merely normal, but Wizard Boy wasn't used to it. He tugged on Priestess's sleeve, looking a little panicked. "Er, uh, h-hey. D-don'tcha think we should st-stop them or something?"

"Oh, they're good friends," she said with a smile, and that was it.

The boy looked at the two demi-humans in disbelief. The various passersby took note of them but didn't seem unduly bothered; it was all just another day for a bunch of adventurers.

Wizard Boy looked desperately at Goblin Slayer, but he was acting as though none of this affected him, and Lizard Priest was doing the same.

"Indeed, even so. Here, give me one of those," Lizard Priest said. He appeared to be buying something with cheese on it. He ate it in a single gulp and announced, "Nectar! Mm, sweet nectar. If anyone were to ask what is my joy in life, I would have to answer: it is this."

Absolutely beaming (yes, lizardmen can beam), he nodded happily. "I suppose, as the song said, a night loving an adventurer is never just a night."

"Well, uh, I mean, I understand that, but…"

The Earth Mother was the goddess of the harvest and closely related to marriage and childbirth. Priestess exhaled and shook her head, just trying to clear her mind for a moment.

After all, there was serious work ahead. She had to focus.

She gripped her sounding staff with both hands and took a deep breath. She reviewed the procedure in her head. *All right.*

"Er, well then, Goblin Slayer, sir. Shall we go?"

"Yes." He nodded briefly, prompting the slightest of smiles from Priestess. It seemed she had been right: no problems with the first step.

"Awesome! So we're getting right down to kickin' some goblin ass, huh?" Priestess didn't know what exactly Wizard Boy thought was going on, but he struck the ground emphatically with his staff.

"Er, I'm afraid not yet…" she said.

"Don't be stupid," Goblin Slayer said, less diplomatically than Priestess. "We have to gather information. We're going to see the quest giver."

§

First, we should observe their skills.

Wizard Boy's power and Priestess's ability to command. It was the perfect opportunity to discover both.

There were no objections to Goblin Slayer's proposal, and soon the party set out with the red-haired boy in tow.

The quest this time came from the foreman leading the work on the training facility, an important figure within the Carpenters Guild. He was seated in a tent on the edge of the building area, a dwarf with a black beard who looked as craggy as if he had been carved from stone.

He poured something from a beautiful glass carafe into some cups and offered them to the adventurers. It was chilled grape wine, and it felt wonderful on throats that were dry from all the talking they had been doing.

"Whyn't yeh put out th'fire wine, brother?" Dwarf Shaman asked.

"Y'damn fool. Only dwarves can start in on the spirits at midday and still keep t'workin'. Yeh've humans there, haven't yeh, brother?"

After this exchange, Dwarf Shaman and the foreman shared some kind of greeting in the Dwarvish tongue. It happened to take the form of three toasts:

"To your long Dwarven beard,
to the gods' dice,
to adventurers and monsters!"

The foreman wiped some droplets from his dark beard and said, "Right, then. Some days ago, a party that's been making a name for themselves took me up on this quest."

Goblin Slayer took a swallow of wine and interjected, "And they didn't come back."

"Sure enough," the foreman replied bluntly.

He was dealing with a Silver-ranked adventurer, but he himself was a dwarf, beloved of steel and fire. There was no way he could fail to recognize the man before him; that equipment was too unique.

"You're the one they call Beard-cutter," he said.

"Yes." Goblin Slayer gave a slow nod. "Some call me that."

"Goblin Slayer...," the foreman said softly, then he smiled and drained the cup he was holding in a single gulp as though it were water. "What do you want to know?"

"Goblins." It was less a question than a statement.

"Yeah. Well, maybe not just goblins but certainly plenty of them." The foreman crossed his short, beefy arms and grunted, revealing canines polished to a sharp point. *Those accursed goblins.* "For now, they're just stealing tools... Well, there's nothing 'just' about that at a construction site, but anyway, it would be trouble for us if they started hurting anyone."

"So it is goblins."

"I know a bunch of laborers aren't like a kidnapped goodwife or merchant. And I know goblin work doesn't pay much."

"Yes. That is the nature of it." Goblin Slayer nodded.

"Hey, Orcbolg..." High Elf Archer jabbed him with her elbow. The foreman frowned to have his conversation interrupted by an elf, but he said nothing. He knew enough of the world to know adventurers had their own ways.

"What is it?" The helmet turned to her with its blunt question.

The elf shook her ears and whispered, "This is all well and good so far, but you're not forgetting that *she's* giving the orders today, right?"

"I'm not."

"...Are you sure?"

"However, I will take over in an emergency."

"Yes, please. I'd very much appreciate that," Priestess said with a smile and a polite bow of her head. "That would be much safer."

This was absolutely how Priestess felt. She would far rather be shown incompetent than see her party wiped by her own fault. Skill might improve with experience, but a fallen companion could not be brought back.

Watching the forthright and brave young woman, the dwarf foreman let out a sound of admiration.

"So then, um," Priestess began.

"Ahem. What can I do for you, m'lass?"

"Thank you, sir. I'd like to take over the questioning, if you don't mind." She leaned in and managed to meet his eyes. "These goblins... er, whatever monsters they may be. Can you describe the ruins they're living in?"

"I can. One of the damn fools who got his tools stolen got all hot under the collar and tried to follow them, but I stopped him." The foreman snorted. He seemed less upset at the goblin who had taken the tools than he did at the carpenter who had lost them.

"That's just how dwarves are," Dwarf Shaman leaned in and whispered helpfully to Priestess. "We don't look kindly on those who treat their tools lightly."

That made sense. Priestess nodded. "In that case, we should certainly bring back any of the stolen tools we can find," she said.

"I'd appreciate that," the foreman said, his face softening into a smile. "And maybe that moron will be more careful the next time around."

Ah, good. Priestess allowed herself an internal moment of triumph. You had to have a good relationship with the quest giver and other locals. That was a thought she had come up with on her own, but it was also one of Goblin Slayer's precepts. Adventurers could never get anywhere without other people's support.

"Anyway, it's a place just a little north of here. I can make a map for you. I suspect it's a—"

"Mausoleum," Goblin Slayer interjected. He took another swig of wine and, apparently oblivious to the looks he was getting, went on. "I've heard it's in a common style, a collection of burial chambers connected by paths."

"Well, now, you know it?"

"Long ago," Goblin Slayer said softly, "I was warned not to go near it."

Then he fell silent again. Priestess blinked at him.

Long ago.

Now that she thought about it, she had spent an entire year at his side, yet she hardly knew anything about his past.

He had an older sister. He's been an adventurer for five or six years. He slays goblins.

She was familiar with some of his personal qualities, like his surprising kindness and consideration for others, but how much did she really know about *him*?

"..."

No. Now isn't the time. It can't be. She shook her head. She mustn't run away from her duties as the point person on the goblin-slaying quest that was fast approaching.

"Ahem," Priestess said. "So is there anything strange about the entrance to that mausoleum? Bones or paintings or anything?"

"The fool didn't mention anything o' the sort, assuming he didn't just forget to see it."

No totems, then.

Priestess tapped a pale finger against her lips and murmured, "Right, right."

That suggested the absence of any shamans, an advanced class. Of course, a year of adventuring had made her painfully aware that they weren't the only possible threat. It was crucial not to underestimate the enemy.

So now, what was important was...

"Do you happen to know the rank and party composition of the people who went in before us?"

"I don't recall who was what rank, but it was a mix of Porcelains and Obsidians. As far as their classes, just judging by what I saw—"

The foreman crossed his arms and looked up at the ceiling of the tent. He searched his memory, crooking his fingers as he listed them off.

"A lizardman warrior and a cleric—a warrior-priest. Then there was a wizard, another cleric, and some kind of thief or assassin."

"Were any of them women?"

"Two of them. The warrior-priest and the cleric—or, er, maybe she was what you'd call an acolyte?"

Something cold whispered in Priestess's gut: *That means we can hope for two left alive… at best.*

She bit her lip, having no choice but to accept the fact.

"Is there a chance you have any potions to spare?" she asked. "We'll pay for them, of course."

They had prepared ahead of time, naturally, but it never hurt to have plenty of healing items. The ability to heal without using up a miracle recommended potions very highly.

"Sure, not a problem," the foreman responded generously. "Anything else you need?"

"Hmm… Well, if there's a doctor around, please have them wait here…"

As they continued talking, Goblin Slayer mumbled a low "Hrm." He turned to Lizard Priest. "What do you think?"

"I think her judgment is correct," answered Lizard Priest, who had stayed out of the conversation until that point. "Two at most. But I'm almost certain they've all been destroyed."

"Wha—?!" Wizard Boy goggled at the cleric's fluent declaration. Lizard Priest's bulbous reptilian eyes turned and stared at him.

"Something the matter?"

"N-no…"

"Mm, indeed? Oh, gracious, there's cheese. What considerate people. Pardon me."

Lizard Priest ignored the boy's disturbed gaze and reached out a scaly hand. He grabbed a serving plate near Priestess and the foreman and pulled it close, happily grabbing some of what was on it. It was cheese, most likely served as an accompaniment to the wine. A smile came over his great jaws.

"Ahh, nectar, sweet nectar! Goodness me. Is this cheese also from your farm, milord Goblin Slayer?"

"Most likely."

"Perfection!"

He acted genuinely untroubled, and as a matter of fact, he was. To the lizardmen, it was simply natural that all living things might one day die. Sooner or later, the moment would come. They might have different ways of life; some might be stronger than others; and each would die in their own way. But those were the only differences.

He swallowed the bulging mouthful of cheese then licked the tip of his nose with his tongue.

"I think we may suspect something besides goblins down there," he said.

"Yes," Goblin Slayer agreed. "If there are no totems, though, it means there probably aren't any shamans."

"Yet, the adventurers failed to return. I should certainly hope it's not another Paladin."

"A hob would be easier prey."

"Or almost any other kind of Non-Prayer."

"At any rate, traps are the real danger."

"A mausoleum will be made of stone. Perhaps we can suppose that there won't be any bursting through walls."

"They've stolen some construction tools, but it's not like working through earth. I suspect we're dealing with about twenty of them."

"Yet, I think we can assume their numbers have been diminished somewhat. I can't imagine five adventurers failed to kill even one goblin."

"Regardless, we haven't time. When they tire of their captives, they will come in force."

"We must deal with them in one fell swoop, then. Do you think we can do it?"

"It will depend on the girl's judgment."

"Even so."

The conversation between them flew so fast it left the boy blinking his eyes wildly.

It was well known that the lizardmen were powerful warriors, but he had never actually seen one up close. And then there was the adventurer talking to the lizardman, with his grimy armor and cheap-looking helmet. He was the one they called the kindest man on the frontier.

There was a major difference, though, between knowing something intellectually and seeing it for oneself. So when he heard High Elf Archer give a lazy yawn, he glared in her direction.

"...What's with you?" he asked. "Don't you do anything around here?"

"When the timing's right," High Elf Archer said. She languidly wiped a tear from the corner of her eye, and her ears twitched. "I'm a scout and a ranger. I let other people handle the rest."

"She's right about that, boy," Dwarf Shaman interjected. He seemed thoroughly into his cups by now; he was pouring himself some fire wine from the flask at his hip.

"H-hey, we're about to start an adventure, here!"

"Don' be stupid, child. A dwarf who's not drunk is like a stone at the side of the road." Then he coughed. Even from where he was standing, Wizard Boy could smell the alcohol on his breath. "For once, I agree with Long-Ears there. Spell casters need to be able to modulate their emotions."

"You didn't need to say *for once*," High Elf Archer said with a sniff. "I only say the wisest and most sophisticated things."

"Seriously?"

"Seriously."

Suddenly, Dwarf Shaman seemed at a loss for words. He opened his mouth to respond but then noticed the boy's disbelieving look.

He cleared his throat once. "Anyhow. We've each our own roles to play," he said.

"Roles?" the boy said, pursing his lips suspiciously. "You mean like how he's a warrior and I'm a wizard?"

"No! Not remotely!" Dwarf Shaman said, gesturing as if he were swatting a fly. "Beard-cutter and Scaly there are our front-row fighters, so it falls to them to work out a strategy ahead of time."

"The girl is doing the talking today because of how we decided to approach this quest," High Elf Archer said, drawing a circle in the air with an extended pointer finger. "Usually she takes care of the cargo, makes sure we have our supplies. All sorts of details."

"You could stand to be a little more diligent yourself, Long-Ears."

High Elf Archer's ears went back, and she growled angrily, but Dwarf Shaman just put a hand on the boy's shoulder.

"Take a good look, boy," he said. "Remember this."

"…"

Wizard Boy studied Dwarf Shaman silently then pushed the calloused hand away. "Carrying the cargo just means doing all the chores, doesn't it?"

High Elf Archer chuckled to see Dwarf Shaman brushed off like this, but the dwarf, undaunted, laughed a great belly laugh.

When Priestess had finished her exchange, the party put their heads together and began to discuss. The boy watched them intently from one side of the tent.

"…If you can slaughter some goblins, isn't that good enough?" he muttered, so softly that no one in the party heard.

§

The mausoleum was buried among some small hills, its mouth yawning open. Above the entrance was a hillock on which grew grass and trees; whether the hill had been built over the entrance or the entrance had been dug into the hill was impossible to say. It had been weathered by far too many months and years.

It was past noon when the adventurers arrived. They were losing the spring light, the sun having passed its zenith, its rays now slanting down over the land. It would be nearing twilight soon, and then all would be swallowed up by darkness.

The perfect moment.

"I get it now," High Elf Archer said to Goblin Slayer with a laugh, her ears twitching with distinct interest. "This is definitely the sort of place kids would come play in."

"Yes. That's why I was told not to."

"But I s'pose yeh did anyway," Dwarf Shaman said with a smirk, as if expecting a story of some youthful mischief. He gave Goblin Slayer a poke with his elbow for emphasis.

Goblin Slayer reached through his hazy memories, trying to recall some distant day. It was more than ten years ago now—no, exactly ten years, and he had been a different person.

"..."

Had he gone in there? He couldn't remember.

He doubted it, though. Doing so would have earned him a severe scolding from his sister. He knew it was wrong to cause trouble for her. So he would not have gone near the mausoleum. Probably.

"Never mind," Goblin Slayer said with a slight shake of his head.

"A'right," Dwarf Shaman said shortly. "Nothing you can tell us about the inside, then?"

"I was told it was constructed of hallways and burial rooms." *Yes.* Goblin Slayer nodded. He remembered now. "That's what my sister said."

She had told him because he wanted to know what was inside. She had researched whose grave it was and then told him.

That was why he hadn't gone inside nor even gone near it.

He wished dearly that he could remember. All of it. He didn't want to forget.

But now his memories were like moth-eaten clothes. The finer details had been wiped out, and everything was ambiguous.

Ten years—ten whole years. To think, there had once been a village there.

"Whatever the case, that was long ago now," Goblin Slayer said. Then he forcefully changed the subject. "So what do you think?"

"Hmm... Well, there aren't any totems, and no guards, either," Priestess replied. She tapped a finger against her lips, taking stock of the ruins before them.

Just near the entrance, she saw the piles of waste that were characteristic of goblin holes. But that was it. She didn't see any of the childish animal symbols that goblins worshipped.

At least we can be pretty confident there are no shamans...

"C'mon, let's just go already! They've got those other adventurers captive, don't they?!"

Priestess felt a slight twinge in her heart at the boy's impassioned exclamation.

He's just the way I was a year ago.

She had been so ready to go along when the boy, the monk, and the wizard had said, "Let's hurry and help those people!"

She still remembered how that had turned out. Even though she didn't want to. It haunted her dreams.

So what about who she was now? She was still anxious, cowardly, and frightened, but…

"Well, but wait." It was Lizard Priest's great hand that came to Priestess's rescue as she stood there caught in the whirlwind of her own thoughts. The clawed, scaly hand rested on her shoulder. "Long has it been said that haste makes waste."

"Right…" Priestess nodded. *Calm down. You can take your time. Be precise.*

First, they needed to…do a final check of their equipment.

"Everyone, is your gear in order?" she asked, checking through her own equipment as she spoke.

She had her sounding staff, and she was wearing her mail. In her bag were her potions, as well as her Adventurer's Toolkit. Mustn't forget that.

There was a whole medley of things, in fact. Wedges and rope, nails and a hammer, chalk and candles, and much more.

Can't leave anything behind.

This was the way they always started, but still, she was glad to see that nobody questioned their temporary leader.

Grimy leather armor, a cheap-looking steel helmet, a sword of a strange length, and a small, round shield, along with a bag full of miscellany.

As Goblin Slayer inventoried his equipment, High Elf Archer restrung the spider's-silk string on her bow. Dwarf Shaman checked his bag of catalysts, and Lizard Priest counted up how many dragon fangs he had.

Only the boy did less: he looked at his staff, and then at his robe, and that was it.

"And what would you have us do next, milady leader?"

"Oh, stop it. You're enjoying this, I'm sure of it." Priestess puffed out her cheeks.

"Ha! Ha! Ha! Ha! Ha!" Lizard Priest laughed, his massive jaws opening.

"*For heaven's sake,*" Priestess muttered, but it was true that time was dear. They had to decide on their formation.

"We may have to modify this based on how wide the passages are," she said, "but since we have six people this time, I think two rows of three, or three rows of two, would be best."

Sounds good. High Elf Archer nodded. Then she pointed to the entrance, eyeballing the size. "My guess—assuming the paths are the same width as the entranceway—is that columns of three would work."

"Hmm. Okay, three rows of two it is," Priestess said, then clapped her hands. If the passages turned out to be a little wide, this would be easier. "If there's enough room to go three abreast, we can interchange our formation if need be."

"Perfect," High Elf Archer replied. "Can't argue with our leader, can we?" She winked and chuckled.

"Oh, stop..." Priestess let out another sigh. "As far as how we'll line up..."

She mulled it over a bit but, in the end, went with their usual formation. Goblin Slayer and High Elf Archer would be in front. Priestess herself and the red-haired wizard boy would be in the middle, and Lizard Priest and Dwarf Shaman would make up the rear. If they encountered enemies ahead, High Elf Archer and Lizard Priest would switch places. If there was an attack from behind, Dwarf Shaman and Goblin Slayer would do so.

This ought to work... I'm pretty sure...

"You're not gonna put the magic users at the back?!"

"Enemies don't just attack from the front, you know," Priestess said, smiling ambiguously and shaking her head. She of all people could not possibly take the rear for granted.

"Oh, and..." she added.

"...What?"

"We have to make sure to cover our scent."

She clapped her hands again. High Elf Archer frowned. The boy made a sound of incomprehension.

They had three people there wearing fresh, clean clothes. In contrast, they only had two perfume pouches.

And the young women were in no mood to give them up.

§

"GROB?!"

"GROOROB!!"

The adventurers piled into the mausoleum like an avalanche. This complex, the resting place of heroes, was now no more than a hideout for goblins. The coffins had been overturned, the offerings stolen, and all manner of refuse and pollution littered the marble floors.

The warrior was in front. Grimy leather armor, a cheap-looking helmet, a sword of a strange length, and a small, round shield, along with a torch.

"Goblins," Goblin Slayer said. "Five of them."

He had hardly finished speaking when his sword went flying. Its aim was true; it pierced the throat of one of the goblins.

"GORB?!"

The creature had opened his mouth wide, about to call out to his companions, but instead of a shout, a bloodied froth bubbled up out of his mouth. He gave a choked scream as he drowned in his own blood, sending dark flecks flying.

Speed above all was the key to a hack and slash.

"One."

Of course, the other four goblins were not about to remain silent in the face of their comrade's murder.

"GROOR!!"

"GROB! GOORB!!"

Were they calling for reinforcements? No, it was pure murderousness. Revenge. They wanted to swarm the adventurers, beat them down, have their way with them. The goblins' little heads filled with hatred, and with dagger and spear and club in hand, they advanced on the adventurers…

"Make that two!" No sooner had the clear voice sounded than one of the creatures slumped against the wall as if simply tired. His skull was pierced by a bud-tipped arrow; with the bolt lodged in his brain, he twitched once and died.

We hardly need mention that it was High Elf Archer who fired the shot. She jumped gracefully backward even as she readied her next arrow.

"GORO?!"

"Hrmph."

Goblin Slayer raised his shield to cover her retreat, using it to sweep aside one of the onrushing goblins. At the same time, he picked up the club the monster dropped and brought it down on the unfortunate creature's skull.

"Three."

The goblin died without even a squeak. Goblin Slayer gave the weapon a shake to clean off the brains.

Three goblins dead in nearly the time it took to blink. They had taken full advantage of their opportunity.

"Sons of bitches!" One member of their party, his brand-new cape covered in unspeakable waste products, seemed to think now would be a good time to join in. He raised his staff theatrically. "*Carbunculus... Crescunt...*"

"Don't use your spells yet!" Priestess said firmly.

"Wha—?!" the boy exclaimed, but this wasn't the time for argument. Conserving your magic was the most basic of basics. Priestess was thinking fast, sweat pouring down her forehead.

With this group more than any other, she hadn't expected to have to give detailed instructions in the middle of battle.

Take in the whole situation. Even if the battlefield was chaotic, it was much better to do something now than to think of it later.

Imagination is a weapon, too...as he *says.*

All the knowledge she had acquired to this point, the many experiences she'd had, bubbled through her mind. There were two more goblins, closing in on them with crude weapons in their hands. Not counting the one they had entered through, the burial chamber had three doors, one in each direction.

"The doors!"

"On it!" High Elf Archer said. As the elf passed by Priestess on her way to the back, the leader handed over the Adventurer's Toolkit. They would shove the wedges under the doors to keep them shut. It was something only High Elf Archer, with her agility, could do.

"With just the two of them, I think we should be fine for now," she said. After all, Dwarf Shaman could use four entire spells. They would need to have him keep some on hand, just in case.

Just as the boy had been told earlier, sometimes the best thing a spell caster could do was nothing.

"Now then, I should hope that I will have a chance to join the fight," Lizard Priest said, waving his tail.

"The enemy is still numerous," Goblin Slayer replied.

It was at this moment that they needed the fighting strength of their warriors.

Goblin Slayer was in a deep stance, his shield at the ready; he held a club in his right hand. In his own way, he cut a comical figure.

Considering they were fighting goblins, however, no one in the room had the gall to laugh.

"We can hardly be frittering away our time here, in that case," Lizard Priest said, and he was exactly right. He spread his arms wide, and then with claws and fangs and tail, he demolished the two remaining goblins, tearing them limb from limb.

But this merits no special remark.

There were still many goblins to come.

§

"Can we really afford to take our time like this?"

"If we don't go room by room, we could put ourselves in danger."

They had cleaned up the goblins in two or three of the chambers. In this mausoleum, in which several rooms were sometimes linked, the layout was easy enough to follow, but it meant a lot of chambers to check. The constant work of finding and eliminating goblins left them aching to their bones.

Wizard Boy jabbed irritably at the stone floor with his staff, prompting Priestess to take a comforting tone.

"But think about it," the boy said, scowling. "Those captives could be in danger..."

That was certainly true. Priestess, too, was worried about the adventurers who had come before them. There were traces—dried blood here, a goblin corpse there. But no more than that. It wasn't even certain whether or not their predecessors were still alive.

But...almost certainly not, a cold voice whispered deep in her heart.

Still... She bit her lip gently. That was no reason to give up hope.

"How do the other rooms look?" she called to High Elf Archer, pushing the welter of unpleasant thoughts to one corner of her mind.

The elf pressed her ear to a wooden door, seeking a sound; she peeked in the keyhole and finally concluded, "Unlocked and empty." Then, however, she pointed to the top edge of the door with one slim finger. "But look at that."

What appeared to be a piece of string was caught in the gap. If they opened the door, the string would fall, and something might come collapsing down on them.

"A trap?" Goblin Slayer asked.

"Looks like," she answered.

Goblin Slayer *humph*ed softly. He tossed away his spent torch, trading it for a new one, which he lighted with a flint. He pulled out a spear stuck in a goblin corpse, checked the tip, then threw it away. The dagger at the creature's hip would be more useful.

He picked up the weapon and put it into his sheath. It was a bit rusty, but you could still stab something with it. He considered it disposable anyway.

Lastly, he went through the pile of stolen loot and came up with a battle-ax that he liked the looks of. It was a single-handed weapon, but surprisingly heavy.

"Troublesome," he declared, even as he rested the ax on his shoulder.

"Go figure," High Elf Archer said with a shrug of her elegant shoulders.

Priestess pattered up alongside them, standing on her tiptoes to look at the top of the door. The string wasn't very thick, and the construction was quite simple. But that didn't mean they could relax. It might connect to something as crude as a rusty nail, but if that nail happened to catch you in the face, you would still die from it. Or perhaps there was poison involved.

Priestess furrowed her shapely eyebrows. She could think of a number of possibilities.

"Come to think of it…the foreman said the goblins had stolen some tools, didn't he?"

"Not that I want t'think about what goblins might do with good carpenter's tools," Dwarf Shaman growled, his arms crossed. He ran a hand over his receding hairline then inspected the string. "Doesn't look t'me like it's attached to anything all that heavy. Whatever it leads to, it's not very elaborate."

"We could also consider taking a different route." Lizard Priest slapped his tail against the stone floor. "There were two other doors besides that which led us to this one. The goblins don't seem to know we're here yet."

"Hmm…"

What to do? Which direction to go?

With the party's collective gaze on her, Priestess rifled through her bag and took out the map. It was a simple, hand-drawn affair, in quill pen on sheepskin. This party didn't have a dedicated cartographer. If they went through some of the sealed-off chambers to come around to the booby-trapped room…

Her thoughts were interrupted by the boy's shout. "Arrrgh! I can't stand it anymore!!" He was no longer trying to hide his annoyance as he pointed his staff at the door. "This is where the goblins live, right?! They don't even know how to set a real trap!"

"Oh! No, wait! Don't just—"

"Outta my way! I'll open that door!"

High Elf Archer may have been Silver-ranked, but the boy was still easily able to pull her aside.

"Wha—? Oh, uh, ummm—!"

She had to stop him. Yet, despite this desperate thought, Priestess couldn't seem to form even a full word. What should she say, and how should she say it? Now that she thought about it, she realized everyone had simply obeyed her orders to this point. She didn't have any idea how to deal with someone who refused to listen.

"..."

Priestess looked desperately at Goblin Slayer, but he said nothing. She didn't know what expression was hidden within that steel helmet. Did he appear disinterested? Or...

If... If he gives up on me...!

The thought was more than enough to shake Priestess to her core. A cold, quiet voice began to taunt her from somewhere in her mind.

What should I do? What should I do? What should I dowhatshouldIdo-whatshouldI...?

Her thoughts raced, but she couldn't say anything. She reached out, hoping to at least hold him back, but the boy was already opening the door...

"Eeyaaaahhhhhh?!" he shrieked as he saw something tumbling down.

His scream echoed around the burial chamber; it seemed loud enough to reach the very depth of the mausoleum. Wizard Boy fell backward, scrambling out of the way of the falling object.

"Wha-wha-wh-wh-wha-wh-what the hell is that...?!"

It was a hand and an arm. They had been torn off so violently that they almost looked like they had been put through a meat grinder. They had once belonged to a woman.

They were lovely limbs with well-developed muscles, but now they looked tragic. It was almost impossible to contemplate what must have befallen their former owner.

"A bit of goblin mischief," Goblin Slayer said with a cluck of his tongue. "They just wanted to *frighten* us."

"U-ugh ..." Priestess moaned involuntarily. She felt something bitter and acidic rising up her throat; with tears in her eyes, she swallowed it back down.

This was no time to be losing her nerve. Hadn't she seen plenty of similar things before?

She desperately told herself to keep control. She gripped her sounding staff as firmly as she could in her shaking hands.

"I've got a bad feeling about this," High Elf Archer said, giving Priestess an encouraging pat on the back. She didn't look much better than her leader; she had flipped up her collar to hide her pale face and lips. "With that scream, there might as well have been an alarm on that door."

"I think that was the idea," Goblin Slayer murmured with no sign of agitation; he took up a fighting stance with his ax in hand. "I believe we will soon have company."

"I can't be sure, but—"

"—GY-GYAAAH...!!"

High Elf Archer had just been giving a flick of her long ears when a woman's high-pitched scream echoed through the mausoleum.

All the adventurers froze, but only for an instant; a second later, they had each readied their weapons.

The only exception among them was Wizard Boy.

"...It came from over here!"

"No! You can't go alo—"

The boy rushed off, paying no heed to the voice that tried to stop him. He kicked down the door of the burial chamber, pushing into the next room, turning this way and that until he found what he was looking for.

"This has to be it...!"

He rammed the door with his shoulder, forcing it open.

The moment he did so, a wet, choking stench assaulted him. Part of it came from the goblin waste that was scattered everywhere. Some came from blood and vomit.

Then the boy saw them.

The goblin.

And the woman.

The woman, tied to a chair with bits of wire that bit into her pale, soft skin and flesh.

Her eyes, open as wide as they could be, streaming with tears.

The ax in the goblin's hand, covered with dark red stains.

And then the woman's bloodied hand.

The red liquid that dribbled along the chair's armrest.

And in the pool of blood, several pale, dainty...

"Ee—yaaaaaaaaaahhhhhhhhh!!" the boy howled.

He was still bellowing as he fell upon the goblin, battering it with his staff. His heart and mind were aflame with rage, and the fire of his emotions spontaneously caused words of true power to weave themselves on his lips.

"Carbunculus… Crescunt… Iacta!! Fly, O sphere of flame!"

The Fireball streaked through the air, trailing a burning tail. It flew true, slamming into the goblin's skull. Brains and blood and shattered bits of bone erupted everywhere, and the now headless goblin collapsed to the ground.

"*Pant, pant, pant*… Take…that…!"

It was…nothing. Nothing at all.

He had killed another living being without so much as laying a finger on it. It didn't feel real.

He had sent a goblin to its doom in a single stroke, just like he had wanted—it was surreal.

The entire interrogation room, the whole awful scene, swirled around him; he couldn't quite grasp it.

"Anyway, I have to help her… Hey, you all right?!"

But he should have paid more attention to what he had done.

The only spell he could use was Fireball, and he could only use it once per day.

He should have remembered the alarm earlier. And the fact that this was a goblin nest.

"Ahhh…hhh… Errr…g…"

"Just hold on! I'll get you out of here right away!"

The boy was focused completely on cutting the wire that bound the woman's limbs to the chair.

That was why he didn't notice. The boy didn't register the obvious fact that there must have been something there that had wiped out the other adventuring party.

"…Errgh… Nngh… Ah…"

"—?!"

It was no skill of his, but sheer luck, that sent him tumbling backward, just avoiding the club that came smashing past him an instant later.

"Wh-whoa—?!"

The blood drained from his head. He discovered that at times of true panic, one's legs become unreliable.

"OLRLLT…?"

He saw a massive, lumpy shape covered in old scars. He smelled a body odor strong enough to make him nauseous.

The creature's bald head seemed like the very embodiment of stupidity, and its face bore an unrestrained, moronic grin.

It had arms the size of tree trunks, and it carried a huge club. And the innumerable nails that studded the club, there to rend and tear flesh, spoke to the murder in the monster's heart.

A troll.

The creature hefted the club as if unsure why its attack had missed. The boy caught sight of some dark red stains on the weapon, and bits of hair that looked like they belonged to a woman…

"Errg… Ugghh…!"

The boy clenched his jaw to prevent his teeth from chattering. Holding out his staff, he stood.

Behind him was an injured, barely conscious, captive woman.

He couldn't run away. Not even if he wanted to. And yet, what was he to do?

As a wizard in training, the boy was naturally familiar with trolls from an academic perspective. Of course he was.

They were huge. Powerful. Stupid. And they had regenerative powers—dealing with them demanded fire or acid.

There was a problem, though.

He was out of spells.

"GRORB!"

"GRB! GROBRORO!!"

And that was not all.

He heard the cackling of goblins echo around the burial chamber, and he knew that things had just gotten worse.

They had put out the bait, and he had swallowed it hook, line, and sinker.

Why would they go out of their way to torture a captive in a place like this? And (as it happened) immediately after some stupid intruder had been screaming, no less!

The doors on every side of the burial chamber opened. Goblins came tromping in, chuckling all the while.

I shoulda listened when that elf suggested circling around the other way…!

But it was too late for regrets now.

This was a trap. One designed to catch adventurers who were advancing room by room.

By the time he realized this, the spell-less young man had only one course of action left.

He licked his dry lips. He took a deep breath and put it all into shouting:

"Stay back! It's a trap—!"

This would be the boy's final action.

An instant later, a hand ax came flying, an arrow whistled through the air, and a Swordclaw flashed.

"GRBRR?!" Screaming and shouting, the goblins collapsed like wheat under the scythe.

"There are twenty of them. Seventeen left."

The voice was as calm as a wind blowing under the ground, and with it, Goblin Slayer leaped into the fray. His empty right hand moved as precisely as a machine, drawing out his dagger and transitioning instantly to a strike at the neck of a confused goblin.

"GROORORB!!"

"Hmph… Four. Sixteen left."

The rusty blade, unable to withstand the force of the impact, shattered and went flying, but it was enough to deal a critical blow to the goblin's spine.

Goblin Slayer gave a click of his tongue and tossed the hilt aside, grabbing instead the sword carried by the collapsing goblin. He drew it by giving the monster a careless kick as it died. He rotated his wrist, taking up a vigilant fighting posture.

"Alive?"

Wizard Boy nodded repeatedly. "Uh, y-yeah… I'm—"

"Not you," Goblin Slayer said coldly, cutting him off.

"I believe he's curious about the young lady over there," Lizard Priest said, scuttling over and taking up a defensive position in front of the relieved boy.

"Yeah!" the boy exclaimed, swallowing heavily. "She's alive! Of course she is!"

"I see," Goblin Slayer said, and from behind his visor, he fixed a reproving gaze on the boy. Not that Wizard Boy was actually sure quite where the man was looking behind his metal helmet. But he thought he felt it. He closed his eyes and tried to offer an excuse.

"I just… I wanted to help her as soon as I could—"

"There are women on our side as well," Goblin Slayer said, his voice sharp and cold. "Two of them."

This caused the boy to draw a sharp breath and look in the women's direction.

"Ugh. This is why I hate goblins…"

"…Hrk…"

High Elf Archer was pale from the sight of the torture chamber, but she let off one arrow after another to keep the troll at bay.

Beside her, Priestess could only offer a sort of stricken gasp; the hands that clutched her staff trembled gently.

"But…!" The boy was about to offer a rebuttal, but Dwarf Shaman came bounding up and shouted angrily, "This is no time to chat, boy! Grab the girl, chair and all, and let's get out of here!"

The two warriors and the ranger carved a path, and the shaman and the priestess followed it.

"We're outta time!"

And indeed they were.

"GROROB! GROB! GROORB!!"

"OOOORLLLLT!!"

Their escape route was gone.

Sixteen goblins. One troll. It wasn't precisely a multitude, but the adventurers were surrounded.

Slowly but surely, the monsters advanced, wicked smiles appearing on their faces as they grew ever more sure of victory.

The adventurers circled up to protect the boy, the acolyte who had been taken captive, and Priestess.

"But how are we supposed to carry her…?" The boy hesitantly put a hand to the chair; several indecipherable moans came from the woman's mouth. His hand came away covered in slick, sticky blood. It was enough to make the boy's stomach twist; he felt as if he might vomit then and there.

Lizard Priest, observing him, rolled his eyes in his head, a wide field of vision being a special trait of his people. His tongue slid out of his mouth.

"Don't forget the fingers. If all goes well, we may be able to heal her."

"Oh…!"

The boy tossed himself to the ground, searching quickly through the red liquid.

The rusty ax had cruelly hewn off flesh and bone together. But he didn't have time; no time. The fingers would've been so easy to overlook, but he made sure he found them, counted them, and wrapped them in a cloth.

He tried to wipe away the sweat on his forehead with a grimy, bloodstained hand. He bit his lip hard.

"I've got 'em!"

"Excellent! You, take that side—yes, that one!" Lizard Priest commanded.

There was a clatter as the chair was picked up, mingling with the woman's moans.

High Elf Archer kept them behind her, shielding them, her bow drawn and her ears flapping.

"They're still coming from deeper in!" She glanced at Priestess. "What do we do?!"

"Oh—ah—!"

Priestess found herself unable to speak immediately. Her hands froze on her staff, which she gripped so hard that her hands hurt and her knuckles turned white.

What to do? What was the right thing to do? Fight them here? Or try to break through?

She had to come up with an answer, right away. Yes, and yet—but—

We've fallen into a goblin trap.

Not just fallen into it, run into it.

It was she who had said, *Let's follow him!*

There was no regret. Of course not. But it was enough to make her legs feel unsteady.

She could see Female Wizard, the poison dagger buried in her.

Fighter, being torn to shreds by the little devils.

Female Monk, trapped, beaten mercilessly, violated in the most awful ways.

Calm down. Each time she tried to push away a memory, she simply found the next one waiting for her.

The time the goblin champion nearly crushed her—the terror, the pain, the despair.

The spot on her neck where she had been bitten throbbed.

"Uh… Um…um…!"

The goblins, closing in. That gigantic troll.

Priestess was dying to speak, yet her tongue refused to move.

Tears began to well up at the edges of her eyes; her teeth wouldn't stay still, setting up a terrible chatter.

And all this when she know as well as anyone that this was absolutely not the time for such things…!

"Milord Goblin Slayer!"

Her salvation came in the form of Lizard Priest, who quickly sized up the situation and then called out.

"Right," Goblin Slayer answered dispassionately. "May we?"

Even now he looked for her consent. Priestess nodded weakly. She didn't know what else she could possibly do.

Goblin Slayer's instructions were swift and curt. "Use Holy Light. We push through to the inside. I'll leave the front line to the rest of you. I'll take rear guard and deal with that giant, growling thing."

"Excellent!" Lizard Priest answered promptly.

"R-right!" Priestess, on the other hand, fought to push down her sense of how pathetic she was.

Wizard Boy, working hard to bring the chair along, was agog. *He would deal with it?!*

"You're a warrior, right?! That thing's a *troll*!"

"Dummy," High Elf Archer said, puffing out her small chest knowingly. "It's times like this that Orcbolg is at his best."

Lizard Priest chuckled. This man was not going to be defeated by goblins.

Priestess, however, did not laugh. If she could do nothing else, she would at least perform the duty she had been entrusted with.

She gripped her staff in both hands. Raised her consciousness, appealing directly to the gods in heaven.

"O Earth Mother, abounding in mercy, grant your sacred light to we who are lost in darkness!"

And just so, she was granted a miracle.

"GGRORRRROOB?!"

"TOOLR?! OORTT?!"

There was a flash of blue-white light, like an exploding sun. It seared the eyes of the goblins and the troll.

Priestess, her small chest heaving with the exertion of this soul-shearing supplication, shouted, as much to inspire herself as anyone else, "Let's go!"

As she started running, her staff held high, Lizard Priest appeared alongside her.

Goblins poured out from the burial chambers, filling the path, filling their vision. Lizard Priest lashed out with claws, claws, fangs, tail, sweeping them mercilessly aside.

Following behind him along the path he carved were Dwarf Shaman and Wizard Boy, carrying the prisoner along with them. They had no leeway to cast spells.

High Elf Archer had her arrows constantly at the ready, peppering the road ahead with covering fire even as she ran.

And then—

"A troll?" muttered Goblin Slayer, left behind at the rear. "Not a goblin, then."

"OOOORLLT!!"

The spikes in the monster's club glinted as he brought it down. But blinded as he was, his strength availed him little. Without a hint of panic or even hurry, Goblin Slayer jumped back. He searched through his item pouch and pulled out a small bottle.

When the container smashed against the troll's skin, sending shards everywhere, it did the creature no harm at all.

Of course, it didn't have to.

The important thing was what was inside the bottle.

"TOORL?! TOORRL?!"

An unidentifiable viscous black liquid clung to the troll's giant body. The stuff gave off a nose-prickling smell. The troll flailed about, desperately trying to wipe away the clinging substance, splashing it around.

The monsters had no idea that the stuff was Medea's Oil, petroleum-based gasoline.

"Good-bye."

Without a moment's hesitation, Goblin Slayer pitched his torch at the creature, turning around in the same motion.

"TOOOOROOOOROOOOOORRRT?!?!"

"GROROOB?!"

Howls and bellows came from the troll, totally enveloped in licking flames, and the goblins whom he was catching up in the conflagration.

Goblin Slayer was already running the other direction; as he went, he grabbed a weapon from one of the dead goblins his companions had left behind. It was a hand spear. He held his sword in his left hand and the spear in his right, crouching low as he barreled along.

"That caught perhaps half of them. Meaning..."

The spear went flying. It slammed straight through the stomach of a goblin who had braved the flames, doing him in.

"GGRORR?!"

"That makes fifteen."

Goblin Slayer spun neatly, setting off after his friends once again.

There was no mistaking the route. Doors were left hanging open; goblin corpses were scattered everywhere. He had only to follow the sounds of battle. His real problem was the goblins who continued to pop out from side doors.

"GBGOR?!"

"GRORB! GORORRB?!"

Arrows came flying from afar, cutting them down. That was three more. Eighteen.

Goblin Slayer ran onward, jumping over the bodies that thumped to the ground in front of him.

Soon he spotted High Elf Archer, her braided hair bouncing behind her like a tail.

"Orcbolg, what's going on? I heard some kind of *fwoosh* from back there!"

"It was an emergency situation."

"You could at least give us a little warning!"

"I hadn't thought that far." As he ran, Goblin Slayer turned, as if springing an ambush from midstride. "Nineteen."

The goblin, who had finally caught up with him, was caught off guard by the half turn. A sword was buried ruthlessly in his throat. When it twisted, the goblin frothed blood and died. A kick to the monster's chest freed the blade again.

"How is it up ahead?"

"Just the usual! *Yargh! Blargh!* All kinds of craziness." High Elf Archer fired off two or three more arrows as she spoke, trusting to luck to land a hit. Three goblins collapsed to the ground, writhing, bolts sprouting from their eye sockets. Twenty-two.

"So do you have a plan?" the ranger asked.

"Of course." Goblin Slayer had completed a change of direction in the time it took the elf to kill those three monsters; now he was jogging alongside her. "I always do."

§

There was only one door in the burial chamber to which the adventurers had fled. The other three sides of the room were just walls. All that remained there was the scattered detritus of goblin life.

The room was entirely extraneous to the goblins, who thought about nothing except how to take advantage of exactly what they had on hand at any given moment.

As they set down the woman, still tied to the chair, Wizard Boy suddenly exclaimed, "We've just let 'em corner us—!"

"Oh, that is not necessarily the case," said Lizard Priest beside the entranceway, fully on guard. He held a Swordclaw, which he had already honed with Sharp Tooth. He was bleeding: he had literally bought their escape with his blood.

"But where are Goblin Slayer and—?" Priestess, for her part, was braced against the innermost wall, breathing heavily. Maintaining the Holy Light miracle, even as they rushed through the maze, was a lot to ask of such a physically frail young woman. Her face was pale, bloodless with exhaustion.

Dwarf Shaman rubbed his bloody hands together then found a potion in his item pouch.

"I'm sure Long-Ears and Beard-cutter will catch up with us soon enough. Here."

"Thank you…"

Holding the potion in both hands, Priestess opened the bottle and drank it slowly, letting each sip moisten her lips. Each time she swallowed, she felt a bit of warmth return to her body. It was not as restorative as a miracle of the gods, but the salutary effects of a potion were nothing to sneeze at.

She closed her eyes and let out a breath. Yes, she felt a little better now. Priestess adjusted her grip on her staff.

"…We have to tend to this woman, right away…," she said, but as she was on the verge of casting Minor Heal, Dwarf Shaman stopped her.

"Take it easy. You need your rest. She's not going to die of these injuries anytime soon."

The petite cleric wobbled a bit then slid down the wall and onto the floor with a dull thud.

"Thank you," Priestess breathed again, but Dwarf Shaman waved her off with a "Think nothing of it."

Whatever else, Priestess would find it very difficult to reattach the severed fingers at her level of skill. Meaning it would be vastly better to save the miracle.

"You okay, kid?"

"Yeah, no prob…!"

"Good," Dwarf Shaman said flatly. No doubt he could see right through the boy's show of bravado. His eyes narrowed. "Just a word of advice," he added. "No one's going to be able to help even if you wind up in a pinch later, because you're too exhausted."

"…I am *not* exhausted!"

Unlike that girl over there, he seemed to imply—but even this boy couldn't bring himself to say as much aloud.

He, too, went over and leaned against the wall, although he kept his distance from Priestess. He dropped his eyes to his hands. The blood had dried on them in crimson splotches; he rubbed his hands together to try to take off the stains.

Clerics should huddle in the back row and say their prayers.

Now he realized what idiotic things he had said. She had given orders, held her staff high to give them light, and run as hard as any of them.

He glanced to the side, where he could see Priestess, still breathing hard and downing her potion. Even Wizard Boy could understand that she was trying to restore her vitality so as to be ready for the next fight.

His lips opened partway then closed. His tongue felt too large for his mouth. He swallowed some saliva and tried again.

"I'm…sor—"

"They're here!" The sharp voice of Lizard Priest cut him off.

Wizard Boy blinked several times, turning to stare into the darkness of the hall they had come by. He quickly discerned the light of a torch coming nearer to them.

"Dammit, Orcbolg—it's still alive!"

"It does seem to have been more resilient than I expected."

High Elf Archer came bounding into the room, as elegant as a deer. Goblin Slayer ran in after her.

And behind them…

"OOOLRTTTTR!!"

The giant troll was puffing smoke and swinging its club.

Simple weight gave the adventurers an advantage in speed. But if either of them lost their footing and fell, that would be the end of it.

Goblin Slayer and High Elf Archer ran as only those could who heard a massive club smashing into the walls and floor immediately behind them.

"I'm so tired of this!" High Elf Archer exclaimed as she burst into the burial chamber. "The heck is that thing?! I'm sick of this! I wanna fight a *cool* monster for once!"

"I think the cool ones are all even stronger than this," Dwarf Shaman added.

"Myself, I would well prefer a dragon," offered Lizard Priest.

Dwarf Shaman knew, however, that as long as they were bantering or complaining, there was really nothing to worry about. He let out a breath. "So. What do we do, Beard-cutter?"

"I'm thinking about it," Goblin Slayer said, looking around the room at his party.

Lizard Priest, Dwarf Shaman, and the red-haired boy all looked fine. High Elf Archer was breathing hard, and Priestess was fatigued.

Goblin Slayer reached into his item bag and took out two bottles by feel alone, passing them to the girls.

"Drink these."

"Wha…? Ah…"

"A Stamina potion, eh? Thanks."

Priestess seemed a little confused, but High Elf Archer gladly uncorked the bottle and downed the contents.

They each had their own supply of these potions, but at that moment, there was no time to quibble about what belonged to whom.

"O-okay, then… Thank you…" Priestess hesitated far more than High Elf Archer had but eventually brought the bottle to her lips. This was her second Stamina potion. The increasingly healthy glow of her cheeks contrasted with the dark expression still on her face.

"Good, we're all ready," Goblin Slayer said, catching the change in her out of the corner of his eye. "I want water. Can you produce it with a spell?"

Although the question hadn't been directed at him specifically, Wizard Boy made an uncomfortable noise. Fireball was the only spell he knew, and he had already used all the magic he could that day. He somehow found it deeply humiliating that this man knew all that.

"There'd be no point, learning a spell like that…" the boy found himself saying, almost pouting.

"Is that so?" Goblin Slayer responded.

Taking in the situation, Dwarf Shaman quickly interjected, "Water? Well, if rain is good enough for you, we can do that. It'll be a bit weak, though, there bein' a ceiling here and all."

The roaring and rumbling of the troll was getting closer. "Ready," Lizard Priest whispered.

"But listen, Beard-cutter. You can't just play one of your usual tricks now."

"It doesn't matter," Goblin Slayer said brusquely. "A shower will be enough."

"Right, then."

"And we will need Holy Light again. Can you do it?"

"I..." Priestess's voice was trembling, and she had to bite her lip to get the words to come out. "Yes, I... I can. I will!"

"Good." *That settles it.* No sooner had Goblin Slayer made this pronouncement than their enemy was upon them.

"OLTROOOR!!"

The rooms and passages of the mausoleum were large enough for a troll to move about easily. Who had the builders imagined was going to visit this place?

"Eeyah!"

"Look ou—"

Priestess was just a hair too late in crouching out of the way, and High Elf Archer jumped to cover her.

The metal spikes of the club grazed her hair, slicing through the ribbons she had used to tie it back.

"Are you all right?!" Priestess asked.

"Don't worry about me!" High Elf Archer shouted, her hair in disarray. "Just do it!"

"O Earth Mother, abounding in mercy, grant your sacred light to we who are lost in darkness!"

She raised her staff as high as she could from where she had been shoved to the ground, offering supplication to the merciful goddess. And of course, far be it from the Earth Mother on high to deny the soul-enervating request of her devoted follower.

"RRLLRTTOOR?!"

There was an explosion of light like the sun. The flash filled the chamber, flooding it with irresistible illumination.

The troll stumbled back, and immediately, Goblin Slayer could be heard to shout, "Water!"

"On it! *Go now, kelpie, it's time to get busy! Earth to river and sea to sky, turn all a-tizzy!*" Dwarf Shaman intoned, clasping a tiny horse figurine he pulled from his bag of catalysts. No sooner had he spoken than there was a high-pitched whinny, and a wet wind galloped through, quickly turning to a drizzling rain.

As Dwarf Shaman had said, the act of summoning a kelpie to produce precipitation was nothing more than Call Rain.

"All yours, Beard-cutter!"

"Next… This." As he spoke, Goblin Slayer took a leather pouch from his item pouch and tossed it at the troll.

"ORLTLRRLR?!"

The monster immediately began bellowing. Its lumpy gray skin began to crack and shatter even as they watched, starting with the scorched parts.

When someone is attempting to clear some land and needs to get rid of a huge boulder, sometimes the rock will be heated very hot, and then cold water will be applied to it. This causes the stone to crack, after which it can easily be broken down with a hammer.

And what about the troll? It was made of rock, said to turn to stone if exposed to the daylight. And it was just like that hypothetical boulder.

"TLRORL?!"

The troll, however, did not understand what had happened. To think mist should descend upon it just because it had been splashed with a little water!

"TTLLOOTTTTTL?!"

"Simple, but surprisingly effective," Goblin Slayer remarked, observing the troll as it clutched its face and thrashed around.

It wasn't entirely clear that even Goblin Slayer understood the science behind what he had done. But what mattered was the outcome of his actions.

The fire powder—what the alchemists called saltpeter—absorbed the water and the heat of the troll, accelerating the cooling process.

"…Where in the world did he learn to do that?" High Elf Archer asked with a touch of annoyance.

"…Oh!" Priestess found herself thinking back to their visit to the water town.

I do remember him asking how to make ice treats…

"ORLT?! TOORLRLOT?!"

Perhaps this was evidence that healing powers or no, being shock-cooled immediately after being superheated was too much to take. The troll, distressed that its wounds showed no signs of regenerating, began flailing about madly with its club.

With a hissing chuckle, Lizard Priest twisted his jaws into a beastly smile. "Most unbecoming, that. Shall we put him out of his misery?" He jumped at the monster, followed quickly by a bolt from High Elf Archer.

"Whatever that large creature is," Goblin Slayer said, flinging his weapon away but immediately picking up another sword from among the detritus. "Once we finish it off, we will go kill all the goblins."

The fate of the troll was always going to bear closely on what happened to the remaining goblins. Amid all this, though, the young boy, chased to the back row, was watching Goblin Slayer with absolute intensity.

I see now. He's right—what I said to that girl was terrible.

But who was this man, who seemed to regard a troll as little more than a nuisance yet was so eager to hunt down goblins?

Yes, the young man had been careless. He had acted like the rookie he was. He had a share in the responsibility and the blame.

But I just can't admit that this *man of all people was so right…!*

§

"Oh, come on. If a dwarf doesn't give the toast now, when will it ever happen?"

"Right, very well then. Here's to our safe return—to that acolyte's future—and to a whole hell of a lot of dead monsters!"

Hear, hear! Their voices rang out, followed quickly by the clatter of cups and the splashing of wine.

There's a reason *adventurers* and *alcohol* both start with the same letter; they're inextricably linked.

Many parties were relaxing at the Guild tavern after another day's work.

Goodness, but the foe that day was tough. Well now, who would use this enchanted sword they'd found? Gracious, that village girl was pretty.

The worst part was when you missed with that attack. But then there was that finishing blow. Lots of chances to use spells.

A celebration of their victory had to come first. Then, a careful consideration of what could have gone better. They laughed off their companions' mistakes and showered their successes with praise.

They divided up the loot they had gotten, conferred about whether to sell or to use any equipment they had obtained, and spoke excitedly of their next adventure.

By convention, adventurers didn't argue or complain about fairness during the adventure itself. No one wanted to have a falling-out in the middle of a dungeon. Such details were reserved for the "after session," the time after an adventure was over. During this phase, the party let it all hang out, so that nothing would be left unsaid, so that, if they should die the next time out, they could do so without regrets.

Goblin Slayer's party was very much part of this tradition.

"What's wrong with you, Orcbolg? I know you're not much for talk, but you could at least come up with *something* at a time like this!"

"Is that so?"

"It sure is!"

Even though High Elf Archer was only sipping her own watered-down wine, she was more than happy to pour for others as they drained their cups. It was less out of a sense of service than personal amusement—not, perhaps, the best side of her personality; but then again, perhaps the drink was already going to her head.

In contrast, Goblin Slayer quietly poured the wine through the slats of his visor, just as always.

"Pardon me very much, milady server, but could I trouble you for some sausage?"

"Sure thing, master lizard! The usual?" Padfoot Waitress came working her way through the crowd of adventurers, weaving between seats and tables. "And cheese on top, right?"

"Ah, sweet nectar! Yes, indubitably!" And then Lizard Priest, having ordered a snack to go with his drink, slapped his tail on the floor. All this was just as usual, but…

"Ahh, come now, your cup is getting lonely! Drink up!"

"Right…"

Priestess, for one, did not look herself, sitting with her shoulders slumped.

In fact, it was normally she who assiduously attended to everyone, making sure all the cups stayed full. Otherwise, High Elf Archer could be expected to be altogether intemperate with both her food and her drink.

"I just… You know, today…" Priestess sounded like she might break into tears at any moment. Her gloomy look was not best suited for a cleric, let alone for a celebration like this.

Then again, it was hard to blame her. It was her first experience of leading a party, and it had been going reasonably well—until she fumbled it. It worked out, because one of her other party members had been able to take over. But if he hadn't, they would certainly all have been wiped out.

Just like her first adventure.

"Aww, c'mon! We're all still here, aren't we? So don't sweat it!" Elves, who lived for two thousand years, were not inclined to be worried about such trivial details. "What, did you expect to jump in and be able to manage things perfectly?" High Elf Archer's tone and expression (witness the great twitch of her ears) made it clear how silly she thought this was. "That's beyond even an elf. If you meet an elf who can do that, tug on their ears, because I guarantee they're stuck on."

"For once you're making real sense, Long-Ears!"

"Pfft! I *always* make sense!" she replied, puffing out her small chest.

But it only lasted a moment. Her eyes drifted half-shut, and she turned her red face to the other side of the table.

"Anyway, what about you?"

In addition to Goblin Slayer and Priestess, there was one more person at the table who wasn't saying much. It was the young man, who was resting his chin on one hand sulkily and pushing a piece of sausage around his plate with his fork.

It made a certain sense: this had been his first adventure, and he had almost nothing to be proud of. He had rushed ahead in a surfeit of valor and run straight into a trap. His magic had been the ace up his sleeve, and he had used it at the wrong time.

His experience seemed almost the polar opposite of the glamorous adventure that so many dreamed of.

Well, I guess that's reality for you. High Elf Archer heaved a sigh then went back to nursing her drink as if she had lost interest.

"There is no need for such consternation," Lizard Priest said. "You returned safely from your first adventure, and that is reason enough to celebrate."

"He's got that right, boyo. Not everyone runs into a troll the first time out." *For better or for worse.* Dwarf Shaman pounded the pouting boy on the back and took a gulp of wine.

"If that stupid troll hadn't been there," the boy said, "then even I wouldn't have had any trouble with those goblins..."

"Only one thing to do, in any case," the dwarf said, pouring liberally into the boy's cup. "Drink up! This is some decent wine."

The boy eyeballed the glass as if it might bite him then swallowed it in a single gulp.

"Guh?! *Cough! Hack!* Ugh!" The boy choked on the throat-searing alcohol.

"There now, see? Ain't a lot as goes right the very first time you try it!" Dwarf Shaman's laugh was both a little bit mean and a little bit encouraging. The boy shot him a resentful look and opened his mouth as if to say something.

Before he could speak, however, he found his mouth full of sausage, pulled off a heaping plate of the stuff.

"Come, now, soothe your tongue with a taste of my cheese-covered sausage."

The meat, so warm it was steaming, was partially buried in gooey, melted cheese. Lizard Priest happily grabbed some of his own portion (noticeably larger than the others') and stuffed it into his mouth. The skin of the sausage crackled as he chewed; his mouth filled with rich juices. The saltiness of the condiments brought out the sweetness of the cheese, a perfect combination.

"Nectar!" he exclaimed, bringing his hands together as if in worship. Then he offered a plate to Priestess. "Have some. Delectable, I assure you. And auspicious, besides. After all, a delicious meal is the most heartening thing after a difficult experience."

"I guess you're right..." With much hesitation, Priestess brought her fork toward the sausage. She speared a piece and brought it to her mouth, which opened just enough to take a little nibble.

"I also...wanted to do better back there."

"Ha! Ha! Ha! Ha!" Lizard Priest laughed jovially. Priestess glanced up at him. He was standing; he claimed his tail got in the way when he tried to sit in a chair. It only served to emphasize how tall he was.

Priestess puffed out her cheeks just a little bit, earning an approving nod from the lizardman.

"That fire in the heart is a good thing. If you have no desire to do a thing, then you never shall do it. What is progress but the attempt to move ever forward?" One scaly finger pointed up, drawing a circle in the air. "The nagas, my fearsome ancestors, first crawled in the swamps before walking on the land with four legs, whence they became nagas."

This was a lizardman myth. Priestess wasn't familiar with it.

Detritus in the sea became fish, then the fish emerged onto the land, trod upon the soil, stood up, and finally became the nagas that ruled over all.

It was the lizardman way of speaking of progress, or perhaps evolution; their culture encouraged them to always be moving forward.

Although all this was quite interesting, Priestess wasn't entirely sure what it meant for her, and she ended up smiling ambiguously.

I can at least understand that he's trying to encourage me.

"Hey, by the way," High Elf Archer said, breaking in just as Priestess was taking a mouthful of sausage so she didn't have to say anything committal. No doubt the elf hadn't intended to help the girl out; she just had a tendency to jump to whatever subject came into her head. "What about that, you know—the acolyte girl? What happened to her? Will she be all right?"

"Oh, yes," Priestess said, nodding quickly and wiping the fingers that had been at her mouth. "They managed to reattach her fingers. Once she's rested, they'll think about what to do next."

"That's great to hear. I mean—I know it's still rough, but as long as you're alive, there's always something else you can do."

For High Elf Archer, it was just a passing comment. So it was all the more surprising when an answer came back at her.

"Sometimes you're alive and there still ain't shit you can do!"

It was the boy.

He was staring at High Elf Archer as intensely as if he could destroy her with the power of his glare.

"She was defeated by *goblins*, wasn't she? She'll never live that down. No way."

"Wh-what's your problem?" the elf girl said, pursing her lips and looking slightly cowed. "I don't think it's as sure a thing as—"

"Well it sure was for my big sister!" the boy shouted, pounding the circular table with his hand.

High Elf Archer sat back in shock, her ears wilting against her head.

The dishes rattled, the food spilled, and the wine overflowed when the boy struck the table. Lizard Priest quickly started picking up the biggest plates, Dwarf Shaman helping him. They seemed to have appointed themselves guardians of the drunken young man.

Eh, the young'uns are so often this way with a bit of wine in 'em.

This was better than keeping his feelings inside. That, at least, was the dwarf's appraisal.

"She lost to the goblins! The things they did to her—!"

"Older sister?" a voice said, very quietly.

Reflexively, the gaze of all the adventurers seated at the table turned to the speaker. It was Goblin Slayer, who until that moment had been quietly drinking his wine.

"You have an older sister?"

"I *had* an older sister!" the boy shouted. The alcohol had stirred up his emotions, and now the words came in a torrent. "And I'd still have her, if she hadn't died after a goblin stabbed her with a poisoned blade!!"

"Huh...?"

No one quite seemed to notice the blood drain from Priestess's face at that remark.

Her thoughts were a dizzying mixture of *Of course* and *It can't be…*

Her hands quivered ever so slightly. Her throat trembled as she swallowed some saliva; it sounded terribly loud to her.

A poisoned blade. Killed by a goblin. Red hair. A spell caster.

How could she ever forget?

"My sis was amazing! If those goblins hadn't used poison, she woulda beaten 'em!" the boy said with a sort of half groan. Then he threw his cup as hard as he could.

Oop. Lizard Priest grabbed it with his tail.

"But those bastards from the Academy, they just…!"

"They can all go straight to hell."

With these last words, almost a whisper, the boy slumped down on the table.

Did the voices of the other adventurers in the tavern only seem to subside for a moment? Or had they heard the boy yelling? Was anyone else in the room looking at him?

Well, even if they had been, they wouldn't have said anything.

Becoming an adventurer was all about being responsible for oneself. Everyone had some burden they bore or some hope they embraced. They sought riches, or fame, or martial renown, or discipline, or money, or dreams, or ideals, or faith.

Though no two were alike, the weight of what was in their hearts was all the same.

How could you compare the desire to put food on the table for another day, and the desire to plumb the depths of unknown ruins? What difference was there between a beginner fighting giant rats in the sewers for all they were worth, and an old hand going toe-to-toe with a dragon?

That was why nobody said anything.

The exception—the only exception—was the man who, despite being an experienced adventurer, continued to hunt goblins.

"Is that so…?" Goblin Slayer muttered quietly, his own voice a groan much like the wizard's.

He picked up his own cup and took a swig.

Then there was a clatter as he stood up from the table.

"I'm going back. Find him a room. It doesn't matter where."

There was a quiet click of his tongue. The boy had not yet gotten a room at any inn.

The adventurer pulled a single gold coin from the pouch at his hip and tossed it on the table.

"This should cover the expense."

"Sure, we'll take care of it." Dwarf Shaman nodded but didn't say anything else. He picked up the coin with his thick fingers.

"Oh..." Priestess seemed like she was maybe, perhaps, about to say something to the man as he walked by. Her mouth opened, but nothing came out except, in a very small voice, his name. "Goblin Slayer, sir..."

"Get some rest."

She found a crude leather glove placed on her delicate shoulder.

By the time she moved to place her own small hand over his, he was already gone.

She looked this way and that for him; she saw him heading for the doorway with his usual nonchalant stride.

"Hold on, Orcbolg!" High Elf Archer shouted, her voice cutting through the hubbub of the tavern. "What about tomorrow? Are we taking a break?"

The answer was short and cold. "I don't know."

Just as he was pushing through the swinging door of the Guild, Goblin Slayer ran into another adventurer coming in.

"Yikes! If it ain't Goblin Slayer!" a handsome but tough-looking man exclaimed. It was the spear-wielding adventurer.

Maybe he had just finished an adventure himself. He was covered in dirt and dust, and smelled faintly of blood.

"Don't just jump out at me like that, man, you scared the sh—"

Whatever he had been about to say, he swallowed it. Instead, he looked intently at Goblin Slayer's cheap-looking helmet.

"...What's wrong?" he asked. "Something happen?"

"Nothing."

Goblin Slayer practically shoved Spearman aside as he left the Guild.

Spearman stood there in the doorway, looking after him as if he couldn't believe what he had seen.

He had never known Goblin Slayer to shove anyone before.

§

There's nothing adventurers like more than good drunken reveling.

The carousing from inside the Guild came through the walls and windows to lend an air of jollity to the night.

If an adventurer were to be curled up in some back alley, somewhere so dark even the light of the twin moons didn't reach it, who would notice?

Cheap-looking leather armor and a grimy helmet. Even a freshly minted newcomer would have fancier equipment.

It was perfectly common: a new adventurer, awash in the relief of surviving an adventure, proceeds to get dizzyingly drunk.

"...An older sister, he says?" the adventurer growled, throwing aside his helmet.

Had he thought he had been able to accomplish even one thing?

Had he thought he had succeeded at doing even one thing right?

"...Idiot."

He ground his teeth and clenched his fists, but it did nothing to alleviate the feeling that there was a lead weight in his stomach.

Unable to resist the wave of nausea, he vomited in the alleyway.

INTERLUDE

Of Two Women

"There, all finished."

The faint warmth she had felt in her neck dropped away, along with the softness at her back.

Noble Fencer shivered, sorry to feel them go, and slowly opened her eyes.

She was in a courtyard bathed in bright sunlight, an invigorating breeze blowing through. She was at the Temple of Law, in the water town.

"...It never quite goes away, does it?" she said.

"That's how *curses* are."

The answer came from a woman of indeterminate age standing behind Noble Fencer, who had been treating her until a moment earlier. The woman had a strikingly voluptuous body, covered only by thin cloth.

In her hand was the sword and scales. The only thing that might be considered to besmirch her otherwise irreproachable beauty was the wrapping that covered her eyes.

"I must apologize. If I had a little more power..."

"...Not at all. You've done so much for me." Noble Fencer gave a deep, reverential bow to Sword Maiden, the archbishop of the Supreme God.

Looking at the bandage over the priestess's eyes made Noble Fencer embarrassed to complain about her own scar.

"...Everything is thanks to you, Archbishop. I'm alive and able to be with my family because of you."

"I should hardly say so," Sword Maiden said, her lips forming a perfect curve. "It wasn't me who rescued you..."

"...You're thinking of *him*."

"Yes, I am." Sword Maiden put a hand to her generous chest and let out a sigh as if she might melt. "He who kills goblins. All I did was make a request of him."

"...Yes. But of course," Noble Fencer said, her own mouth curving upward slightly into a characteristic smile. Her left hand moved to touch the silver dagger hanging in her belt, almost a caress.

It had been months since the battle on the snowy mountain—and it was not by her own strength that she was still here.

In fact, the same could be said of almost everything in her life. How many things had she really done on her own? Her parents, her party members, Goblin Slayer—and of course, all the friends she had made in that frontier town. The priestess who was like an older sister to her; that cheerful elf; the receptionist and the farm girl. The thought of them all made her heart sing.

And with that warmth inside her, she was sure she would be all right.

"...That's why I want to do something by my own hand next time."

"You mean for everyone's sake?"

"No," Noble Fencer said. "...I don't know whether it will end up being for everyone or not."

Sword Maiden nodded, as if to say that was very good.

It was all well and good to hope you could do something for the benefit of the world. But there were no guarantees that whatever you did would, in fact, be for the world's good.

Righteousness was also danger. That was precisely why the Supreme God had handed down his laws.

Noble Fencer understood this all too well. What she had thought was right had been a mistake. The brand on her neck was the proof.

What could she do for the repose of her party's souls? And for all those who were just becoming adventurers?

"...But I'll certainly give it everything I've got."

"Of course. I'll certainly give you any help I can, feeble though it may be." Noble Fencer found Sword Maiden's quiet smile deeply encouraging. This was the hero who had ended the war ten years before and, indeed, the Archbishop who had the ear of kings and kingmakers alike. "Feeble"? Hardly. But Noble Fencer didn't want to impose, either.

"Incidentally..." Lost in thought, it was a moment before Noble Fencer realized that Sword Maiden had moved almost uncomfortably close to her. "What *do* you think of that man?"

"...I'm sorry?" Noble Fencer said, blinking. Sword Maiden's unseeing eyes seemed fixed on her. Noble Fighter felt as if she had been hit with Sense Lie as she said, "How do you mean...? What...?"

"Only just what I said."

"...I owe him my life." Noble Fencer answered without hesitation. Touching the dagger at her belt once more, she said, "...Not just him. His party, too. I even gained some friends, thanks to them."

"Is that true indeed?" Sword Maiden seemed at once reluctant to speak but also joyful.

With no small hesitation, Noble Fencer looked at Sword Maiden to find the other woman nodding and smiling at her.

"I see. What a blessing you had to encounter them."

"...Yes, ma'am!" Noble Fencer answered happily, sticking out her own not inconsiderable chest.

There were few among her own deeds that she could take pride in, but that meeting, at least, was different.

There was a spring in Noble Fencer's step as she walked through the halls of the temple, Sword Maiden following at a slight distance.

Behind her, the priestess was smiling happily, but Noble Fencer had no idea of the real reason why.

CHAPTER 4

The Men with No Names

Hardly a week later, people started using the new training grounds, even though they weren't actually finished.

The early summer sunlight bathed the grassy hill, and a pleasantly warm breeze came blowing through. What better weather could there be to tempt one to work and sweat?

"Yikes—ow! Watch out, now my hand is numb!!"

"Don't drop your shield hand! You want me to split your head open?!"

"Yipes! Ack! Waah—!"

Metal rang against metal in the circle of white sand.

The complex (one might almost say magical) training facility was still under construction, but even a total greenhorn could put up a fence. The circular space for mock battles was the first thing that had been finished, and eager young hands were already putting it through its paces. After all, the area behind the Guild building was too confined, and it was nice to have some loaner equipment on hand to try.

"Your hand is numb? I don't care if it *falls off*! Don't lower your shield! Your shield needs to be your most faithful companion in a fight!"

"Couldn't we, y'know, take this just a little slower?!"

At the moment, it was Female Knight and Rhea Fighter—the young fighter dressed in leather armor and carrying a round shield—who were competing in the ring.

Well, *competing* might have been a strong word. Female Knight had the duel by the scruff of the neck and was enjoying herself. As for the rhea fighter, it was all she could do to squeal and get her shield up to block the incoming attacks.

And she needed to: the practice blades might not carry an edge, but getting hit with them could still leave one with worse than a bruise.

"What's wrong? Get on your game! If you can't stand up to this, how are you ever gonna deal with a dragon's teeth and claws?!"

"I'm just Porcelain! I don't wanna think about any dragons!!"

"Don't you know the parable of the random encounter with the dragon? Whoop—there go your feet!"

"Eek!!"

An exemplary sweep from Female Knight took Rhea Fighter's feet clear out from under her, sending her tumbling gracelessly to the sand.

Laughing uproariously, Female Knight pressed her advantage, lashing out with the hilt of her sword. One blow from a hilt like this, with the sword held in reverse and raised above the head, could be critical.

Gasping and shrieking, Rhea Fighter tried to escape the trap, only to stumble again.

Female Knight was ruthless, or perhaps lacked something in sympathy; in any event, she came on without mercy. It almost crossed the line into cruelty. And she wondered why no one wanted to marry her…

"Whoa…"

"Yeah, holy crap."

Rookie Warrior and the red-haired wizard looked on, their expressions stiff, trying not to think about the fact that it would be their turn next. They had never realized that sitting outside that circle, trying to steel themselves for what was coming, could be a form of training itself.

Where did they think they were—the impregnable Great Labyrinth in the land of utmost cold? It would be impossible to go there, or to get back.

"Hey, don't get distracted, you punks."

The butt of a spear gave each of the young adventurers a gentle

©Noboru Kannatuki

bonk on the head. And who should be holding that spear but Spearman, dressed not in his usual armor but in civilian clothes, a silver tag hanging around his neck.

"It's easy to get distracted by girls. Believe me, I know. But if you don't focus, next thing you know, you'll be dead."

"Uh, that's not what I was doing."

"Yeah, and I don't really have the same problems you do, Spearman..."

One grumbled as the other chuckled to himself. "Listen, you two," Spearman started with a frown. "I don't know what you think of me, but you don't sound like you're ready to learn anything."

"Yeah, but," Rookie Warrior said like it was the most obvious thing in the world, "you're always getting shot down by that receptionist, right?"

"I only just got here, and even I know about it," the wizard added.

A vein in Spearman's temple made a visible twitch, but it's possible neither of the boys noticed.

"Oh, I see," he said with a stiff yet endlessly kind smile. "Aren't you kids clever? Well, you're not the only ones who can play that game."

"?"

The two of them looked at him questioningly, whereupon Spearman stuck up his pointer finger as straight as a spear and continued, "On *your* recent adventure, you went rushing in, used up your magic, and ended up not being able to do jack."

"Erk..."

"And *you've* always spent all your time hunting giant rats, so you didn't have the endurance for a longer battle and drank your entire reward in Stamina potions."

"Guh?!"

These things were both true. Embarrassing secrets the boys would rather not have broadcast too widely. Nobody knew except their party members, and...

"Th-the receptionist? She told you...?"

"Darn straight. She asked me to look out for you guys, make sure you had the physical strength you needed." Spearman chuckled quietly then rose as easily as a ghost and took up a fighting stance. Rookie Warrior and the wizard boy both settled into deep stances, looking as terrified as if they were preparing to battle a warrior back from the dead.

"Let's play hide-and-seek. I'll be the hunter and you'll be the hunted."

It was only as Spearman spun his weapon with a flourish and resumed his stance that the boys realized how angry he was.

"Yikes, let's get outta here!"

"Y-yeah, gotta go!"

Rather than apologize or reflect on what they had done, they elected to speed off like hares at the sight of a hound. It was undoubtedly the right decision.

"Hey! You're not getting away that easy!"

The boys set off running around the training area so fast that they left their equipment (including the wizard's staff) lying on the ground. Spearman went storming after them.

Construction workers, along with adventurers on break, watched the commotion wearily. Of course, everyone knew that Spearman was not serious. He was maintaining a speed that would allow him to catch the boys if they flagged even slightly—but judging such a thing was impressive in itself.

All those watching privately agreed that despite his appearance, Spearman was good at looking out for others.

Instruction at this place would generally be handled by retired, high-ranking adventurers. But there was nothing to stop active adventurers from providing a little mentorship of their own. Maybe just to pass the time, or even to supplement their own training.

The training ground wasn't even finished yet, and already adventurers happily used it as a place to congregate and talk.

"..."

Goblin Slayer watched all this without a word, his hand moving restlessly. He was sitting in an open field, neither part of the completed training area nor the part still under construction.

Birds went singing through the blue sky, and the breeze sent gentle ripples through the grass.

If one were to look in his direction, one would have seen two young women waiting anxiously for him to finish what he was doing.

One was the rhea druid, the other the apprentice cleric who served the Supreme God.

"This is how you do it," he said, at last showing the girls the product of his labors. They blinked at it.

It was a simple sling, a strip of leather tied to a small stone so that it could be thrown.

"Huh? Is that all there is to it?"

"It is surprisingly straightforward."

"Yes," Goblin Slayer said with a nod. "Shepherds sometimes carry them to discourage wolves."

"It looks like something you could make in a hurry if you needed to."

"All you need is some string. Ammunition is easy enough to come by. There's nothing to lose by learning how to do it."

This had all started when they had seen him pitch a stone at a certain festival. It had seemed to them like the perfect skill for two people who stood on the back row and needed a way to defend themselves.

When Guild Girl mentioned that there were two young adventurers who wanted to learn to use a sling, Goblin Slayer surprised himself with how readily he replied, "Is that so?" and agreed to help them.

Now Goblin Slayer got to his feet. "Swords are often proclaimed to be the best weapon for humans, but slings are better," he said, slowly starting to twirl the device. He made sure he went gradually enough that the two beginners could follow his every move. Given that in battle, heft, spin, and strike were usually a single motion for him, this was a display of considerable care.

"Humans are unsurpassed in throwing, whether stones or spears. Our bodies are built for it."

He raised the sling higher, slowly increasing the rate of rotation, picking a target. Mindful of the possibility of an accident, he aimed directly away from the training ground.

Over in the weeds, a dummy had been dressed in armor and helmet—castoffs from the Guild workshop. It was not very tall—to represent a goblin's height, needless to say.

"This is the result."

As he spoke, Goblin Slayer let the stone fly; it whistled through the air and *whack*ed into the dummy's helmet. The headgear rolled into the grass, where Goblin Slayer walked over and collected it, casually tossing it to the two girls.

"Wow!"

"Eek!"

The girls couldn't help but cry out. It was only natural: the stone had punched clear through the helmet's metal exterior and leather lining and was rolling around inside the bowl. What would have happened to the skull of anyone wearing this particular helmet when it was hit by that stone didn't bear thinking about.

"In this way, even someone as relatively weak as a rhea should be able to deal with at least one encroaching enemy."

"*In any event, my own teacher was a rhea.*" This near whisper brought a series of blinks from Druid Girl.

Goblin Slayer approached them with his bold stride, collecting the stone from inside the helmet. It was sharpened, like an arrowhead. Something he had picked specifically for throwing like this, focusing on power over midair stability. He added softly that such preparations were sometimes effective.

"If you can keep away that first enemy, it's possible that your party members will come and help you."

"Only...possible?" Apprentice Cleric asked doubtfully.

"Yes." Goblin Slayer's tone was utterly serious. "It simply represents one more card you can play at your moment of need. If that's enough for you then practice with it."

"Mr. Goblin Slayer, I really think you have a harsh way of saying things," Druid Girl said reprovingly. *No wonder that sweet priestess of yours always seems so stressed.*

"Is that so?" Goblin Slayer asked, genuinely perplexed. The two girls let the matter drop, picking up slings. They wound up the strings with a great deal of "Is this right?" and "How about this?" before lobbing their own stones at the dummy.

Some of their shots landed, and others missed. Some didn't even go the right direction. But Goblin Slayer made no move to say anything about any of their efforts. If they had questions, they would ask him. Otherwise, it was best to let them focus on their practice. That was how Goblin Slayer had been taught, and he felt he should do the same.

Those who don't try will never be able to do.

Now, at last, he thought perhaps he understood what his master—Burglar—had meant.

And was he, finally, able to do it?

He had no answer. He had no way to answer.

Goblin Slayer let out a breath, sitting down where he was almost as if in resignation.

At that moment, however, a voice interrupted his thoughts. "Heh-heh-heh! Don't you all look very dedicated." A shadow fell over him.

"Oh…" Goblin Slayer turned to see Guild Girl, holding an umbrella and smiling.

"…So you came."

"Of course. Just to observe, or maybe…well, not inspect. But yes, I'm here."

She plopped herself down next to him, arms around her knees. She was in her usual work clothes. Maybe they were a little bit warm for the start of summer, because a trickle of sweat ran down her forehead.

It was clear enough that bureaucratic work such as hers could not be done in just any old clothing. She may also have been a bit shy, but in any case, she wasn't about to open her collar or lie back on the grass.

"…Aren't you hot, Goblin Slayer?"

"No," he said with a shake of his head. "Not especially."

"Really?"

"What would I gain by lying about it?"

The answer didn't seem to make Guild Girl remotely happy; she sniffed and muttered, "Forget it." After a moment, she asked, "What do you think of our Obsidian and Porcelain adventurers?"

"Hmm," Goblin Slayer said, watching the girls practice their slinging.

They were certainly enthusiastic. And serious. They were good girls.

But that was no guarantee that they would survive.

"I don't know."

"Oh, you…" Guild Girl puffed out her cheeks and raised her pointer finger, shaking it slowly, reproachfully. "You're supposed to answer a question like that with something banal and inoffensive!"

"Is that so?"

"It is. Especially when your answer's going to be written down."

"I will remember that," Goblin Slayer said and rose. He could feel Guild Girl looking up at him.

It was time.

"Hey, everyone! How about some lunch?"

"Fresh from the farm!"

The clattering of a cart could be heard, accompanied by women's voices: Priestess and Cow Girl.

There had been no specific decision about this. It wasn't a formal arrangement. They had no obligation to bring lunch.

This was a simple act of good-heartedness.

Goblin Slayer was profoundly grateful that Cow Girl's uncle would do something like this for the adventurers. The conceited thought that it might all be for him never once crossed his mind.

"Oops, I better go and help," Guild Girl said. She brushed grass and dirt off her skirt as she stood up. She yawned a little, folding up the sun umbrella and clasping it to her side. Then she pattered off through the grass like a small bird.

"Oh, that's right," she said, turning back with a smile. The wind played with her braids. "Should we classify this under 'visiting men on duty'?"

Goblin Slayer didn't answer. Instead, he turned to the girls, hard at work on their slinging and said, "Take a break."

Both of the young women were red in the face from exertion. They nodded eagerly and headed over to the cart. He watched them go then turned his back on the growing crowd of adventurers gathered around the food and began walking away.

He felt a slight twinge of regret for having been asked to help with training like this and for having accepted.

"Hey, Goblin Slayer!"

It was Spearman who stopped him. He hadn't noticed the adventurer come up alongside him.

Spearman watched Guild Girl go, her braids bouncing, then he exhaled and looked square at Goblin Slayer's helmet.

"Where's the big guy at?" he asked, meaning Heavy Warrior. "Where'd he go?"

"He took the other children to a cave today."

Half-Elf Fighter and the rather quick-witted Scout Boy had gone with him. No adventure was ever totally without risk, but nothing was likely to happen on an expedition like that.

Goblin Slayer was quiet for a moment then asked softly, "What do you think of that boy?"

"Ahh, the wizard brat?" Spearman smiled ferociously.

The boy was just then over at the cart, getting a bottle of lemon water that had been cooled in the well. The fervor with which he drank it down suggested how hard Spearman had run him.

"He's got guts. Can't speak to his magical abilities, though."

"Is that so?"

"What's gotten into you, though?" Spearman said with a sharp sidelong glance at the grimy steel helmet. "Mentoring at the training grounds? I thought you were focused on that cleric of yours."

"That is not necessarily the case," Goblin Slayer said brusquely, and then he began to stride off.

He seemed intent on leaving the area as quickly as possible. That left Spearman to look up at the sky, unsure quite what to do.

"Sigh…"

The sun was dispiritingly high. It looked like it would be another hot summer.

"…Hey, you free tonight?" Spearman asked.

"Hrm…" Goblin Slayer grunted. He glanced in Cow Girl's direction; she was looking back at him. She smiled, waving a hand she held at her hip. The two of them seemed to be talking, somehow.

Then Goblin Slayer nodded. "…Yes. I think it's all right."

"Let's go get a drink, then."

"…You mean alcohol?"

"Does a man drink anything else?"

Goblin Slayer had some trouble grasping what Spearman meant, or perhaps what he intended. What possible benefit was there in inviting him for a drink?

"You're inviting me?"

"You see anyone else around here? Let's grab the big guy, too. Three men. No holding back."

"...I see."

"Come on, humor me."

Goblin Slayer gazed silently up at the sky. The sun was past its zenith, shining down on the gentle slope. In this place, it was easy enough for him to read the passing time, no matter the season.

It was his older sister who had taught him to do this.

He could never forget.

"...Very well."

"Great," Spearman said, smacking Goblin Slayer on the shoulder with his fist. "It's settled, then."

§

The clear blue sky seemed to extend forever.

The boy lay panting in the grass; he could feel the little green blades pressing into his sweat-covered back and cheeks.

He lay on his back, spreading his arms and legs wide, gulping oxygen into his lungs. It was lack of oxygen that made one short of breath. If you breathed, you would get oxygen. That was why the breath became ragged.

The early summer breeze blew sweetly across his face as one thought circled around and around in his mind: he was most certainly not pathetic.

Spells depleted the user's strength, and adventures frequently included a lot of tromping through fields and mountains.

Why? Well, horses were expensive. Horses had to have feed, stables. They needed shoes and equipment.

If you were only going from town to town, post to post, maybe it wouldn't matter so much. But adventures commonly took people to remote underground labyrinths, or supernatural lands untrod by human feet.

It would be hard enough with a horse or a personal carriage, and in some ways, renting one would be worse. Brave adventurers with long experience said that adventure was a walking trade, and it was absolutely true. Hence, a wizard needed stamina as much as any warrior. He knew that.

Yes, of course he did—and yet… And yet…

"It just doesn't…"

"…S-soooo tired…"

Yes, their opponent had held back. But there was a difference between Porcelain and Silver. Between the tenth rank and the third.

The second voice, joining in the boy's complaint, came from Rhea Fighter, splayed out beside him on the grass. She was a mess, having been worked to the bone by Female Knight until a few minutes prior. She had tossed aside her armor, shield, and sword, perhaps unable to bear the heat, and now lay spread-eagled in the grass. Her chest (not that large, but pretty big for a rhea) heaved up and down.

The boy glanced over, but when he caught sight of her sweat-soaked shirt, he forced himself to look back at the sky. He felt a little embarrassed, and a little bit as if he had done something wrong.

His head throbbed with the heat and the pace of his breath, but he managed to move it just a little. When she was done, it would be his turn with Female Knight.

"S-so… Did you…get the hang of it…?"

"…I dunno."

In other words, it had been nothing more than a session of being smacked around and falling down.

Wizard Boy grimaced and let out a groan, but Female Knight didn't seem to think she had been especially mean to the young adventurer. At the very least, it could be considered training in how to keep your defenses up even when confronted with an overwhelmingly strong opponent—so it was all fair game.

Spearman would no doubt feel the same way if anyone asked his opinion. Strength and endurance were even more important than quick thinking, when it came down to it. Adventurers who seriously hunted dragons and ogres would naturally outclass a couple of Porcelains.

So yes, the mentors held back. But…

"…Aren't they hot like that?" the rhea girl said.

"No clue."

A short distance away, Rookie Warrior rested his head on Apprentice Cleric's knees. Everyone looked absolutely exhausted. Maybe

Druid Girl had gone with Scout Boy, because they didn't see her anywhere.

Rhea Fighter grumbled that she should have practiced slinging, too, but the wizarding boy gave a click of his tongue.

"There's nothin' to learn from a guy like *that*."

"You think so? He is Silver-ranked, after all."

"But he never fights anything but goblins."

"*And he's obsessed, and stubborn, and you never know what he's thinking*," the boy added in a pouty mutter. "Goblins? An adventurer should be able to kill a goblin in one hit."

"Even I wouldn't lose to a goblin in a one-on-one fight," the rhea agreed.

"Right? 'Goblin Slayer,' my ass!"

"They call him that because he kills goblins, don't they?" This rebuttal came not from Rhea Fighter but from Apprentice Cleric. "Look, I'm not saying I don't have my doubts about him." She ran a hand through Rookie Warrior's hair as she spoke, and he made contented little noises in response. "But I don't think someone who's done nothing should go around criticizing someone who's actually done something."

"..."

"I heard you didn't even manage goblin slaying."

"You can just shut up!" The boy spat at the sky. "I hear you never hunt anything but giant rats, yourself."

"I mean...that's all we're capable of right now," Rookie Warrior said, almost in a whine. Unlike the rhea fighter, he was still wearing his armor, sword, and club. He had simply loosened the fasteners of his equipment ever so slightly to allow his body to relax.

"We've finally gotten to where we understand how to attack and defend against giant rats. But if there's even three of them at once, we're pretty much done for."

"But rats are poisonous, right?" the rhea girl said. "Isn't fighting them all the time dangerous?"

"Well, that's why antidotes and potions keep draining our wallets..."

"The next time my level as a cleric increases, I plan to ask the deity for the Cure miracle."

Then, she said, the two of them might be able to save a little money and get better equipment. Change his sword for something with a broader blade, maybe get some mail for better protection. Helmets were hard to see out of, but maybe they could at least get a sturdy cap of some kind…

"…Pfft." The boy seemed to find none of this remotely interesting. He clicked his tongue dismissively, at which Rhea Fighter shot him a look. "Whatever," he muttered, looking away so she couldn't see his eyes.

"Hello, everyone! How about some lemon water?" Priestess appeared, strolling up the hill, smiling widely. She was carrying a huge basket filled with small bottles and packages of food. "I have some snacks here, too…"

She was not eagerly received. Maybe nobody felt like eating after dashing around or swinging their weapon all over. Rookie Warrior just groaned, "Urrrgh," and Rhea Fighter said, "I think I might just throw up anything I eat…"

Apprentice Cleric just shook her head silently, perhaps unwilling to be the only one to eat.

"Er, but… If you don't eat, you'll never make it through the afternoon," Priestess said, knitting her brow. Obviously, though, she couldn't force them to take the food.

Wizard Boy certainly had no specific intention of helping Priestess, who stood there looking quite at a loss, but nonetheless, he raised his hand and said, "I'll eat."

"What, seriously?" Rhea Fighter asked.

"Yeah," the red-haired boy replied, lurching upright out of the grass. "I learned once that…if you don't eat after you work out…you'll never gain any muscle."

"Crap, really? I better eat, then."

"…Okay… Me too…"

"I guess I'll have some, too, then. Thanks."

Lunch consisted of simple sandwiches: bacon, ham, vegetables, and some cheese squeezed between a couple pieces of bread. All the same, the salty flavor was very agreeable to their sweaty, enervated bodies.

At first, the group intended to have something to drink with their food, but soon, they were ravenously wolfing down the provisions.

She really does understand, doesn't she? Priestess found herself thinking with some admiration.

That farm girl had been helping Goblin Slayer out for years now. She knew exactly what adventurers would need after a hard morning of training.

What they needed…

"My sis was amazing! If those goblins hadn't used poison, she woulda beaten 'em!"

"Right," Priestess said quietly, strengthening her resolve. Then she sat down next to the boy.

"How are things? I mean…how are you feeling?"

She was simultaneously asking everyone there and him alone.

"Sooo tired!" Rhea Fighter answered immediately.

"Yeah!" Rookie Warrior added, audibly exhausted.

"I'm managing, somehow," Apprentice Cleric said with a touch of pride.

"……"

The red-haired boy, however, didn't say a word; he merely snorted.

"Um…" Priestess said.

He brushed me off.

Her brow furrowed awkwardly, and she decided to just change the subject. Rather than standing frozen, waiting for inspiration to strike, it was better to act immediately. That was something she had learned from Goblin Slayer.

"Hey," Priestess said, fixing in on Rhea Fighter. "I don't seem to see the rest of your party around…"

"Oh, that. Our leader was the second or third son of some noble house somewhere," Rhea Fighter said, taking a big bite of her sandwich and chewing noisily. "But then his big brother went and got himself killed, so suddenly there was no heir, and the family wanted our leader back. And that was the end of our party."

"Ah…"

Well, such things certainly did happen. Second or third children—anyone but an eldest son, really—could find themselves in a socially unpleasant position. If they wanted any role besides standby in case anything happened to the oldest child, they had to go out and get it themselves. They might be able to get their parents to grant them a bit of land, but otherwise, establishing themselves through martial deeds was an option or, perhaps, marrying into another house…

Knights' families were especially severe this way. Knighthood was, in general, a single-generation title. Parents couldn't pass it down to their children. An eldest son might be granted opportunities for service and training, a chance to make his name, but any children who came after him were unlikely to be so lucky.

Hence a good number of adventurers came from families of such standing. There was no distinction between men and women here. Second and third daughters of noble houses were a copper a dozen among adventurers.

And the survival rate of these self-proclaimed knights-errant was remarkably high. They had equipment, they had know-how, and sometimes they were even versed in swordsmanship, all of which contributed to their durability.

But once in a while, something would happen to the eldest son, and then these adventurers would be called back to the families they had left. For the party leader in question… Well, the path to become the family patriarch had opened to him, and he hadn't even been injured in the meantime, so he could count himself lucky.

For whether or not one had family connections, quality equipment, knowledge, experience, or skills, inevitable death still always waited in the wings.

"I guess it's not like he's going to have it easy, exactly."

Nobles have their own problems and all, Rhea Fighter thought to herself. She spoke so knowingly that it was comical, and Priestess couldn't help but giggle.

At the same time, she was a little worried. This meant that this young woman was going to embark upon a dangerous path all alone. As she recalled, rheas reached adulthood at around thirty, so strictly speaking, Rhea Fighter was probably older than Priestess.

"Isn't soloing difficult?" Priestess asked.

"It's not easy, but hey—I have my dreams!" Rhea Fighter answered, puffing out her chest proudly. "I'm gonna be big! So big, no one will care that I'm little!"

"Man, I hear that," Rookie Warrior said, shoving the last piece of his sandwich into his mouth. "When I said I was going to become the strongest guy around, they laughed at me. Said I was too rustic for that!"

"Yeah, exactly!" the rhea girl said, clapping her hands.

"Of course they laughed," Apprentice Cleric said. "If *you* turn out to be the strongest, think how much worse the other country rubes will look!" She smiled with a hint of pride; in some ways, it was seeing him excited like this that made her proudest of all. "Heh-heh! Bet now you're glad you decided to come with me on my training!"

"I'm glad I didn't leave you all by yourself. It would've been dangerous."

"I'm sorry, *who* didn't leave *who*?"

"Guh?"

"What, don't want to admit it?"

And on and on they went, arguing.

Priestess squinted happily; she felt like she was seeing something rather joyful. The two arguing children reminded her of her own party members.

"What good friends you are," she said.

Absolutely not!—was something they could hardly say in response.

The two of them looked at each other; each muttered something then shut their mouths.

The conversation broke off there.

A gust of wind caressed cheeks gone red from exertion.

".........I just don't get it," the boy growled. "But anyway, I gotta focus on killing some goblins, and killing them right. That's my priority."

That'll show the punks who laughed at my older sister.

Priestess wasn't quite sure what to say to this display of vitriol. She had been an adventurer for less than a year. She hardly had enough experience to go offering unsolicited advice. Especially, she felt, when it came to this young man's feelings.

That was why—

"I knew—"

That was why she bit her lip as she spoke.

"I knew a wizard, once."

Her throat constricted, and her voice trembled. She had to get ahold of herself.

"She said that...she wanted to fight a dragon one day."

"...A dragon?"

Dragons—true dragons—were utterly terrifying foes. They weren't like the creatures that sometimes skulked around fields and mountains. They overflowed with power. They had strength and stamina, intelligence and magical power, authority and wealth.

That was precisely why dragon slayers were so much praised and held in awe.

"That's... It might as well be a dream. It's impossible."

"Of course it was a dream," Priestess said with a smile, no edge in her voice. "It doesn't have to be anything more than that."

Yes—yes, she was sure of it.

That time, the moment they visited that first cave, was still there.

Just because the party was immediately shattered...

...doesn't mean the value of what everyone said just disappears.

Now Priestess thought she could understand that, at least a little bit.

It was a precious thing—not something to mock or ridicule.

No matter how unrealistic, no matter how out of reach, no matter how likely to fail.

Dreams were dreams.

It wasn't a matter of whether they could be realized.

They were absolutely not something for goblins to trample on.

"..."

The boy found there was nothing more he could say. Or perhaps he intended to say something, but before he could open his mouth again:

"Hello, all my cute little newbies! Looks like you're working hard!"

A high, clear voice, pleasing to the ear, came rolling over the grassy plain.

They looked toward town to discover three unusual but familiar figures coming toward them.

"In the afternoon, your favorite elf will take you on a tour of some caves!"

"Who's anyone's favorite elf, Long-Ears?" From beside the ranger,

Dwarf Shaman gave her a pointed elbow to the ribs. "I grant it's our day off, but I happen to know you were asleep until practically noon."

"You know what they call the time before noon? *Morning.* At least among elves."

"I guarantee that's not true."

The friendly banter continued as they got closer. Priestess glanced at Rookie Warrior and Apprentice Cleric as if to say, *See?* Neither of them would quite meet her gaze. But never mind them.

"Caves? Does that mean…goblins?" Priestess asked.

"Oh, please. Are you *trying* to sound like Orcbolg?" High Elf Archer waved a hand as if she were shooing away a bug.

"I'm talking about a bear's den—well, former bear's den. Hibernation season is over and he's out and about for the spring, so it should be a good way to get used to spelunking."

Priestess nodded in understanding. Unlike sewers or fields, there was a knack to moving and using weapons in caves. If the kids could practice doing those things in a cave with no monsters, it could only benefit them.

"Er, let it be said that we have yet to take our lunch," Lizard Priest said, bringing his hands together in a strange gesture. His breath came out the nostrils situated on his huge jaws. "And it appears you have prepared meals. With your indulgence, perhaps we may partake…?"

"Oh, sure. It's sandwiches," Priestess said. She dug through her basket and produced several wrapped lunches. "They have ham and bacon, vegetables… Oh, and cheese."

"Ah! Truly a gift from heaven! Nectar! What a fine and wonderful thing this is!"

"We have some that are just cucumber and cheese, if you like. And there's wine, too."

"All right!"

"Ho-ho-ho! Aren't you the thoughtful one. Thank you, don't mind if I do!"

Priestess set down the basket, and her three friends dove for it, each eager to be the first to get their food. She gave a wry smile at the sight. Even as she watched them, the early-summer breeze came up again.

Priestess clutched her hat so it wouldn't fly away, closing her eyes to appreciate the wind sprites as they brushed her cheeks.

"Oh, what about Goblin Slayer—?"

Is he going to have lunch?

Before she could finish her question, Priestess looked around: she didn't see him anywhere.

Huh?

Then she spotted him—in the distance, talking to two other adventurers, Spearman and Heavy Warrior.

"Hrm," Priestess breathed, almost as if imitating him. She was a little bit lonely—but a little bit glad.

"...Heh-heh."

Yes, there was no question: this was a good thing.

§

"I'm going, then," Goblin Slayer said to Cow Girl. He was in his room performing a quick check of his equipment. "I'll be late tonight. I won't need dinner."

He put his sword at his hip and affixed his shield to his arm, put on leg protection and hung his item bag from his belt, then finally put on his helmet.

He was dressed and ready to go out on an adventure, but Cow Girl was used to all this. "Okay, sure," was all she said in response.

He had been off helping to train some novice adventurers, and yet this was what he did the moment he got home. The fact that he came home at all—was it his way of trying to be considerate?

"Uncle said he had some errands to run, so he'll be late, too. I guess I'll just stay here allll alone, all by myself..."

"Don't forget to bar the door. Keep the fence gate shut, and close the shutters on the windows."

"I know about all that. You're such a worrywart." She chuckled, and Goblin Slayer fell silent. She took the opportunity to brush some dust off his armor.

He went "Hrm"—did this displease him?—and then turned his head from side to side, checking his helmet's mobility.

"So I know I'm ready," Cow Girl said. "But what about you? Do you have your purse? That's the most important thing, you know."

"Erm..."

He obediently rifled through his item pouch. The little bag of coins was there.

"I have it."

"Good, then!" Cow Girl took him by the shoulder and made him turn around. She adjusted the frayed tassel on his helmet. "I can come get you if you get falling down drunk," she said, "but just try not to cause too much trouble for your friends, okay?"

The word *friends* caused Goblin Slayer to cock his head slightly, but after a moment, he responded, "Okay," and nodded. "I don't intend to."

Goblin Slayer carried no light as he walked the road from the farm to the town, then through the town to the tavern. Traversing night-dark fields was very much part of his training, and once he reached town, he didn't need a light anyway.

The special confusion of a bustling town at twilight greeted him; it was a situation he was not familiar with, and he proceeded silently through it.

People pushed and jostled. Not just adventurers, but travelers, as well as the workers building the training facility, were everywhere.

Goblin Slayer made his way along, glancing this way and that, until he saw the sign he had been told to look for.

"...Hmph," he grunted as he pushed his way toward it, finally extricating himself from the crowd. At the same time, he reached a hand into his item pouch, making sure he hadn't been the victim of any kind of pickpocketing. All was well.

The sign bore the inscription THE FRIENDLY AX and was itself in the shape of a hatchet.

Goblin Slayer pushed through the swinging door and was instantly enveloped in an ear-shattering cacophony. The cavernous interior was illuminated by the reddish glow of lamps, and all the many round tables were full.

The building itself was smaller than the Guild branch office, but then again, that was a multipurpose structure. From the perspective of the old system, under which places like this had a tavern on the first floor and an inn on the second, the Ax was fairly large.

It used to be that adventurers' lodgings doubled as places to find work—but now that was part of history. The Guild system had been widely adopted, and adventurers, who had previously been little more than a bunch of street toughs, had acquired a certain kind of public status.

Even today, there were a few shops that worked with the Guild to offer quests, but for the most part, adventurers' inns had fallen into decline.

Then again, it was said that the legendary tavern The Golden Knight never assigned so much as a single quest, but still…

"Hey, Goblin Slayer! You made it!"

As the armored adventurer lingered just inside the door, a powerful voice called out to him. His helmet turned, scanning the inside of the bar as if taking stock of a cave he had just entered. There—there was the source of the voice.

In one corner of the tavern, in a seat from which he could see the entire room, sat a handsome and tough-looking man, currently waving his arm.

"Over here, over here!"

"You're late, man! We've already got started!"

"Sorry," Goblin Slayer grunted.

The cup one of the men raised was already almost half-empty, and some of the snacks were clearly missing. But the biggest hint was that both adventurers' faces were already flushed.

Goblin Slayer seated himself somewhat awkwardly at the circular table.

The other two men were dressed in civilian clothing; Goblin Slayer alone was wearing his armor. It was impossible not to find it slightly humorous. Unlike the way so many young people envisioned things, adventurers didn't normally go around town in full gear.

Yes, Spearman and Heavy Warrior were both canny enough that even now they each carried a short sword at their hips, but it was probably overkill. The little glances that came their way were probably from travelers who were unaccustomed to adventurers.

These three men were of some renown: The Frontier's Baddest, Spearman. The Frontier's Kindest, Goblin Slayer. And the leader of The Frontier's Coolest Party, Heavy Warrior. (The reason they couldn't be called "famous *faces*" was because of one of them in particular…)

"Why did we not go to the Guild tavern?" Goblin Slayer asked.

"Because I don't want rumors spreading that I was having a rowdy party with some guy who won't even take off his armor," Spearman shot at him.

"He's just saying that," Heavy Warrior said immediately. "He's embarrassed to be seen drinking with you."

"Is that so?"

"*Especially* by Miss Receptionist, if ya know what I mean."

"Aw, shut yer trap!" Spearman growled. Then he jerked his thumb at the menu on the wall. "Anyway, hurry up and order something."

"Yes," Goblin Slayer said, studying the menu. There were at least a dozen kinds of alcohol alone, from ale to fire wine to grape wine.

"……Hmmm," Goblin Slayer muttered.

"Listen up," Spearman said with an exasperated sigh. "Times like these, you don't think about it. Just go with an ale!"

"An ale, then."

"Good! Hey, Miss! Three ales!"

"Taking charge, huh?"

Heavy Warrior couldn't suppress a smile and a quiet chuckle.

"What?" Spearman demanded with a glare, but the warrior calmly replied, "Nothing."

The server placed three brimming mugs of ale on the table with a practiced hand. "Here you go, three ales! Enjoy!"

The waitress was a centaur, still young. One would have to be careful not, in a drunken lapse, to call her a Padfoot. Centaurs were quite a proud people and had no such soft thing as pads on their feet.

It was probably the same with minotaurs, some of whom became Pray-ers. Not that minotaurs as a group usually worried about such details…

But to get back to our story.

The waitress set the cups down, her generous bosom bouncing, then walked away (on all four of her feet), her tail swishing. It was impressive how readily she could weave through the crowded tavern with such a large build.

Watching her muscular behind closely, Heavy Warrior breathed, "I know boobs are good, but a butt is *good*."

"Huh, so that explains why you're so into that knight friend of yours—she rides a horse!"

"She has nothing to do with this." Heavy Warrior paused a moment then said, "Guess we couldn't have a chat like this at the Guild tavern, huh?"

There, you never knew when a woman might be watching—or listening. Heavy Warrior sighed and picked up his ale, sending a ripple through it.

"How about a toast, then?"

"To what?" Goblin Slayer asked quietly. He had also picked up his mug.

"Er… Ah, hell. Too much trouble to think of something. Let's just go with the usual."

Spearman nodded, following the others' lead in raising his drink.

"To our town!"

"To the gods' dice!"

"To adventurers."

"*Cheers!*" they exclaimed and then drained their mugs.

§

Someone—none of them could have said which one—suggested going outside to walk off the drinks a bit.

The streets were packed with people who had enjoyed some wine and were now out on the town. The three adventurers worked their way through the crowds, eventually winding up on the banks of a river.

The river burbled beside them and the stars shone above. The two moons shone down on them.

The evening breeze was pleasant on their alcohol-warmed bodies. It would have been impossible to be in a bad mood on a night like this.

It was only natural to hum a song or two.

* * *

Let the earth turn sour and the wind grow ill
And the world fall dark for all time
There won't be a moment when this shimmering jewel
With four bright lights doesn't shine
For I'll walk the path that seekers will
As I've sworn, with these friends of mine.

To the ends of the earth and the home of the wind,
Though all's a dream, I'll go
Those four bright lights in that gem never end
Or gutter or burn down low
And as for us, we'll never forget
Our friends as we walk the road.

It was a half-forgotten song of military valor from long, long ago. A bard with his lute could make it sound beautiful and brave, but three drunken adventurers were lucky even to qualify as out of tune.

"The hell?" Spearman seemed to have had his fill of singing after a couple of verses, because he broke off in the same register as the tune.

His glare settled on Goblin Slayer. Something was bothering him.

"What're you gonna do?"

"What do you mean?"

"You know what I mean!"

Ahh, he's gone, Heavy Warrior thought, looking up at the stars.

Should they have brought along that witch? Bah. She would probably just be staring off into the distance. Maybe smiling ambiguously. No, you couldn't count on her at a moment like this.

"I mean the receptionist, dumbass! Plus you've got that elf and your farm girl and that priestess! You're crawling with ladies!"

"..."

Goblin Slayer didn't speak for a moment. Finally, he said quietly, "I don't think anything will be possible until all the goblins are gone." He paused another moment. "I..."

Then he fell silent. Spearman gave him a sidelong glare.

That was understandable enough.

It wasn't too difficult to guess what kind of a past a man named Goblin Slayer must have.

Hence, Spearman gave a dramatic sigh then shrugged his shoulders with exaggerated annoyance.

"There it is."

"A goblin?"

"No, you nut." Spearman snorted. Heavy Warrior laughed out loud.

Then the muscular fighter nodded and said, "Hey, it's not like I don't get it."

"Oh yeah?"

"Yeah. It's like..." Heavy Warrior made a broad gesture at the sky, as if searching for something invisible. "It's like, a man wants to be free, right? King of his own domain."

"A king, huh!" Spearman smirked as they walked along. He wasn't making fun; it was a grin of understanding. "Sounds good to me. There's that old story about the mercenary who became a king."

"Too bad I ain't got any smarts," Heavy Warrior said, giving himself a tap on the side of the head.

"If you study, you will gain some," Goblin Slayer said. "You have money as well. You must have a certain intelligence."

"Problem is, I don't have the time." Heavy Warrior shrugged, and the sword on his belt, which he diligently wore even when drunk, rattled. "And you can't start studying *after* you become a king. That would just mean you were a stupid king, and nothing's worse for the people than a ruler with no brain."

"Yes."

"But if I start studying *now*, I won't be able to go on adventures, and that'll put the rest of my party through hell."

"I see," Goblin Slayer said. He crossed his arms and mumbled thoughtfully. Finally, he produced his conclusion: "It's difficult."

"You got that right," Heavy Warrior said soberly. *Hard enough to make you give up your weapons and equipment and everything.* His voice, however, was light and cheerful. The way the edges of his lips turned up was proof of a smile.

"Not that things are boring the way they are."

"Plus, you've got your lady knight, huh?" Spearman interjected.

"Shaddup!" Heavy Warrior gave him a kick.

"Ow!" Spearman exclaimed. The muscles of a trained warrior practically qualified as weapons themselves.

Heavy Warrior ignored the shouting, leaning on the railing of the bridge they were on. Goblin Slayer stood just beside him.

"I doubt it's such a bad thing."

"..."

"I'm sure it isn't."

"Guess not," Heavy Warrior said, meeting Goblin Slayer's somber words with a sly smile. "...Yeah. I guess I wouldn't mind having her along, either."

"Feh! You unattached guys have all the luck!" Spearman said with a click of his tongue. He leaned back against the railing and looked up at the stars. He squinted to see a light, at a height just past their reach, beyond the far side of the sky.

"You're just greedy," Heavy Warrior teased him.

"You idiot," Spearman shot back. "As a man, you're born wanting two things: beautiful women and the utmost strength. What else could you aim for in life?"

"You're sounding like one of our kids again..."

Did he mean Scout Boy or Rookie Warrior? To seek to be known as the strongest of all adventurers was a privilege granted to youth.

"Yeah, the strongest, that's right," Spearman said, almost pouting. "Because I believe that when I am the strongest, I'll be able to do anything." He spat up at the heavens—not that it would change the rolls of the gods' dice. "Women will love me, people will thank me, and I'll be able to do the world some good. Nothing wrong with that, right?"

"Love you? Actual women?" Heavy Warrior snorted. Maybe it was some gentle payback for earlier.

"You better believe they will!"

"Hmm," Goblin Slayer muttered. "I cannot picture it."

"Aw, you be quiet!" Spearman glanced at Goblin Slayer while keeping his face skyward. As usual, the adventurer was wearing his metal mask. His grimy steel helmet. There was no way to know what expression lay behind it.

©Noboru Kannatuki

I'll bet our dear receptionist would know.

It was just proof of how much and how often they had talked together. Spearman wondered: if *he* put on a helmet, would she know what his expression was?

He sucked in a deep breath then let it out. "And what about you, Goblin Slayer?" he asked. "What did you dream of when you were a kid?"

"Me?"

"Think there's anyone else around here who kills enough goblins to go by that name?"

"...I suppose you're right."

Goblin Slayer lapsed into silence, staring into the river. Even in the light of the twin moons, it looked dark and black, like spilled ink.

Where did the river come from, and where did it go? He remembered asking his older sister once.

She had told him that it came from the mountains and went to the sea. He had once thought that he would follow it back to its source, just to see it. But he seemed unlikely to get the chance now.

"...I wanted to be an adventurer."

"Huh!" Spearman said, giving Goblin Slayer a jab with his elbow. "Well, that's one lifelong dream checked off the list, isn't it?!"

"No," Goblin Slayer said with a slight shake of his head. "It is difficult."

"It is, huh?"

"Yes," Goblin Slayer nodded. "It is not so easily done."

That right? Heavy Warrior added to himself. He let out a long breath. "What you wanna do, what you gotta do, and what you can do don't always line up, do they?"

"It's enough to make a guy nuts," Spearman agreed.

The three men went quiet then, looking up at the moons. The wind blew across the river, pregnant with the promise of summer.

What we wanted.

To be renowned warriors. Great heroes or kings; part of history and legend.

To find some item from the Age of the Gods, rescue princesses, fight dragons, and save the world.

They'd wanted to explore hidden ruins, discover the secrets of the world and bring their truths to light.

They had wanted to be surrounded by gorgeous women, loved and admired—and just as smart as anyone they might meet.

They longed to wield weapons they had well and truly mastered, performing feats of strength that would be spoken of for generations to come. Someone who people would point to, no matter what the task, and say, *Him. He can do it.*

Most likely, they realized, at this point, that such stories were not to be theirs.

They were Silver, the third rank, the highest rank of adventurer to be out in the field. And that meant something to them. They never dismissed that achievement or felt it was so much trouble to be Silver that they would have been better off staying at Bronze or even Steel rank.

And yet.

And yet, truly…

"So, well…"

He was Goblin Slayer.

He was not the red-haired boy.

That was reason enough.

"…At the very least, I want to let her do what she wants to do."

The men all nodded.

CHAPTER 5

THE TRAINING FIELD ON THE EDGE OF TOWN

"...Come again?"

Dwarf Shaman was in the Guild tavern, stuffing hot mashed potato into his face. It was a bit too early for lunch—the meal in question might be considered a late breakfast. "Y'want me?"

"Yes."

Across from him was a man in grimy leather armor and a cheap-looking steel helmet: Goblin Slayer. There was no sign that he had eaten or was eating anything.

Goblin Slayer put a hand to his helmet as if he had a headache and drank some water through the slats of his visor.

"Will you do it?"

"Sure, I don't mind, but..."

Dwarf Shaman ate another spoonful of mashed potato. Dwarves were known as gourmands who would try anything, and as such were greatly welcomed in any dining establishment. The food just had to taste halfway decent and be in plentiful supply. If the flavor happened to be especially exquisite, that was a bonus.

High Elf Archer, if asked her opinion, might have characterized this as a lack of restraint, but Dwarf Shaman would probably have replied that elves simply had no imagination.

Regardless, the spell caster was quite happy to eat a mountain of mashed potatoes with only a bit of salt for flavor.

"Potato?"

"Mmf, mrf… Yes! I was in a potato mood today," he replied, coughing indelicately as he took another mouthful. "Not going to have any, yourself?"

"I have goblin slaying to do."

"That so?" Dwarf Shaman took Goblin Slayer's cup, filled it to the brim with wine, and pushed it back at him. "Well, drink up. You can spare a few minutes with me, can't you?"

"Mm." Goblin Slayer gulped down the contents of the cup. Dwarf Shaman watched him with a smile.

"I get the impression that me and our brash friend practice slightly different kinds of magic," Dwarf Shaman said.

"I don't know the specifics, but I suspected as much," Goblin Slayer replied.

"And I think you might be better off asking someone other than me for this."

"That will not do," Goblin Slayer slowly shook his head. "You are the most capable spell slinger I know."

"…"

Dwarf Shaman's hand froze as he reached for another helping of potatoes. He swirled his spoon (which had previously been making ceaseless trips into his mouth) in the pile of food, rather tactlessly.

After a while, he sighed.

"Well, no sayin' no t'that, is there?" he said. He shot Goblin Slayer a resentful glance. "I'll bet y'could say the same thing to that witch lady."

"I certainly could not," Goblin Slayer said softly. Even Dwarf Shaman could guess what he meant by that.

"Sorry. That was a poor thing to say, even in jest."

"If it's too much, feel free to refuse."

"A foolish thought. I only ever turn down work from people who don't like dwarves."

Then Dwarf Shaman set to eating ravenously again. He didn't even bother to clean off his beard but veritably poured mashed potato into his mouth, like wine into a barrel.

When he had at last made a dent in the quantity of food, he tossed aside his spoon.

"But, Beard-cutter, I want you to tell me one thing."

"What?"

"Whatever brought this idea on?"

Goblin Slayer went silent.

It wasn't such an unusual story. He was a warrior; he had little aptitude for magic. When he needed someone talented in such arts, why not turn to a shaman?

But that was not what the dwarf was asking. Even Goblin Slayer understood that much, as he looked over Dwarf Shaman's beard to meet his eyes.

"I am Goblin Slayer." He took a swallow of wine as if to wet his lips. "And he is an adventurer."

"Fair enough." Dwarf Shaman gave a snort and leaned his small frame against the back of the chair. It creaked under the weight of his heavy girth. "When our long-eared friend gets wind of this, I don't think you're likely to hear the end of it anytime soon."

"Is that so?"

"I should think."

"I see."

Dwarf Shaman pushed his empty plate toward Goblin Slayer and waved his hand.

There was now a collection of five or six empty plates, and the waitress—this one padfoot—appeared and ferried them away to be washed.

"Anyway, I accept. But I might…need you to wait for a little while."

"I don't mind. I told him to come this afternoon."

Goblin Slayer poured some water as he spoke. He swirled it around, watching the tiny waves run along the edges of the cup.

"…Do you think he'll be there?"

"Heh! We could bet on it, if you like." Dwarf Shaman smirked and rubbed his hands together. It was a dramatic gesture, like a magician preparing to show off his next trick. "Now, then. I think I need a few more drinks before I go. And then a nice, easy walk." He pounded himself happily on the belly. "I've eaten just enough, after all. Not too hungry, not too full!"

Goblin Slayer didn't say anything but set his empty cup on the table.

§

"......"

The boy was standing in the training grounds; they were still under construction, so a good portion of the area looked like little more than a grassy field.

He was the very picture of being forced to do something involuntarily. His cheeks were puffed out, he looked pouty, and he had his chin in his hands as he looked up at the man who had called him.

"...What, not off killing goblins?"

"No." The man in the grimy leather armor and steel helmet shook his head. "I intend to go once I've collected you."

"I don't recall anyone asking you to look after me."

"Is that so?"

"Yeah!"

"Sorry."

The nonchalant attitude got under the boy's skin and angered him.

What a guy to be in a party with!

If it had been he who wound up in that group—well, he couldn't have categorically refused, but it would have been awfully unpleasant. How could that priestess do it? Or that elf, or that lizardman? Or—

"Ah, there y'are. Excellent, that's a sign of promise."

Or the dwarf, who was now trundling across the grass.

He was grinning, though the boy couldn't imagine what was so funny, and taking swigs from a jar of wine that he kept at his belt.

Yes, he was Silver-ranked. No doubt he was a very capable magic user.

But still, that didn't mean the boy wanted to have to learn at his feet.

It didn't, and yet...

"..."

The boy came back to himself at the sound of his own gnashing teeth.

"Good. May I trust you to handle this, then?" Goblin Slayer asked Dwarf Shaman.

"I'm sure you may. And don't you go getting yourself worked over just because you don't have a spell caster along."

"Of course not."

"And treat me to some wine sometime."

"Very well."

As the boy watched, the two men conducted their conversation in short bursts, almost as if they could read each other's thoughts. He fixed them with a glare, indignant at being unable to join the talk.

Goblin Slayer turned toward him. "Listen to what you are told, don't cause trouble, and get serious."

He practically sounded like an older sibling giving instructions to their kid brother. The boy just snorted. Goblin Slayer seemed to take this for acceptance, because he turned around. Then he set off at his usual bold, nonchalant stride.

"Hey, wait—!"

"Eyes on me, boy, I'm the one you ought to be worried about."

The boy couldn't shake the sense that he was being left behind, but Dwarf Shaman grasped his shoulder. His small but rough hand was strong enough that his grip almost hurt.

"Have a seat, boyo. It makes a difference whether you try to learn sitting or standing. You don't use your head the same way."

"...Fine," he responded, adding to himself petulantly, *I just have to sit, huh?* and setting himself down in the grass.

From a distance away came enthusiastic voices and the clanging of weaponry. Added to that were laborers carrying materials and working their tools.

The sky was blue, the sunlight warm enough to make one sweat. The boy let out a bit of a sigh.

Dwarf Shaman noticed it; he slowly sat in the lotus position and grinned.

"Right, then. I'm no expert, but... How many spells can you use and how often?"

That was the one question the boy least wanted to answer.

"Fireball. And…just once." He spoke quietly, sticking out his lip. "…But you know that already, right?"

"Y'blamed idiot." A fist came down on the boy.

"Gah?!"

"I'm tellin' you, you're dead wrong."

The boy groaned, holding his throbbing head where he had received the blow. Weren't spell casters supposed to be physically weak?

No, wait, this one was a dwarf. Dammit. The boy grunted. Differences in race couldn't be taken lightly.

"Er… Ergggh. That frickin' hurt… You coulda split my head open!"

"A spell caster's head shouldn't be so hard to begin with! You might be better off if it split open."

"…I thought dwarves were normally warriors anyway."

"We're monks, too, if you didn't know. And why not? We have wits to spare, and spirit, too."

"I—I guess I have heard about the Dwarven Sages…"

"They're just a story," Dwarf Shaman said, sighing deeply. "Listen," he said, whispering as if to impart a secret. "Fireball is not the only spell you have."

"Huh?"

The boy spontaneously forgot the ache in his head, his face a mask of surprise. Three fingers appeared in front of his eyes.

"*Carbunculus*—fiery stone. *Crescunt*—arise or become. *Iacta*—shoot or release. That's it, isn't it?"

"Uh."

"You bring together three words of true power and they become Fireball. See what I'm saying?"

"Yeah, I know that, but…"

He swallowed the rest of what he had been about to say.

It was so obvious.

The spell he had learned consisted of three words of true power, woven together to create a single spell.

That meant power resided in each of the words individually, as well. How much simpler could it be?

Each word might contain far less power than the complete incantation. But still, anyone who reacted to an obvious but new teaching by saying "Yeah, whatever…"

…would just be an idiot.

Dwarf Shaman observed the boy's face stiffen, whereupon he smiled broadly. "Excellent! Looks like the first cracks have appeared in that skull of yours. Now, what are the implications? Tell me what you think."

"…Create fire. Expand. Throw."

"See! Now you've got four options."

"Four?"

"You can cast your Fireball, or you can set something on fire, or cause something to swell, or shoot something."

Though I suppose shooting a swelling ball of fire is still the main thing.

The boy stared at his palms. He cocked his fingers, counting.

Four…

He had been under the belief that a Fireball was all he was capable of—and yet all this time he'd had *four* spells?

"Hey…"

"Hrm?"

"Is it really supposed to be this simple?"

"Changing the way you look at the world isn't— Well, I suppose that's not quite what we're doing. We're just making sure how many cards we have in our hand."

With that, Dwarf Shaman pulled a deck of playing cards seemingly out of thin air.

What was this—a sleight of hand? The thick fingers moved so fast they were almost invisible as he cut the deck and fanned out the cards.

"Low cards are still cards, no?"

"I guess…"

"No need to guess! They are."

He reformed the deck and then, like magic, it disappeared.

He didn't pause for a moment to call attention to this act of prestidigitation but instead whispered conspiratorially, "Say, boy, do you remember a certain very lovely magic user? A witch?"

"…Yeah," the boy said, blushing as he pictured the buxom spell caster. "I know her."

"She uses *inflammarae* to light her smoking pipe."

"...Wait, seriously?"

It was the first completely honest reaction the boy had shown all day, and no wonder. If anyone had done something like that at the Academy, the professors would've had their head.

Magical spells were composed of words of true power, able to alter the logic of the world and manipulate the very way things *were*. They were not to be used lightly—weren't experienced adventurers always saying things like that?

Don't let down your guard. Don't hesitate to kill. Don't use up your spells. And stay away from dragons...

"Anyhow, I think you understand that it isn't best to just pop off spells left and right like that. But think about it." Dwarf Shaman crossed his arms and made a thoughtful noise; the boy still didn't quite follow him. "Say you're out in the rain, you don't have any flint, and all your fuel is wet, but you just *have* to build a campfire. That's when you'd use it."

"...Well, yeah, I guess."

"But if you're really clever, you could build a fire another way in that situation and save a spell."

If you combine branches and bark you can sometimes get a fire going, and often branches you dig up out of the ground will be dry. And depending on how carefully you pile up your firewood, sometimes a wet branch can dry out as the fire burns, making it useful fuel.

Having more than your share of brains is the best way to look after your spells. Any sufficiently advanced skill is indistinguishable from magic.

"The only difference is the method," said Dwarf Shaman.

Each method is an alternative, and alternatives mean, in turn—

"More cards in your deck."

"..."

"And another thing..." Dwarf Shaman ignored Wizard Boy, who had his arms folded and was grumbling. He then pulled the cork from the jar at his hip. An expansive smell of alcohol, the unique aroma of Dwarven fire wine, drifted out. "A spell caster's job isn't to chant spells."

This caused the boy to blink in confusion.

"It's to *use* them."

"…? And those are different how?"

"If you can't figure that out, you won't get anywhere."

Riddles like this were at the heart of what it meant to be a wizard.

What weight was there really in the words of those who always went around proclaiming that they had the truth?

And what value was there really to the truth that one had?

Thus, a wizard would laugh. Laugh and say, *Maybe, maybe not.*

"Only a know-nothing amateur would think that a wizard is doing nothing more than lobbing a ball of fire or some lightning at his enemies."

And then Dwarf Shaman grinned like a shark.

§

Goblin Slayer struck a flint, lighting his torch on the sparks. The smell of burning pine resin mingled with those of damp and mold, as well as less wholesome odors wafting around the cave.

This seemed like it would be as good as alerting the goblins that adventurers had arrived, but strangely, goblins frequently failed to react to the smell of a torch. The smell of women, or children, or elves was much more likely to draw their attention and provoke an attack.

Goblin Slayer's hypothesis was that goblins couldn't distinguish the torch from the rest of the rotten stenches in their home. At the same time, he believed there was nothing better to minimize the smell of metal from armor.

"Ugh… This is just soooo unfair…"

And one must not forget to cover the aroma of elf.

High Elf Archer's face was daubed with muck, and she wept and simpered. She looked vastly less than pleased as she rubbed mud all over her ranger's garments. Her long ears drooped pitifully, trembling.

"Why am I the only one who has to get covered in this stuff?"

"Because you will agitate the goblins."

The answer was curt. High Elf Archer hugged herself and shivered. Since she had joined up with this obsessed adventurer, she had seen more than a few victims of "agitated goblins." She even recalled once when she herself had nearly been killed by them, a position she didn't want to imagine being in again.

If she wanted to avoid that fate, she had to take the appropriate measures.

And so, looking thoroughly pathetic, she continued to paint herself with the vile effluent at the entrance to the cave.

"What happened to the sachet of herbs you used last time?"

"...I ran out." High Elf Archer's expression was vague, and she looked away evasively. "...Of money."

Apparently even High Elves, with bloodlines that reached back to the Age of the Gods, were subject to such ordinary problems. Maybe that was part of the reason she had joined a party where she was going to do nothing but goblin slaying, a job she detested.

It didn't particularly cross her mind to be grateful to Goblin Slayer.

"Just as with your arrows," he said softly, "it's important to manage all your resources."

"I told you, I hate money!"

"Is that so?"

"You use it, then it's gone!"

"Yes, that's true."

"But then it never grows back!"

"Right."

"I just don't get it...!"

"I see."

Her ears bobbed up and down in anger; Goblin Slayer listened impassively.

What mattered to him were the drawings the goblins had left on the cave walls. The crude, cartoonish forms of unidentifiable animals were painted in a dark crimson.

He looked at them, confirming that he saw no relation between these drawings and the brand that had been used by the goblin paladin.

"Simple totems." Goblin Slayer rubbed at one of the symbols, which had been painted in the blood of a living creature. Dried blood flaked off the wall, leaving reddish grime on the palm of his gauntlet. "There is a shaman here."

"Hmm." High Elf Archer didn't sound especially interested. She pulled the bow off her back and readied an arrow. "How many?"

"Fewer than twenty, I suspect," Goblin Slayer said, guessing based on the amount of pollution outside the cave. "Are you in?"

"Let's do it," High Elf Archer replied, puffing out her scrawny chest. "If they think they can take us lightly just because there's only two of us, they've got another think coming."

Only two.

Yes, this time it was just a pair of adventurers who were going to challenge the goblin nest: Goblin Slayer and High Elf Archer.

Dwarf Shaman was helping the boy, while Lizard Priest and Priestess apparently had some sort of business to attend to together.

When it came to facing down twenty goblins, a warrior and a ranger did not make the best pair.

But nonetheless, goblins had appeared.

And he was Goblin Slayer.

The quest was exceedingly simple—practically off a template. Some goblins had shown up on the fringes of a village. The villagers had sought to simply leave them alone, but that had only allowed them to multiply.

Crops had been stolen. Livestock made off with. A girl who went to pick herbs was attacked, kidnapped.

Please, please help her. The reward was a pouch of grimy, rusty coins from at least two generations ago.

But there was no reason to ignore them.

A stereotypical case. A pitiful reward. But so what?

The enemies were goblins. What more reason could he need?

Goblin Slayer certainly couldn't answer that question.

"You're conscientious if nothing else, Orcbolg," High Elf Archer said, glancing back at him with a smile. "I notice how when there's a chance of rescuing someone, you never use poison gas or water or fire."

Although when it was too late, or after they had helped the person, he was merciless. High Elf Archer gave a little chuckle.

"Here, take this. A little something for your belly."

She tossed him something: some of the elves' secret food, small fried treats.

High Elf Archer herself was already nibbling on some of the stuff like a squirrel or some other small animal. Goblin Slayer's helmet turned toward her.

"With you around..."

"What?"

"With you around, it is always lively."

"...Is that a compliment?" She glared at Goblin Slayer suspiciously, scuttling up to him like a little bird. She looked deep past the visor, her ears drooping in time with her eyebrows for a moment. "That's not your way of saying I need to shut up, is it?"

"I meant only what I said."

"...Well." She spun on her heel, leaving the noncommittal word hanging in the air. Her hair fluttered along behind her like a tail.

She darted deeper into the cave, free as the wind, but still...

"Heh-heh!"

Her ears bobbed happily, something that could clearly be seen even from behind her.

Of course, the two were not in as easy a mood as their banter suggested. Anyone who wasn't a complete beginner would know that they were on enemy ground in a place like this.

Goblin Slayer shoved the baked treat through his visor, drawing his sword even as he chewed.

High Elf Archer's superlative senses caused her ears to flick each time she heard a noise.

The lighthearted chatter—even if it was High Elf Archer doing all the chattering—was a way of preserving their sanity.

The proof came a moment later, when High Elf Archer suddenly stopped in her tracks.

"They're quick."

"Yeah. But I didn't get the feeling they were watching us."

They needed no words. Goblin Slayer already had his weapon at the ready, and High Elf Archer was as taut as a drawn bow.

"If you kidnap a young girl, it's only to be expected that adventurers will come."

The battle between goblins and adventurers had been going on since time immemorial. Over a dizzying accumulation of ages, even the goblins had managed to learn something: *adventurers will come.*

They always came. They came and killed and took what belonged to the goblins. Therefore, the goblins would kill them.

It was a total failure to reflect on their own actions or to take any kind of caution that made goblins what they were.

"Which direction?"

"Right." High Elf Archer closed her eyes, her ears fluttering. "Five or six of them, maybe. I hear some weapons, too."

"What about in front?"

"Nothing for now."

In other words, there would be no attempt to catch them in a pincer movement. Goblin Slayer snorted, then took his sword in a reverse grip, holding it by the blade and taking up a stance.

"They always think ambush is a skill that belongs to them alone."

The next second, Goblin Slayer took his sword and slammed it into the earthen wall as if he were chopping firewood.

"GROOOORB?!"

The earth, shallow now from being dug out, collapsed inward, raining into the side tunnel. The goblin at the head of the digging party opened his eyes wide, completely flummoxed.

They were supposed to surround the stupid adventurers, beat them, humiliate the woman, make her bear their—

Goblin Slayer landed another blow to the creature's head, putting an end to his plans—and his life.

"One. We'll hit them from this direction. Let's go."

"It's awfully tight. Hard to shoot in." Of course, even as she complained, High Elf Archer fired off three arrows simultaneously over Goblin Slayer's shoulder, piercing three goblins.

"GROR?!"

"GOOBBR?!"

One took the arrow to the throat; the monsters to either side were caught in the eye, one left, one right. They collapsed, and Goblin Slayer struck their corpses.

"Four…"

A sword covered in brains up to the hilt wasn't going to be much use. He kicked over a goblin that now had a blade sprouting from his forehead, taking up the spade the monster had been using as a weapon.

"...Five."

The fifth goblin attacked him. He blocked the blow from the monster's pickax and, in the same motion, took the torch, which he held on the same side as his shield, and brought it down into the goblin's face.

"GROORRORBRO?!"

There was a crackling sound and the hideous stench of cooking flesh. Goblin Slayer watched the monster with the fried face cry out. The counterattack's failure would soon be discovered, he assumed. A scream would make scant difference now.

Goblin Slayer was utterly without mercy: he thrust the spade into the goblin's neck.

"GROORB!!"

The final goblin howled even though nothing had happened to him yet. He threw away the hatchet he had been holding and tossed his arms over his head. Slobbering and sniveling, he prostrated himself before the adventurers.

A creature we missed at the mausoleum?

Goblin Slayer cast aside the broken torch and picked up the crimson-stained hatchet. He put it into his belt, pulled out a new torch, and lit it from the old one.

"Now, then."

"GOR?!"

Goblin Slayer gave the creature a kick; it shrieked and tumbled on its behind. But it quickly resumed its pathetic groveling, scraping its head against the ground.

He was begging for his life. Did he have a modicum of intelligence? Was he calculating what would be in his best interests? Did he have a notion of surrender?

Given that he had been at the back of the group, maybe he had a certain status even among goblins.

Then again, he was physically the smallest. A child, perhaps...?

"Orcbolg..."

"Yes."

High Elf Archer's voice was shaking. Goblin Slayer nodded silently.

That young goblin was trying to draw a poisoned dagger from his belt.

Around his neck was a necklace.

A necklace he had gotten by stealing.

The objects on the necklace had been pierced by an awl, sewn together. They had been chopped off by a hatchet. Ten freshly cut fingers of a young woman.

To this goblin who cowered and simpered, all the while hiding a dagger at his back, Goblin Slayer had one simple thing to say.

"We kill them all."

§

"Come to think of it..."

"Hmm?"

"This may be the first time it's been just the two of us."

"Ah, indeed, I think you are right about that," Lizard Priest said, his tail swinging gently.

It was afternoon at the training grounds. Although the facilities were nearly half-finished, the place was still open to the elements.

Novice adventurers, as well as laborers, lounged here and there on the grass, eating their lunches.

It wasn't guaranteed that food would be provided, and even if it was, physical activity made a body hungry.

"Even the gods and spirits cannot cure an empty stomach," Lizard Priest mused.

"You're forgetting about the Create Water and Create Food miracles," Priestess said.

Not that I have them yet.

"Ho-ho," Lizard Priest laughed appreciatively. "If I changed religions, the available blessings would change as well, I see."

"That's true. Although I don't think I can do any more praying today..."

Why had the two of them come to the practice grounds? The answer was training, combined with performing some healing.

It wasn't just inexperienced adventurers who were at risk while practicing. If anything, the people working on the construction of the facility were probably in greater danger.

Bumps and scrapes, of course, could be treated with simple first-aid, but broken bones could affect so much more than just the construction. Calling on the gods for a Minor Heal miracle could make all the difference.

At length, the two clerics settled on the outskirts of the field to have their food.

Priestess sat with her knees drawn together and undid the parcel that held her lunch. It was bread and cheese, along with watered-down wine and several pieces of dried fruit.

"My," said Lizard Priest, peeking at her provisions from where he sat cross-legged. "Will that be enough for you?"

"Yes," Priestess answered. It wasn't so much about a balanced diet; she just tended not to eat that much. "I've, ahem—" She looked away from him, her cheeks turning a little bit red. "I seem to have put on a few pounds since becoming an adventurer."

Lizard Priest opened his great jaws and cackled. "Ha-ha-ha-ha-ha-ha! Never fear! Surely that is from building muscle."

"I think it might be because there are so many good things to eat in this town..."

"I should think, child, that a little meat on your bones would be for the best. You're rather too thin."

"The Chief Priestess told me the same thing..."

At a certain age, perhaps even cleric girls worried about these things. It probably didn't help that there were so many attractive women around her, like Cow Girl, Guild Girl, and Witch.

Priestess let out a small sigh then quickly offered a prayer of thanks to the Earth Mother for her food.

Lizard Priest, for his part, made one of his strange palms-together gestures and opened a pouch made from an animal skin.

"Oh," Priestess said. Her eyes widened a bit, and then she smiled gently. "A sandwich, huh?"

"Heh-heh-heh-heh-heh."

Lizard Priest made an expression that was perhaps a full-faced grin then rolled his eyes and held up the sandwich triumphantly. It consisted of thick bread slathered in butter, surrounding slices of seared beef.

What really drew the eye, however, was the cheese, so much of it that it threatened to be more than the bread could contain. It practically buried the beef; the cheese was obviously the star here. It was the exact opposite of a normal sandwich, in which the beef would be the main component and the cheese just an addition.

"One's favorite ingredients, arranged just as one pleases. This is true freedom." He sounded as happy as a clam, and Priestess couldn't resist a smile.

"I can't say I don't understand..."

"Mm. If food is indeed culture, one would need a truly enlightened civilization to produce this." As he spoke, Lizard Priest gobbled the sandwich down. Half of it was gone in one bite; two chomps later, it had vanished.

"Ahh, nectar! Delicious!"

"Heh-heh. You really do like cheese, don't you?"

"Indeed. It makes me grateful to have ventured into the human world."

Smack, smack. His tail slapped the ground in a display of high spirit. Priestess followed its movement.

She opened her own mouth, much less wide than Lizard Priest, and began putting torn-off pieces of bread into it. As she chewed, a nutty flavor filled her mouth. She accompanied it with a swallow of grape wine.

"What kind of food did you eat back at your home?" Priestess asked.

"We were warriors and hunters, you see. We ate birds or animals that we caught." Having finished his first sandwich, Lizard Priest was reaching for his second. "The young warriors ate with the young warriors, the more experienced with their own cohort. And the superiors ate with the superiors." Holding his sandwich in one hand, he smacked the grass with the other. "We ate on the ground or on the floor, just like this."

"You didn't all eat together?"

"If a king or a general were to come among the common soldiers, how could they relax?"

"I see."

"Banquets, now those were different. When we would achieve a victory in battle, fires would be lit in the public square, and everyone would sit down together."

In her mind's eye, Priestess found she could picture a scene from a land she had never been to. A great crowd of lizardmen gathered at the foot of a huge tree in the rain forest, raising their cups and drinking their wine, celebrating together.

In the midst of it all, a great beast roasted on a spit, brave warriors cutting off hunks of meat and raising their voices. For some reason, one of them in particular was joyfully taking mouthfuls of cheese… But that was probably just an imaginative detail on her part.

If nothing else, though…

"It seems very festive."

"I should say so," Lizard Priest said confidently. "At times, we would also go in search of corn or potatoes…"

"Ooh. Potatoes go well with cheese, you know."

"Oh-ho!" Lizard Priest leaned forward suddenly, his eyes gleaming and his jaws open. It was no wonder Priestess drew back a little with a frightened yelp.

"I should like to hear more on that topic!"

"Er, well, I—back at the Temple, I used to cook them together…"

Cut the potatoes, mix them with a sauce of milk, flour, and butter, then sprinkle cheese over them and bake them in the oven. The result was a rich meal for winter festival days or any kind of celebration.

"Everyone gathered in the Great Hall, offered up our prayers, and then ate together."

"That is most excellent…!"

Both the recipe and the meal, he meant.

"To share a meal with one's fellows," Lizard Priest proclaimed, "is to deepen one's ties to them."

"Yes," Priestess nodded, smiling. Then she thought of something and cocked her head at him. "Oh, if you want, we can cook it together when we have a chance."

"I should like that," Lizard Priest replied.

That was when a bright, cheerful voice reached their ears: "Hey, looks like you've got something good to eat there!"

Priestess looked in the direction of the voice. The first thing she saw was a pair of bare feet. Small but muscular, they led up to legs covered in short pants, and then a light shirt. She was hot and sweating, fanning at her collar to get the air moving. It was Rhea Fighter.

"A sandwich? Lucky you! Can I have a bite?"

With a grunt, Lizard Priest flung the rest of the food into his mouth, waving his tail in an intimidating manner as he chewed.

"Among the teachings I received, there was no such thing as the sharing of food."

"Aww…"

She didn't actually look that disappointed, though, and soon Lizard Priest rolled his eyes in his head.

"Well, not like I didn't bring my own lunch!" she said. "Can I join you?" She laughed openly and held up a parcel in her hand. It was wrapped neatly in a red handkerchief and was startlingly large.

Priestess, who had been chewing on some dried sweet beans, swallowed her mouthful and made an affirmative noise, nodding. "Oh, yes. I don't mind."

"Nor am I bothered."

"Don't mind if I do, then!" The rhea girl flung herself down in the grass next to them, busily unwrapping her lunch. It was a pile of fluffy pancakes, cooked to a golden brown color not unlike that of a fox pelt. Each one was as big as a person's face, and there were one, two, three, four—five!—of them.

Considering a rhea's physical size, this was equivalent to enough food to feed a dwarf.

She took out a bottle and popped the cork, pouring thick, rich honey over the pancakes, then she dug in.

Priestess found herself blinking. "You've got quite an appetite, haven't you?"

"We eat five or six times a day!" *Can't always get all your meals during an adventure, though…* The girl licked clean a honey-sticky finger. "So I have to make sure I eat enough at once that I don't starve between meals!"

"Ha-ha-ha..." Priestess laughed noncommittally. She had the distinct sense that the rhea would have eaten just as much even if she were getting all her meals.

"By the way," Priestess said, "you're solo right now, aren't you?"

"Sure am. So I was thinking maybe I'll hunt some rats next or something."

Cleaning the giant rats out of the sewers was a basic task for beginning adventurers. That didn't mean it was an especially popular job—people felt it wasn't adventure-y enough. No one became an adventurer just to fight overgrown rodents. They wanted to do battle with terrifying monsters, delve dungeons, and get loot from treasure chests. That's what adventuring was all about.

But it wasn't easy to do any of that solo.

"Plus, this place is crawling with fledgling warriors." *No party for me.* She laughed.

As great as it was to join forces with some people you got along with and go adventuring, by the same token, it could be painful when you were left on your own.

If it weren't for Goblin Slayer...

What would have happened to her?

That was what was in Priestess's mind.

It was such a strange thing. If those three people hadn't called out to her on that day, where would she be now?

If she hadn't gone on an adventure with them, she wouldn't be here at this moment.

It was all because of that adventure, and all the fighting that had come after, day upon day piling up. The tiny decisions she had made, one second at a time, had produced this exact instant.

"Um..." The thought caused the words to come out of her mouth almost of their own accord. "If you like, why don't you...try adventuring with us?"

"Adventuring?" The rhea looked at them, a bit baffled. "What about your armored buddy, Goblin Slayer or whoever? Don't think I've seen him around today..."

"Oh, umm..."

"As it so happens," Lizard Priest said, leaning forward and picking up the thread from the momentarily inarticulate Priestess, "in order to advance in rank, she must demonstrate her abilities and, as such, is seeking temporary adventuring partners." As he spoke, he chewed and swallowed another sandwich noisily.

"Most likely, we'd only be together for one quest..." Priestess said apologetically.

"Hmm." Rhea Fighter crossed her arms and looked into the distance.

Beginning adventurers were sometimes called "the mob," and in that group, human and dwarf warriors were plentiful. A great many of them were solid and strong, either because they had trained hard or because they were born that way.

"I'm just warning you, I'm really nothing special," Rhea Fighter said with a faint smile. Yes, she had trained, but she lifted one of her arms to demonstrate that it was still smaller than that of a human or dwarf. "I mean, I'm a rhea. I don't have really good equipment. And I'm just a warrior."

Then leather armor. A sword and shield. Decent equipment, but definitely on the small side.

In light of her skills and strength and equipment, there were probably lots of warriors better than her.

"Are you sure about me?"

"Ah, but," Lizard Priest said, nodding somberly, "you have luck."

"Luck...?"

"Call it a convivial relationship with fate. No?"

"Absolutely!" Priestess immediately agreed with Lizard Priest. She puffed out her little chest as best she could. "Like how you asked us about our potions? That's why...!"

That's why I asked you.

"Huh, so you remember that?" Rhea Fighter said and nodded. "...Well, fine then, all right. But I have to say, I think it's gonna be a liiiittle difficult for just you and me." *So*—she clenched both fists and raised them high. "Let's invite some others, too! Just leave it to me—I've got some great ideas!"

"Oh, I'll come, too!"

Once the idea was in her head, Rhea Fighter moved startlingly quickly. She was off like a hare; Priestess belatedly rose to go after her.

As she went scurrying away, Priestess spun around and bowed deeply to Lizard Priest.

She fully understood that the naga cleric had engineered this on her behalf.

It had been a full year since the four of them had become a party.

Lizard Priest gave her an encouraging wave, as if to say, *Don't worry about it*, and she nodded at him again.

"Heeey, let's move! Everyone will start training again once they're done eating!"

"Right! Sure! Sorry, and thank you…!"

"Yaaah!" Well ahead of Priestess, Rhea Fighter was giving the red-haired boy a kick.

When Priestess caught up, she bowed repeatedly and explained what was going on. Dwarf Shaman laughed uproariously. In that interval, Rhea Fighter spotted her next targets and went barreling off toward Rookie Warrior and Apprentice Cleric.

The latter was objecting that they were right in the middle of lunch, when Priestess came up with Wizard Boy in tow, once again bowing and apologizing.

"Ahh, luck is a virtue, and virtue is luck," Lizard Priest said happily as he ate and observed the goings-on.

They had been together for a whole year, after all. He was well acquainted with the girl's personality, with her goodness of heart.

Well, then.

His mind worked as he finished off his final sandwich.

What about the virtue of milord Goblin Slayer, the strange fanatic at the heart of our party?

§

Chirp, chirp. Chirp, chirp, chirp, chirp.

Cow Girl was roused from the depths of sleep by the canary's tweeting.

"Hrn… Hmm? Hmm?"

She rubbed her eyes and blinked several times. She gave a big stretch and realized she was sitting in a chair in the dining area. She must have stretched out on the table and then fallen asleep at some point.

The sun was already well and truly set, leaving the interior of the room dim; the only light was the faint shimmer of the twin moons.

On the tabletop was a cup of black tea, which had gone completely cold.

She must have fallen asleep waiting for him.

"Hmm… At least I don't have pillow marks," she said, massaging her stiff cheeks. As she did so, a blanket fell from her shoulders.

Her uncle must have put it there. Although it was early spring, the nights were still cold. Cow Girl picked it up and folded it.

"I'll have to thank him…"

As she did this, the canary continued to chirp noisily, flapping around its cage. Cow Girl quickly lit a candle, placing it in a candle-holder and making her way over to the cage.

"What's up? Are you chilly? Or maybe hungry?"

The tone she adopted, as if she were speaking to a small child, was probably only natural. She leaned forward, peering into the cage; the canary cocked its head and peered back.

She could just make out the silhouette of herself in her nightclothes wavering in the window's reflection.

Maybe I ought to go sleep in bed.

The thought made good sense, yet she just didn't feel like it.

Maybe I should start going with him…

She went over to the window, put her chin in her hand, and sighed.

No, impossible. A fantasy that faltered at every point.

True, she was rather muscular—as much as she hated to admit it, her body was better built than most girls her age. But even so, that didn't mean she would be able to use a weapon or face down monsters.

Most of all, though, was that if she were to start going places as well, perhaps he just wouldn't come home anymore…

"…Whoa, don't get a big head, now." Cow Girl couldn't resist a chuckle.

That was when it happened: with a rattle and a clatter, the door opened. The night air came drifting in, along with a strange smell. An odor of iron. Mud and sweat and dust, along with blood.

Even without looking, Cow Girl knew immediately: it was *his* smell.

"Welcome home!"

"...I'm back."

The response to her gentle voice was quiet, dispassionate, and blunt.

He closed the door behind himself as he came in, trying as hard as he could to be quiet, but the noise was still just a little bit loud. Cow Girl turned, smiling softly, and his helmet shook doubtfully.

"You've been awake all this time?"

"Nah. I just woke up."

"Did I wake you?"

"No, no. Don't worry about it. Somebody got me up at just the right moment." She pointed at the birdcage and added, "Huh, little buddy?" to which the canary responded, *Chirp!*

"This bird's really something. It knew you were home before you came in."

"Hmm," he grunted softly, pulling out a chair and sitting down heavily. Cow Girl thought he could at least afford to take off his weapons and armor, but she didn't say anything. She pulled herself away from the window, grabbing an apron that hung in the kitchen and tossing it on over her nightwear.

"Dinner?" she asked, glancing over her shoulder at him as she tied the apron string behind her.

"Let me see," he replied, and then, "Yes, please." Finally, he added quietly, "Anything is fine."

"I've got stew ready to go."

After a moment's pause, "...Is that so?" he replied with a predictable nod.

It took time to relight the oven fire and warm up the stew.

"Oh, you may want to wipe down your armor a bit."

"Is that so?"

"Yeah. There's a hand towel over there you can use."

"Ah."

He obediently began to wipe the grime from his helmet and armor, although his movements were rather rough. Of course, these were not stains that were going to come off with a little rubbing, but it was enough to satisfy Cow Girl.

When she set the stew down in front of him, he began shoving it through his visor like a starving man.

It was already spring, and there was no longer a need for such warm foods, yet she still made stew. Yes, very unsophisticated.

"It's all the time these days, isn't it?"

She sat across from him, supporting her head by putting her hands against both cheeks.

"What is?"

"That you go out." Cow Girl grabbed a napkin and leaned over the table, mopping a stray bit of stew off his helmet. "It's all those goblins—or, well, I guess you've got that training area now, too."

"Yes."

"Are you busy?"

"...No," Goblin Slayer replied after a moment's thought. The helmet tilted as if he wasn't quite sure. "...I wonder."

Hmmm. Cow Girl sat back in her seat, chin in her hand, and observed him. Obviously, she couldn't see the color of his eyes, which were hidden behind his visor.

"I knew it," Cow Girl said, giggling a little in the back of her throat. "You don't want them building something there, do you?"

Bull's-eye. His spoon stopped halfway to his mouth. "It is not... exactly that I don't want them to."

Hrrrm. He tried to act as if he was thinking.

His body language hadn't changed a bit from when they were younger. He had always struggled to hide when he was upset.

"It's a lonely feeling, isn't it?"

"..."

"And you're worried about that girl, aren't you?"

"....."

"You're worried, but you can't think of a good way to help her out."

"........"

"And in the meantime, goblins will be up to their tricks..."

"..........."

"You get anxious when you're not doing anything."

He tossed down the spoon in his hand, still silent. Then he sighed deeply and finally spoke. "...You know me well."

"I ought to. We've been together for years." Finally, she couldn't restrain the laughter, and she winked at him.

From inside the helmet, his gaze was fixed on her. It made Cow Girl sit up straight in her chair.

"Do you not think anything of it?"

The question was brief, but she was probably the only one who could understand what he was thinking when he asked it. In fact, she wasn't completely sure that even she understood.

Her uncle, however, was not a resident of that little village. The only two remaining were him—and her.

"I'm not...saying it never bothers me."

"..."

"I remember...splashing in the lake and lots of other things."

She remembered.

The voices of her parents, with their little brick house.

The friendly warmth of the stone wall when it had been sitting all day in the sun.

The wind on her face as she ran along the little path through the village. The sound of the adults' hoes and plows as they worked the fields.

The creaking of the poorly wrought bucket as it came up from the well full of cold water.

That little tree that stood on top of the hill, and how her heart pounded when she hid some treasure in its hollow.

Those feelings she had when the two of them watched the bright red sunset spread from the far side of the horizon out over the entire world.

How the grass tickled her back when she lay out on the plains, staring up at the two moons until late into the night.

The pain of the slap her father gave her, angry at her for coming home so late. The loneliness of the attic where she had shut herself up in anger.

How her mother's home-cooked breakfasts smelled, the scent wafting up to her after she had dozed off upstairs.

She remembered it all.

It was a world that no longer existed anywhere, except in her heart, and his.

"But I've started to think, maybe it just is what it is." Cow Girl smiled weakly. "That's how everything goes, right? The world keeps turning, we keep living. The wind keeps blowing and the sun keeps rising and setting."

Fwip, fwip. She made circles in the air with her pointer finger.

It had been so long since that day and yet not long at all.

Ten years, eleven. Enough time for a child to grow up. For the look of a place to change. And towns, too, and people, and everything else.

Everything in the world continued on, changing, never resting. Even thoughts and memories.

Was there anything that didn't change? Perhaps change itself was the only thing that didn't change.

I'm not even sure if change is bad or good.

"All that means we need to accept change."

"…Is that so?"

"Yes, it is." Cow Girl nodded as if to emphasize her own point. "I'm sure of it."

"I see."

That was all he said; then he fell silent.

A great many things had happened, he thought.

A year—it had been a year since he went on that adventure to save that priestess girl or, more accurately, to kill goblins.

He had met High Elf Archer, Dwarf Shaman, and Lizard Priest. He had fought that monster whose name he could never remember.

He'd done battle with a goblin army that attacked the farm. Spearman, Heavy Warrior, and many others had helped him emerge victorious.

Then there were the goblins who had appeared in the sewers beneath the water town. The fight with the champion. Sword Maiden.

The autumn festival was another occasion that showed him how many friends he had made.

And in winter, they had gone to the snowy mountain and fought the goblin paladin.

There was an unmistakable difference between his previous self and the way he was now. Otherwise, would he ever have considered looking after that boy?

The path of life was full of crossroads and forks. He could choose any direction he wanted now.

"..."

Still.

Still, yet...

And I'd still have her, if she hadn't died after a goblin stabbed her with a poisoned blade!!

"...It isn't yet possible," he—Goblin Slayer—murmured quietly.

"...Mm," Cow Girl said. She nodded, somehow sadly. "...I see."

"I have no proof, but I think the goblins are on the move again."

Goblin Slayer picked his words carefully, thinking hard as he spoke.

Goblins had stolen construction tools. They were appearing with impunity near the training grounds.

Were they simply interested in the unusual spectacle of the training area being constructed?

Not possible.

It was a warning, a sign.

The thought might seem alarmist, but in his mind, these things were connected.

It was not clear whether this was the doing of fate or of chance.

The one thing he was certain of was that he would have to fight the goblins.

"That's why I believe I have to do this."

"Yeah. Yeah... I know."

Their eyes met. Cow Girl's gaze wavered with anxiety. His, from deep inside the helmet, never flinched.

Her throat tightened. What should she say, and how should she say it? Several times, she opened her mouth then closed it again.

"I'll be...waiting for you, okay?"

"Yes."

Then Goblin Slayer rose from his chair. He left his empty bowl on the table.

She heard the door shut, and then she was alone in the kitchen again.

Cow Girl turned her face away from the unsteady candlelight, clutching her head as if she wanted to curl into herself, but instead, she lay out on the table again.

The soft twittering of the canary was no comfort to her.

§

For the next three days, nothing happened.

Adventurers spent their time on adventures, or training, or deepening friendships.

It was certainly a meaningful time, no question.

The flow of time can no more be reversed than the current of a river. Even the gods themselves cannot take back a roll of the dice.

That was why it was certain that goblins would appear. Fate? Or chance?

It happened three days later—at twilight.

CHAPTER 6

To Each Their Own Battle

It was one of the laborers who noticed it first.

"Hrmph, and just when I thought I was done for the day."

With a shovel on his shoulder and a long look at the setting sun, he heaved a sigh.

He was a worthless layabout of a man; he had no desire to enter the service of some merchant household, nor did he have the money to live a life of luxury. Thus, he found himself working with his spade in hand and only the sweat of his brow for company, but even so, he was ill content.

Damn, but I do like me them lady adventurers.

They may not have been dressed in the most beautiful clothes, but they moved around so freely. And then there were the girls in loose robes, the wizards and clerics. They were completely different from the prostitutes who went about in their makeup and perfume.

Of course, the really high-class courtesans were a breed apart, but they were also out of reach for man like him.

And then there were the other adventurers, the ones who shared their food and their beds with those women.

How easy their lives must be. Living just as they pleased, dying just as they pleased. It was enough to make a man jealous.

"They've got a good thing going. A li'l hack and slash, monster slaying, and treasure-chest plundering, and bam, you're rich."

Granted, even this man understood that things were not really so simple. But everyone wants to think they are somehow special, that they will uniquely succeed. And everyone wants to look at things in the way that most benefits them.

This man, who sat there playing with the idea of being an adventurer, was no different.

He didn't have to be a huge success. He didn't care if he never became a renowned warrior. All he needed was a bit of decent equipment, the chance to save a village or two, and maybe earn the thanks of the local girls…

Ah, or perhaps he could buy some noble girl who had fallen into slavery and look after her. That might be good. He could find a beautiful wizard woman to be his party member and slowly gain more and more companions. All gorgeous women, of course.

He would find secret caves no one else knew about (not that he knew about them at the moment, either), and that was where he would make his fortune. And finally, he would set up house with his favorite woman, coming home from his travails and asking her out on an adventure.

"…Heh-heh!"

The man didn't particularly care that his vision of "modest success" lacked something in the way of realism. He was just enjoying an indulgent fantasy.

No one would point and laugh at him for it. As a way of passing the time, it didn't hurt anyone.

Work, drink wine, eat food, enjoy women and friends, complain about the unfairness of it all, and occasionally dream a little. Live. That was enough.

"…Hmm?"

And again, he was the first to notice it.

He looked toward a corner of the training ground, which by now was mostly fenced in and nearing completion.

He saw a pile of dirt he had no memory of.

Dirt was a resource in and of itself, so anytime they dug up the earth, they had to deposit it in a designated location.

"Damn it all, who's been slacking off on the job?"

It wasn't that he didn't understand how annoying the requirement could be. He himself had been known, on occasion, to put the dirt in some convenient location instead of the specified one.

But since he had noticed the problem, it was his responsibility to fix it, and that was annoying.

He entertained the possibility of just pretending he hadn't seen the pile, but unfortunately for him, he had a shovel right there in his hand.

"...Nothin' for it, then," he muttered. What was the big deal? It was just a little dirt. Rather than have a guilty conscience tomorrow, why not do the job and sleep well tonight?

As the man approached the pile of dirt, he thought he caught a glimpse of a humanoid figure on the other side. It was about the size of a child—and the fading light of the sun wasn't enough to obscure the cruel details of its face as it gibbered and grunted.

A goblin?!

The fact that he didn't simply start screaming at that moment was praiseworthy. The actions he took next were also above reproach.

He grasped the shovel in both hands, crept toward the creature as quietly as he could, and raised his spade.

"GROB?!"

The point of the shovel, polished by contact with the earth until it was as sharp as an ax, shattered the goblin's skull. Dark blood and brains sprayed out as the creature collapsed, and the man trampled gleefully on the corpse.

"Ha-ha! How ya like that, you—!"

When he finally pulled the spade back and saw the thread of blood dangling from it, the man frowned. Rational thought reminded him that this was a tool he was going to need the next day. He'd better wash it.

Along with the wave of revulsion, however, came a profound gratitude to his tool: when the moment had called for it, the shovel had served brilliantly to smash that goblin's head in.

"...Where the hell'd it come from anyway? Did it dig this hole or somethin'?"

Flicking the blood off his shovel, the man smirked down into the tunnel. It was a crude but solid passageway. The goblin must have dug it.

The man couldn't see the bottom of the hole. Not just because it was dark down there—the sun was setting even as he stood in place.

"..."

The man shivered. A nameless fear ran along his spine.

"No way. Forget it. I don't need to go down there. This calls for an adventurer."

Let them handle it. It wasn't his job. Still, he would have to report it.

But at that moment...

"Ow...!"

He felt a piercing pain run through his right foot, and suddenly, his vision upended as he tumbled to the ground.

The hell? He forced himself to bend so he could see his foot, where he discovered blood oozing from his ankle.

"GROB! GROORB!!"

Then he saw a goblin holding a dagger slathered in some unidentifiable liquid.

No... Not just one goblin. Ten, twenty of them, snickering under their breath as they emerged from the night shadows.

"...———..."

The worker opened his mouth as if to cry for help, but his tongue seemed to be stuck; he could not make a sound.

A numbing pain came up from his stabbed foot. His throat was dry. There was some kind of liquid in his mouth; he tasted blood. He couldn't breathe. His vision began to go dark.

Why hadn't he noticed there was more than one goblin there?

If he hadn't even seen that, then of course he hadn't spotted the poisoned dagger one of the monsters held.

The man died shortly thereafter.

But of course, he was not the first to die that night, nor would he be the last.

§

"The topic of tonight's lesson is 'Eight Ways to Kill Goblins Silently.' Now..."

That was as far as Goblin Slayer got in his lecture to the novice adventurers when there was a scream.

Adventurers had to deal with the darkness at many times, not just when coming home in the evening.

There was no guarantee, for example, that an adventure might not take place at night. And even during the day, ruins, labyrinths, and caves were often dim.

It was certainly worthwhile to train in the dark hours, with only the light of the moons and the stars.

At the very least, so thought the adventurers gathered there—the red-haired boy, the rhea girl, Rookie Warrior, and Apprentice Cleric. They and about ten others had gathered at the training grounds even after a long day of adventuring.

"Wh-what was that?!"

"That was a scream… Right?"

The young adventurers whispered urgently to one another, their faces tense.

"…"

Goblin Slayer, however, drew the sword at his hip.

He acted quickly.

Ignoring the chattering students, he swept his gaze around the area, looking for the source of the scream.

It turned out it wasn't just *a* scream. After a moment, a second came, then a third.

"H-hey! Just what the heck's goin' on out there—?!" the red-haired boy asked in bewilderment, but Goblin Slayer replied, "Don't panic. Get up against the wall. Form a half-circle surrounding the spell casters. Front row, have your weapons ready."

"Right," Rookie Warrior said, his face a mask of anxiety as he moved to protect Apprentice Cleric. "…Hey," he added, "this isn't some kind of…drill or something, is it?"

"Even if it were," Goblin Slayer said shortly, "we would have nothing to gain by treating it lightly."

"Ooh… I hate this! I don't even know if I'm scared or not!"

Then with a bout of dry laughter, Rhea Fighter picked up her diminutive sword and shield and assumed a fighting stance. Her face was stiff; even in the night darkness, it was obvious how pale she was.

Fear, nervousness—clearly a combination of the two. Her pointy ears, not as long as an elf's, trembled slightly.

"Tsk..." This click of the tongue came from the red-haired boy. He raised his staff and turned to face the other novices, who had yet to fully grasp the situation at hand. "Hey, didn't you hear him? Don't just stand around! Form up!"

"R-right...!"

"Yeah, got it...!"

Maybe the fact that the words were coming from one of their peers helped them. Even those who had been frozen, unable to think or absorb the situation, finally lurched into movement. Each picked up their weapon and helped form the half circle against the wall, although it wasn't very pretty.

"You there, get that shield up! Protect the people beside and behind you!" Apprentice Cleric shouted, whipping into action a group unaccustomed to such maneuvers.

It was surprising, when she thought about it: although she and Rookie Warrior had only really fought giant rats, they were experienced adventurers in their own way. Rhea Fighter and the red-haired boy were the same. They had taken a definite step forward from being pure beginners. After that would come the next step, and the next...

"..."

Goblin Slayer observed them but groaned so quietly no one could hear him. Should he leave the newbies to go check out the situation, or should he stay here and protect them?

Partly, he was unsure... And partly, he found he didn't want to leave them alone.

A foolish thought.

It mystified even him. To neglect to gather information in these circumstances was the same as simply waiting for their collective annihilation. After a certain point, even thinking would become a waste of time. There were some things that shouldn't have to be thought about.

Having reached this conclusion, Goblin Slayer said, "Hold here." He looked around at the young adventurers then said, "If I'm not back in fifteen minutes, you will have to act on your own."

"On our own…?"

"Because it will mean I am dead, or at least heavily wounded." His voice was dispassionate. He forced himself to ignore the chatter this provoked among the students. "Returning to town would probably be the best course of action, but if it appears impossible, stick around here until morning."

Then run. As fast as you can, without looking back.

Several more screams sounded. War cries, bellows of rage. The sound of weapons colliding and swords crossing.

Suddenly, the noise seemed to come from everywhere at once, crashing in on him from every direction. He found that on this spring night, still crisp with the breath of ice sprites, he could not tell what was going on.

The shadow of the half-built building was eerily large. Goblin Slayer let out a breath.

No…

"…One."

Dashing as fast as he could, he nonchalantly raised his right hand and flung his sword.

It flew into the shadows of the materials piled by the building, evoking a strangled death rattle. Goblin Slayer followed it quickly into the gloom, where he braced his foot against the goblin his blade had run through and pulled his weapon back out.

A bloody shovel tumbled from the hand of the dead goblin, clattering as it fell to the ground.

"Goblins. I knew it."

How pregnant with meaning were those brief words.

Goblins hidden in the night, two more of them. Although he couldn't see clearly, their burning eyes were obvious.

Then there was a thick, sticky feeling on the bottom of his foot, and the rising odor of iron.

It was a novice adventurer, collapsed on the ground. He couldn't tell what class, or how old, or what race.

The adventurer had no face.

Something sharp had torn mercilessly through the adventurer's head from the crown all the way down through the face, but the slight swell of the chest and the build of the still-twitching limbs suggested a woman.

"GOROROB!!"

"GROOOORORB!!"

The goblins jumped at him, yammering. Without a word, Goblin Slayer struck at them with his sword.

There was a sound of metal on metal. The goblins were carrying pickaxes. Stolen tools, no doubt.

Without hesitation Goblin Slayer moved in, pressed back the pickax with one hand. But…

"GROB!!"

There was another. He had a pickax, too, and he was bringing it swiftly down.

"Hrg…"

The steel pick of the ax bit through his upraised shield. Such weapons were always strong against armor.

But this was perfect.

Goblin Slayer bent his left arm forcefully, pulling the pickax from the goblin's hands. At the same time, he brought his leg up toward the goblin on his right, slamming a kick as hard as he could between the creature's legs.

"GROOORORORORORBB?!?!"

"Two."

There was a disgusting feeling of something being crushed beneath his foot, but he didn't care about the muffled scream.

He stomped on the writhing goblin's head, his sword humming at the same moment. Just to his left, the now pickax-less goblin was trying to run; he flung the blade into its back.

"GOROORB?!"

"And that makes…"

The creature might not die instantly, but with its spine severed, it wouldn't be able to move.

Goblin Slayer placed the heel of his boot against the back of the struggling goblin's skull and pushed down mercilessly.

The feeling was like stepping on a ripe fruit. He wiped off the blood and brains and continued forward.

He pulled the blade out of the twitching monster, slicing as he went, sending it to its final rest.

"...Three."

He forcefully pulled out the pickax that was still buried in his shield.

There was fresh earth on the pick. The goblins must have dug a tunnel from somewhere in order to attack the training grounds.

Were they so eager to assault this place? To kill the people here?

Goblins.

Goblins.

Goblins.

He didn't like it.

He didn't like any of it.

Heaven and earth spun.

There were four corpses. Three goblins, one adventurer.

Just like that night ten years ago.

He could no longer run from it. Hadn't he known that already?

He was Goblin Slayer.

"...Is there anybody there...?!"

That was when somebody shouted a question and came into the shadows—an adventurer.

Well, it made sense: what else would an adventurer do when faced with someone standing with a weapon in the darkness, the smell of blood drifting all around?

It took the adventurer, who carried a sounding staff, a moment to make out exactly what she was seeing, but when she did—

"Goblin Slayer, sir!"

"Are you all right?"

"Yes!" Priestess gripped her staff firmly with both hands and nodded happily. "I was on healing duty again today. I used up my miracles, so I was resting in my room, but..."

Her gaze took in the fallen goblins...and then the corpse of the adventurer. Her lovely eyebrows knit her face into a frown.

Priestess knelt, unconcerned about the blood that stained her white vestments, and reached out to the body, which continued to twitch reflexively.

"Was it goblins?"

"Yes." Goblin Slayer didn't look at her but only shook the blood from his sword. "Do you have any miracles left?"

"Thanks to that rest, I can ask for three, just like usual."

"Are our other..."—Goblin Slayer almost stumbled over the word—"...friends coming?"

"Probably..."

"Good."

Goblin Slayer finally turned toward Priestess. She looked up at him, her blue eyes visible in the pale moonlight. It occurred to Goblin Slayer how clear her eyes were, like glass beads.

"Can you join me?"

"...Yes, I will." Priestess bit her lip, her voice trembling. She didn't rub at her eyes, because she wasn't crying. "Let's go...!"

"Yes," Goblin Slayer nodded. "We're going to kill all the goblins."

§

Not long after, the two of them arrived at the building that would serve as the training ground's administrative center when it was complete.

Although it was to be the central building, it was not yet finished and felt very much abandoned. There were many gaps in the walls and roof, and the forms of many adventurers who had gathered with equipment in hand could be seen.

Thankfully, it seemed more than a few adventurers had made it through the crucible to arrive here.

"Hey, look! If it isn't Goblin Slayer! Everything okay?"

The first person to greet them was the adventurer who stood guard by the doorway—Spearman. Given how he always seemed ready to jump directly into action, it was actually somewhat surprising to see him standing there.

"Yes," Goblin Slayer said with a nod. He correctly parsed the intent of the question. "The ones I was looking after are all safe."

"Yeah? Most of the kids went back home anyway, it being so late and all."

"Before...it, gets dark...yes?"

There was one other person. A voluptuous witch appeared at Spearman's side, sidling up like a shadow; a pale sphere of light floated in the air near her. A will-o'-the-wisp? No, this was no spirit. Perhaps the Light spell.

No one wanted to risk using fire, even magical fire, in this area. The wind this spring night was strong. If the fire were to catch on anything here, it would be a catastrophe.

"You're both safe..." Priestess, perhaps relieved to see a couple of familiar faces, let out a soft breath.

She finally put a stop to the shaking of her knees, gripping her sounding staff with both hands and managing to look suitably resolute.

"We're here, too!" The clear voice was like an encouraging pat on the back, and it brought a smile to blossom on Priestess's face.

"You're all here!"

"Ahh, and so are you. Though this be ever a place of practice battles, I didn't expect it to become the grounds for a real one."

"Those little bastards made me miss dinner!"

Up came Lizard Priest, who looked the same as always, along with Dwarf Shaman, who was leisurely rubbing his belly.

Priestess was running toward them before she knew what she was doing, when High Elf Archer held her back.

"You really okay? You're not hurt? Those goblins didn't do anything to you, did they?"

"It's fine, I'm okay. Thank goodness you're all safe..."

Thank goodness it didn't turn out like that *time.*

Surrounded by her friends, Priestess found that her eyes were brimming. No one said anything about it. Who in the world could bear to lose their friends twice, or even three times?

"..."

Goblin Slayer watched his comrades for several seconds then slowly turned his steel helmet.

The key was to always be thinking—about what one should, and could, do.

This building was yet incomplete and fragile. They would not be able to barricade themselves in it for very long.

That being the case, they needed firepower. They were not a bunch of novices cowering in a corner. At that moment—

"Hey. Made it here in one piece, huh, Goblin Slayer?"

His eyes met those of a well-built warrior.

Heavy Warrior appeared to have been through a battle already; the faint reek of blood hung about him.

Presumably, of course, it was goblins that he had killed. What else could it have been?

Goblin Slayer glanced around the building to see whether he recognized anyone else.

"You're alone today?"

"She may be a knight, but she's still a woman. There are times when she's indisposed. The brats are keeping her company at the inn." Heavy Warrior's expression contained indescribable depths. He shrugged, causing his armor to rattle. "A party leader has to think about his people's health."

It had been a stroke of luck, really. Feeling indisposed had kept his party at home and, thus, out of this trouble.

"But listen," Heavy Warrior said, grinning like a hungry shark. "When the three most-whatevers on the frontier are all in one place, things are bound to be interesting."

There was, of course, no room for error in this situation. The death rattles of adventurers who had failed to make it to the impromptu base could be heard all around. Each time a goblin howl echoed through the night, the novices in the building looked at one another and shivered.

Adventurers were generally accustomed to being the attackers, not the attacked. Yes, they were occasionally ambushed, and sometimes they took on escort missions. But somehow, deep in their hearts, they continued to believe that they would never really be the hunted.

Priestess could be said to have been unlucky to have had this assumption so violently disproven, but then again, it was its own kind of good fortune.

In any event, if they didn't get out of there—or rather, slay the goblins—they would not live to see the sun again.

All present shared this understanding. Spearman was glancing outside with a sour look.

"Are we just gonna let them put us under siege? Boring. I don't wanna just hole up in here and die."

"What…ever…the case, it might, be best…for everyone to link up, first."

"Yes," Goblin Slayer agreed. "My charges are stationed in the square."

"Need a messenger, then," Heavy Warrior said quickly. "*Situation assessed—goblins. Come join us.* That sort of thing. We have to let all the survivors know and get them here as soon as we can."

"I'll go!" High Elf Archer piped up immediately, raising her hand. "I'm the fastest runner around!"

"Perfect, get on it."

"You can count on me!"

And then she was off like the wind into the night.

Heavy Warrior watched her go then glanced around. Goblin Slayer and his party made five. Then there was Spearman and Witch. And himself.

Depending on how many among the novices could really be counted on in battle, they had about ten people to fight for them. He didn't count the ones who were trying to curl up into little balls. Heavy Warrior made the decision: he wouldn't involve them.

"So, Goblin Slayer," he said. "We're dealing with goblins. Who do you think is leading them?"

"Probably another goblin," Goblin Slayer said without hesitation. "A higher one, I assume, but I doubt another lord has been born. Maybe a clever shaman…"

"Got any proof?"

"If someone other than a goblin were leading them, the goblins would be treated as foot soldiers, not the main force."

It was true. No one but a goblin would think to use other goblins to dig a tunnel to attack the training grounds.

Heavy Warrior nodded. "We have to deal with the small fry, but we also have to make sure we take out the bigger fish," he concluded. "And where would that bigger fish be…?"

"In my estimation, the little devils will have more than one hole,"

Lizard Priest said, his jaw set. He slapped his tail on the ground and raised one scaly finger. "Presumably there will be one in each direction. The quickest solution would be to follow one of them back to its source."

"About that," Spearman said, keeping a close watch outside as he spoke. "How do we know which one goes back to their headquarters?"

"I've the same question. More to the point, most likely they're all connected inside."

In matters subterranean, no one could match a dwarf.

Dwarf Shaman took a swig from the wine jug at his hip then let loose a very alcoholic-smelling burp.

"Chances are they only dug one tunnel then split it off just before the attack. That'd be easiest, after all."

"Sounds good, then. We go down the nearest hole. You good with that, Goblin Slayer?"

"I have no objection."

"Then, the problem, is, those children." Witch gestured meaningfully at the novices. "There are, others, aren't there? What do we, do about…the little ones?"

"Leave 'em, bring 'em, or have 'em run away," Heavy Warrior mused.

Spearman, however, gave him a grin and a poke on the shoulder. "I've gotta think a broadsword won't do much good in a tunnel…"

"Aw, screw off!" The reminder of Heavy Warrior's past failure struck a nerve. "But hell. I always liked being aboveground better than below it. I'll take the kids. You handle the dirt."

"Right," said Spearman.

"No problem," Goblin Slayer added.

The veterans had calculated all this in the blink of an eye. Although she was no longer exactly a beginner, Priestess found she couldn't have gotten a word in edgewise. Unlike High Elf Archer, who might have chosen to refrain, Priestess couldn't have spoken up if she wanted to. (Anyway, the elf seemed to see insouciant interjections as her role.)

It was a variety of opinions and perspectives that led to a sound conclusion. Objections and dialogue were not the same as denying what someone else was saying. But right now, perspective—something rooted in genuine experience—was what Priestess overwhelmingly lacked.

But…

What was it? This inarticulate anxiety?

Although she couldn't put it into words, it may have been some sort of hint from the gods.

She thought of the alarm that had welled up in her when her party entered the cave on that first adventure. The mounting panic building in her little chest—the feeling that she had to do *something.*

Things would end badly if she just let them go on. She had to do something.

But what?

"Oh."

The sound escaped her mouth the moment the possibility occurred to her.

The collective gaze of the other adventurers pierced her, prompting her to blush a little bit.

"What is it?" Goblin Slayer was the first to speak. "Goblins?"

"…Uh—um!" Her voice was shrill. The focus on her became even more intent. It was enough to make her want to run away. "The other new adventurers, they've already gone home, right?"

"Yeah," Spearman nodded. "All but the ones who wanted to practice night fighting. Gone the moment the sun set."

"Where do you…suppose they are now?"

"What're you getting at?" Heavy Warrior said, eyeballing her. He certainly wasn't intentionally trying to frighten her, but circumstances were what they were. His very seriousness, his intent not to overlook any idea or information whatsoever, was itself intimidating.

"Well, um…"

Priestess flinched back.

Was there actually any value in her giving her opinion?

What if it turned out to be nothing but a flight of fancy?

What business did she even have thinking she could—?

"Just tell us." Goblin Slayer's voice was soft, dispassionate. Absolutely the same as ever. Priestess gulped; she gripped her staff harder to hide the trembling of her hands.

She took a breath in then let it out.

"...The goblins... I think they must be after the novices on their way home, too."

"*What?!*" Heavy Warrior exclaimed in spite of himself. His armor clattered, causing Priestess to flinch for a second. But she didn't stop speaking. She mustn't.

"Isn't it strange? I know goblins are cowardly, scheming creatures."

Because somebody taught me as much.

Taught her to think like a goblin. How they lived. The fright of them.

"If I were a goblin, the last place I'd want to attack is a building full of strong adventurers."

And also, how they could use a large army as a diversion...

That was something he had said back when they fought the goblin lord—how long ago had that been?

She was still learning. She had experience yet to gain. But she did have *some* experience.

She herself just hadn't realized it.

"...I believe she's right," Goblin Slayer growled quietly. "I overlooked that."

"And I...I have an idea."

Once Priestess had started speaking, the rest was easy.

Not that it made it simple to express her ideas clearly and succinctly, but speech itself came readily to her, and she didn't hesitate.

"And so I'm—I'm going now."

With everyone around focused completely on her, Priestess outlined her plan.

"Our adventurer friends include, um, two warriors, a cleric, a wizard..."

She counted on her fingers. Rookie Warrior, Rhea Fighter. Apprentice Cleric and Wizard Boy.

"I think just having me, another cleric, there could turn the tide. So..."

I'm going to help them. I want to go.

These earnest words caused the Silver-ranked adventurers to look at one another.

"…Time, is short…is it, not?" Witch glanced outside and gave a single seductive laugh but spoke encouragingly.

"I've got no idea what this girl is or isn't capable of. So I'll abstain," Spearman added quickly.

"…Makes sense," Heavy Warrior said. Then he squinted at Priestess, looking her over, up and down her willowy frame. "There's always a chance that divide and conquer is the whole idea. Think you can handle this?"

"As for me, I have faith in her," Lizard Priest said with a thoughtful nod and a roll of his eyes. He winked at Priestess. "We must strike at the heart of the enemy, but we must by no means abandon our young adventurers to do so. I think this is a fine ploy."

"Perfect for a promotion test, I'd say," Dwarf Shaman chuckled, stroking his long white beard. "D'you agree, Beard-cutter? Gotta push 'em out of the nest some day, eh?"

Goblin Slayer, sir…

Priestess looked at the man in the grimy armor beseechingly.

Now that she thought about it, she realized that this would be almost the first time she had gone on an adventure without him since the very first adventure she had been on.

Could she do it? She herself?

Priestess would by no means be alone, but she would have to rely on her own strength.

Could she fight the goblins?

Everyone kindly told her they believed she could do it. Even High Elf Archer, who wasn't there, surely would have agreed.

It made her very happy; what more could she wish for than that?

And yet…

If this person says I shouldn't or can't…

Then she would just have to quietly accept it. That would be best for everyone, she was sure.

But what he said was not what she feared.

"Can you do it?"

"I…"

His question was so succinct, so simple. As he always was.

And yet…

It made her wish all the more to rise to the expectations implicit in it. She had to.

Priestess swallowed the half-spoken words, bit her lip, and then answered almost in a shout, "…I will!"

Goblin Slayer looked at her intently. Whatever was in his eyes was hidden behind his helmet; she couldn't make out his expression, but still…

"Is that so?" He nodded slowly then rendered his verdict. "Then it's decided."

§

"Hraah!!"

"GROBR?!"

In the narrow confines of the cave, the mithril spear tip pierced through the goblin's throat. The long, pole-shaped weapon in Spearman's hands lashed out in time with the sounds of magic, flowers of death blossoming all around him.

One thrust, one kill. Four thrusts, four kills.

The goblins held up flimsy wood boards in place of shields, but they counted for little.

Only an amateur would imagine that the spear could not be used in a tight space like this; in fact, Spearman made it look like it was capable of anything.

Sweep, strike, block, stab. Stab, stab, draw back, and then stab again.

The repeating flurry of attacks was furious enough to control what was happening in front of them.

The buffed spear lashed out with the speed of a whirlwind, painting the walls all around with goblin brains and blood.

The gentle downward slope of the ground did nothing to upset the footing of these experienced fighters.

"Don't you think about getting behind me!"

"Inside! I see six—no, three!"

As Spearman struck an impressive pose, keeping the monsters at bay, High Elf Archer slipped up alongside him and fired a volley of arrows. Three bolts flew as quickly as magic, finding the eyeballs of three separate creatures lurking deeper in the hole.

"GORRB?!"

"GROB! GROORB!!"

There were not six, but three remaining. A simple calculation. If you had no confidence that you could hit, then you couldn't shoot.

"One…!"

That was when Goblin Slayer made his entrance.

The sword was already flying from his hand even as he charged in, slamming it through a goblin's throat.

"GRRRO?!"

The monster clawed at his throat as if he were drowning, but Goblin Slayer ignored him, grabbing a dagger from the corpse of one of the goblins with an arrow through his eye. Then he used it to slit the throat of a monster who had not yet gotten over the shock of seeing four of his companions murdered in an instant.

Blood spewed from the creature with a whistling sound; Goblin Slayer swept him aside with his shield and flung the dagger.

The throw may have been just a bit too strong; the knife missed its mark and lodged itself in a goblin's shoulder.

"GORB!!"

"That's three."

Goblin Slayer, unperturbed, took a hand ax from the goblin drowning in a sea of blood. Then he buried it in the skull of the final goblin, and the random encounter was over.

A party of experienced adventurers needed only a single turn to kill ten goblins.

Spearman put up his weapon—he wasn't even breathing hard—and looked to Goblin Slayer in exasperation. "Hey, you," he said. "You have *got* to stop throwing away all your weapons. It's a waste!"

"They are consumables."

"Have a look around. You know they sell those magical throwing knives that come back to you after you throw them, right?"

"Goblins could use them as well," Goblin Slayer said. "What if they were stolen?"

"We don't have time for this!" High Elf Archer exclaimed. "Will you pipe down and help me collect my arrows?" Spearman was busy looking annoyed, and Goblin Slayer was searching the corpses for weapons.

The three of them seemed carefree enough, but they made not a single unnecessary movement. They scanned the area ceaselessly, checked their weapons, readied what they would need next.

Goblin Slayer groaned softly. The goblins had not treated their equipment politely; everything they had was in dismal repair. There were no good weapons here.

"Goodness gracious," Lizard Priest said with a somber nod when he saw the scene. "What a pleasant feeling of security one gets from having two front-row fighters."

"Says the lizard who's always up front."

"In…deed," Witch mumbled calmly. "One, warrior…for, each of us, no?"

They had left the novices at the training ground in Heavy Warrior's care and headed underground via one of the holes.

Unlike the parties' normal five-and-two split, this time they formed a single group of six people. That meant a different formation from usual, too. Goblin Slayer and Spearman stood on the front row, with High Elf Archer behind them and the spell casters in the back.

Which was more important? High Elf Archer's arrows or Lizard Priest's spells? The answer was obvious.

"I got them," Goblin Slayer said, handing over the arrows.

High Elf Archer looked at them and gave a click of her tongue. "Oh, for— The heads are missing!" She tossed them angrily back in her quiver of bud-tipped bolts. There was nothing to be done about it. "What about you, Orcbolg? Find any good weapons?"

"Beggars cannot be choosers."

"Why'd you let the girl go without me anyway?"

"Are you upset?"

"Not really," the High Elf said, looking away. "But aren't you worried about her?"

"If my worrying would help things go well for her, then I would."

Yeesh…

But no sooner had High Elf Archer breathed a sigh than her ears pricked up, twitching.

"They're coming."

"Direction and number?" Goblin Slayer asked immediately, drawing a small leather pouch from his item bag as he did so.

It was his purse: the coins inside jangled. It carried an embroidered floral design and seemed to be quite old. He cinched the mouth of the purse tightly; it made a sharp noise as he did so.

"I dunno… The sounds are echoing everywhere…!"

"Well, we ain't got time to discuss it in committee!" Spearman said, shaking his weapon to get the grease off. "No matter what, we can't let them get up top."

"Not many choices left. Want me t'do it?"

As experienced adventurers, they were quick to respond to the situation. Even as Dwarf Shaman spoke, he was reaching into his bag of catalysts, readying his spell. Witch calmly brought her staff up and begin focusing herself to intone her magic. Lizard Priest brought his hands together.

"Gracious, goblin slaying does involve the worst of both the troublesome and the unexpected, does it not?" he said.

"You're quite, right," Witch said with a languid chuckle, and then her luscious lips were whispering words of true power. "*Sagitta… sinus…offero.* Gift a curve to arrows!"

A wizard's spells were words that rewrote the very logic of the world.

As an invisible flow protected the party, High Elf Archer and Spearman were shouting.

"They're coming! Both walls!"

"Fall back!"

Showers of stones and dirt came from both sides of the adventurers. At almost the exact same instant, they all jumped back.

"GRORB!! GROOROOBB!!"

"GROOBRR!"

Was this what the word *horde* truly meant?

The average adventurer might expect not to see ten or twenty goblins in his or her life.

But more goblins than that, far more, were now pouring in upon them. The goblins howled like animals, and it was easy to guess what their shouting meant.

Kill them. Steal from them. Get revenge. Revenge for our brothers. Die, adventurers, die!

The men they would slaughter immediately. The women they would rob of every last vestige of dignity before putting them both to the sword.

They would take the one woman's staff, bind her legs, and make her bear goblin young for them until she was too dead to be of any more use. Elf meat, they knew, was soft and kept a long time. They could chop off her arms and legs bit by bit and feast on them.

The women would weep; they would beg for forgiveness; but the goblins would ignore them.

Kill them, just as they would kill us!

"Drink deep, sing loud, let the spirits lead you! Sing loud, step quick, and when to sleep they see you, may a jar of fire wine be in your dreams to greet you!"

No doubt several of the little devils ended their lives never waking up from that dream. Caught up in the mist of wine Dwarf Shaman spat from his mouth, they found themselves under the influence of the Stupor spell.

Stumbling over their now-unconscious vanguard, the goblins began to topple like dominoes. Several were trampled to death as the goblins in the back tried to force their way to the front.

There was agonized screaming and shouting. It was pandemonium.

"Fools." Without hesitation, Goblin Slayer spun his purse, attacking the nearest monster. The speed and the centrifugal force of the coins in the little leather pouch was more than enough to split the skull of a goblin.

And thus the money all the villagers had saved so diligently, to pay for an adventurer to end their goblin troubles, was used to actually murder a goblin. Poetic justice at its finest.

"GRB?!"

"GRORB?!"

One monster found its eyeball popped like a bubble, found itself pierced to the brain, which was then further crushed in from the temple.

Stopping one or two goblins was easy enough.

Goblin Slayer kicked the first one aside, grabbing the sword at the creature's hip in the same movement.

"Hrgh…!"

Another goblin had seized this moment of inattention to jump at him with a poisoned dagger. He met the creature with his shield, sending it flying.

More arrows came raining down, but as they were turned aside by an invisible power, he ignored them. They were no concern of his.

"I'm sending some your way!"

"Aw, don't make more work for me!"

Despite his complaints, Spearman was putting on a display of superb technique. In a single stroke, he stabbed several creatures in front of him, and as he pulled the weapon out again, he thrust the butt behind him. It slammed into the skull of the goblin who had been pushed aside by the shield, crushing in his head and killing him.

"We ain't lettin' even one goblin past us!"

"That has always been my intention."

The two warriors stood back to back, goblins breaking upon them like a dark tide.

When it came to grandiosity and strength, Spearman obviously had Goblin Slayer outclassed. He threshed goblins like wheat with every swipe of his spear.

Goblin Slayer, naturally, restricted himself to making sure Spearman wasn't taken from behind. He finished off anyone Spearman missed, dealt with those in front of him, and passed off to Spearman those he couldn't personally finish.

They hardly thought about defense, leaving Deflect Missile to ward off incoming stones.

They simply focused single-mindedly on their weapons.

But of course, even for Goblin Slayer, things would never be so simple.

"Shaman!"

High Elf Archer's shout cut through the melee. At the rear of the goblin formation stood one monster with a staff, uttering a spell.

Light swelled from his upraised staff then flew outward.

It was the most basic of all offensive spells, Magic Arrow.

It might not be very powerful, but if it hit, in some cases, it could still be enough to turn the tide of battle. What was more, because it was magical, Deflect Missile would provide no protection against it.

Surprisingly clever, for a goblin. But Spearman shouted eagerly, "Take it!"

"*Magna…remora…restinguitur!* An end to magic!"

Witch smiled indulgently and recited a spell almost in singsong. It was Counterspell, and it would resist the words of true power the goblin shaman had spoken.

The moment they encountered Witch's words, the majority of the incoming arrows vanished, only a scant few of them reaching Spearman and Goblin Slayer.

"Could I, trouble you not to, make more work for m…e?"

"That *is* your work!"

Banter for banter. Spearman waded into the host of goblins, even as blood dribbled from a wound on his cheek; it didn't seem to bother him in the least.

"They want arrows? I'll give 'em arrows," High Elf Archer growled, letting her spider-silk string bow do the rest of the talking.

One of the bolts went flying through the dust and the thick air, lodging itself, just as she had intended, in the shaman's neck.

"There!"

"Any injuries?" The question came from Lizard Priest, who was evidently growing bored in the back; he slapped his tail impatiently against the ground. Without Priestess there, he was the party's one cleric, the only one capable of healing miracles. He seemed rather displeased at having to remain so far to the rear, carefully conserving his spells.

"No problems," Goblin Slayer answered briefly, checking himself over. There were places where his poor leather armor and mail had been pierced through; blood oozed here and there, and he felt pain.

In other words, I am still alive.

He continued to work his sword against the goblins in front of him as he groped through his item pouch, relying on the knots to guide him. He pulled out a potion and gulped it down then lobbed the empty vial with his left hand.

"GROORB!!"

"Die."

The goblin had stumbled back under the unexpected blow; Goblin Slayer cut his throat mercilessly. Blood frothed at the creature's neck; Goblin Slayer kicked him away and pulled out his sword, shaking off the gore.

"You have spells left?" he asked, steadying his breath.

"Yes, thank…fully," Witch replied with a smile.

"Us, too," Dwarf Shaman said.

"Shall I produce a Dragontooth Warrior?"

"No," Goblin Slayer said to his friend's question, shaking his head thoughtfully. He grunted softly, looking up at the ceiling of the tunnel the goblins had dug.

"Orcbolg," High Elf Archer said in a resigned tone. "You're thinking of something unpleasant again, aren't you?"

"Yes," Goblin Slayer said with a nod. "Unpleasant for the goblins."

§

The adventurers in the half-built office building began to relax as the sounds of battle grew more distant.

"…Think they went that way?"

"Seems like it."

Maybe we'll be rescued after all. Mom, Dad, maybe we'll survive.

As they looked at one another and whispered, every word was one of fear or complaint.

This isn't gonna help.

Heavy Warrior sighed to himself as he stood in the doorway, looking out. He was losing heart, and he hated it.

It wasn't that he didn't sympathize with the novices.

Anyone, when they failed, when they encountered something difficult or painful, could find themselves cowed. Might stamp their feet in frustration.

Above all, these kids didn't want to be killed by goblins. No one did.

But what was an adventurer who never went on an adventure? Fumble though they might, a true adventurer never gave up until the moment they died.

Even if the next roll of the gods' dice might be critical.

Just then…

Fwump.

There was a sound of heavy footsteps, which caused the ground to rumble gently.

The beginners trembled, swallowing nervously; they shut their mouths and stopped talking.

A dark shadow.

It lumbered past clutching a massive club in its hand.

Heavy Warrior didn't have to plumb the depths of his monster knowledge to know what it was.

"Big, ugly visitor we've got. A hob."

A hob. A hobgoblin.

A higher form of goblin that appeared intermittently. They lacked intelligence and were not particularly elegant fighters, but they did have endless strength. In many nests, they served as the chief, or sometimes as hired muscle.

"Hey, kids. Wanna see something neat?" Heavy Warrior spat into his palm, smeared it on the hilt of his broadsword, then gripped the weapon tightly. "I don't know what the other guys taught you, but I've got just one lesson for you."

Then he casually flung himself out the door.

"HHOOOORRRB!!"

One step, two, three. He advanced straight toward the gigantic goblin.

It was only a goblin. But a goblin nonetheless.

It was no comparison to the goblin champion he had fought before.

Still, a direct hit from those muscles wasn't likely to be a lot of fun. It might even be fatal, depending.

"No matter what overgrown lump you're facing, if you've got enough info on him—"

Who would believe that such a massive weapon could be swung in a circle?

He stepped in.

He let the momentum of his body carry him. If you were strong enough, it wasn't impossible.

His body began to bend.

The two-handed steel sword had cost vastly more than any of his other equipment. The price put it on a different level. And Heavy Warrior—

"—then, boys and girls, you can kill anything—even a god!"

—went in swinging.

§

Goblins only ever have mischief in mind.

Fairy tales tell us that much, but the chance to see it firsthand is rare.

"GROB! GROORB!!"

"GORROOR!!"

How had this happened?

His mind worked quickly as his leather armor, still new enough to be stiff, crunched and cracked. He was supposed to have a sword in his hand, but he must have dropped it somewhere while he was running. Every time he took a step, the scabbard slapped against his leg, reminding him that his head was as empty as the sheath.

The night darkness seemed to be entirely filled with the cackling of goblins.

The shadows of the trees in the light of the twin moons loomed eerily, and a horde of eyes burned like stars in the blackness.

It was something most had seen only in nightmares. Perhaps the beginners—beginners who would not even have a chance to finish their training—had never even dreamed of it.

Not one of them.

Most of them, when they imagined themselves in a crisis, also imagined coolly extricating themselves from it. Deep in a cave, surrounded by goblins? They would think of a clever way to turn the tables.

But never had they imagined that they might be surrounded by goblins on an otherwise perfectly open night road.

"...D-dammit!"

"This way, quick!" someone shouted, and they made a beeline for the woods.

They thought it would give them an advantage over being trapped in the field.

There had been, perhaps, fifteen of them at first. They had been meandering along the road after training, heading back toward town.

There would be more training tomorrow. But they wanted to go on adventures sometime soon. Such had been the subject of their conversation.

And what of it?

A scream had come from the tail of their group. They turned to see a girl ensconced in a dark mass.

"Nooo! No, stop, st—ahh! Gghh… Hrrgh…?!"

They could still hear her screaming as her life ended, her voice thick as she wept and cried out for her mother.

When he dove in and somehow managed to drag her away, it was already over. She was all deep cuts and ripped cloth, bone sticking through torn flesh. Of course she wasn't alive. How could she be?

…After that, all had been chaos.

"Goblins!"

Some people had shouted and run, attempting to flee; others had tried to face the monsters, but one disappeared, then another got separated…

Now only five or six of them were left.

"I thought goblins were supposed to stay in caves…!"

"Well, they're here now, so stop griping!" The warrior running alongside took off his helmet, which had grown too hot. "We just have to make it back to—"

He never got to finish.

A rock came down on his head from above, crushing in his skull.

"Wh-wha—?!"

Above us?!

Another adventurer desperately wiped away the bits of brain that splattered on his forehead then looked up into the trees, where he saw them: the fiery, gleaming eyes of goblins.

"I never heard they could climb *trees*!!" He could count himself lucky that he didn't just burst into tears right there.

He was still only fifteen years old. The strongest boy in his village. That alone had been enough to convince him to leave his hometown behind.

He knew how to swing a sword. Basic scouting, how to pitch a camp—and so on and so forth. He had thought that put him "in the know." He realized too late how wrong he was.

The five surviving adventurers gathered together, trying to keep their knees from shaking.

They held weapons in trembling hands, tried to chant spells with unresponsive tongues, attempted to pray through overpowering fear.

The howling laughter of the goblins came again.

"GOORORB!!"

"GROORB! GRORB!!"

They pointed at the terrified adventurers, closing in and jabbering loudly.

If the adventurers had been able to understand the goblin language, their fear would only have increased.

Two points for an arm. Three points for a leg. Ten for a head. And a torso, five.

No bonus for a man, but ten extra points for a woman.

A most awful way of deciding whom to target.

And all this despite the fact that slings and throwing spears made it impossible to say who had killed what, and they would no doubt simply end up arguing about who had how many points.

The goblins thought this was a wonderful game they had come up with. They hefted their weapons gleefully.

Was this the end?

The adventurers' teeth chattered as they watched the goblins advance.

Up rose the rusty swords, the spear tips, the crude rocks, no hint of mercy—

"O Earth Mother, abounding in mercy, grant your sacred light to we who are lost in darkness!"

That was when a miracle happened.

A flash burst like the sun, assailing the goblins with its power.

"GROOROROB?!"

"GORRRB?!"

The goblins bellowed and stumbled back; then among them appeared a silhouette, and then another.

"Take—*this!!*"

"Yaaaaahhh!!"

Rhea Fighter wielded a one-handed blade, while Rookie Warrior swung his club this way and that.

Their strength was inelegant but effective. *Bash, bash, bash.*

They were like a whirlwind descending upon the goblins.

"GORB?!"

"GOROORB?!"

They might not exactly be able to carve the goblins in two, but if you slice a creature from the shoulder down to the torso, rending bone and flesh along the way, your enemy will die.

They didn't need critical hits against goblins.

"E-ergh, I'm really not used to the feel of this yet!" Rhea Fighter moaned as she pulled her sword out of one of the monsters.

"They're still comin'!" Rookie Warrior shouted back, kicking aside a goblin corpse.

He was imitating Goblin Slayer. If *he* were fighting this fight, he would drop his sword and steal another weapon.

Then again, Spearman would have acted more decisively, picking vital points and stabbing them quickly before moving on to the next.

And Heavy Warrior? He would have swept all the goblins away with one great swipe of his broadsword.

But I guess I can't do any of that, so…!

Thinking of the heights he had yet to reach emboldened Rookie Warrior's fighting spirit.

"Okay, you monsters, bring it on…!"

"Oh, for—! If you lose another weapon, no allowance until we buy a new one!" Apprentice Cleric shouted at Rookie Warrior, then she hurried over to the adventurers, holding up the hem of her vestments so she could run. "Any injured? Speak up! Come over here, I'll treat you! Miracles for the grievously wounded only!"

Several of the adventurers all but crawled over to her. She didn't immediately see anyone in need of emergency care. Nor did there appear to be anyone poisoned.

Still, this was hardly the moment for *Thank goodness we made it in time!*

Ten other young adventurers lay cruelly murdered in the street.

Apprentice Cleric bit her lip and pulled some bandages out of her item bag. She didn't have the leeway to cast Minor Heal on everyone.

"Y-you guys..."

"We've come to—to help you!"

This ringing voice came from the priestess who held up the staff from which Holy Light shone. Her slender face glistened with sweat, and she glared at the goblin horde; it was her unshakable faith that kept the miracle going.

"Everyone together!" she commanded. "We're going to get out into the field! In a confined space like this, we're at the goblins' mercy!"

"But... But if they surround us out there..."

"I'll keep us safe with Protection... Just go!" Priestess shouted, calmly considering how to use her miracles.

Most likely, she would have to overlap two miracles to stave off the goblin attacks as they retreated. She could still only use three miracles per day, so it would be a critical failure to waste even one of them.

No Minor Heal today, either, huh?

She felt a pang at the thought, but this was the best way for her to fight. If she stayed firm in that belief, the all-merciful Earth Mother would continue to grant her light.

"——"

Among the adventurers who had come to the rescue was a single boy with red hair, not saying a word.

The clamor of battle. The shouts of their two front-row fighters. The screams of goblins. The admonitions of the two clerics. The responses of the adventurers.

The boy took all this in, his mouth firmly shut, gripping his staff so hard his fingers turned white.

Why? Because in this five-person party, he had the most firepower of anyone.

I can't use my spell carelessly.

He wouldn't make the same mistake he had last time.

There were so many goblins. Including him, there were only three adventurers who could properly fight, yet the enemy was more than a dozen.

Could he take them all out with a single Fireball? No, impossible. The enemy was too spread out to catch several of them in a single blast.

But using up his spell to take out just one goblin didn't make sense.

He didn't have any time to mull it over, though. There were goblins everywhere, and standing still made you an easy target.

Just like that acolyte they had captured. What would happen to the girls here?

What had happened to his sister…?

Suddenly, Wizard Boy felt his vision grow hot as fire, yet he himself was utterly calm.

That weirdo of an adventurer, Goblin Slayer—much as Wizard Boy hated to admit it, he was always calm. If he let his anger dictate how he used his spell, this time he really would be a lesser man than *that* adventurer.

No—not that Goblin Slayer would say anything. But he would never be able to forgive himself.

So what do I do, then?

There was more to a wizard than flinging balls of fire and calling down bolts of thunder.

So what was there to do—?

At that moment, there was a flash like lightning in his brain.

"Everyone, cover your ears!"

"Wha?! We're—a little busy—fighting, here—!"

"Hurry!"

"Aw, man!"

Rookie Warrior and Rhea Fighter weren't happy about the sudden instructions, but they didn't argue.

There was no time to waste.

The red-haired boy glanced at Priestess, who nodded solemnly at him.

"I'll leave this to you!"

It was just as Goblin Slayer had done for her during the battle after the festival, and again on the snowy mountain.

The use of spells, like so many things, required both the orders and the trust of the party leader.

And the boy she had trusted—the red-haired wizard boy—nodded and raised his staff.

"You too! Do what he says and plug your ears!" Apprentice Cleric shouted at the adventurers in her care.

Rookie Warrior and Rhea Fighter quickly dealt with the goblins in front of them then hurried to make some distance.

I'll only get one chance.

From the boy's mouth boomed words of true power, his spell unleashed upon the world.

"Crescunt! Crescunt! Crescunt!"

It was only three words. An invisible power welled up, floating through the air, spilling out in front of the boy.

What followed was a single sound.

HRRR RRRRRRAAAA AAAAAAAAAAAAA AAH HHHH!!!!

The air shook.

§

It was like killing every bird with a single stone. Cutting the Gordian knot.

Such was the single blow from Heavy Warrior's broadsword, along with the shout he gave.

In a tremendous blow, it cleaved through every inch of the hobgoblin—its club, flesh, and blood alike.

Black blood sprayed everywhere; the creature split clean down the middle before collapsing to the ground.

The astonished beginners could only stare as Heavy Warrior shook off his sword and stashed it once more on his back.

"Oh-ho."

The entire area was filled with a howl that threatened their eardrums.

Somebody's scream? Where was it coming from?

He looked up at the sky, not that he was going to find the answers there.

"Sounds like someone's having a little fun," Heavy Warrior said with a sharklike grin.

§

At that moment, bits of earth rained down from the ceiling, and the clinging moisture of them brought Goblin Slayer to a decision.

"Upward."

He lodged the hand spear in a goblin's throat then kicked the frothing corpse away, letting his weapon go with it. Instead, he grabbed the hatchet from the creature's belt.

Goblin Slayer knew that he was nowhere near Spearman when it came to the use of spears.

"Open a hole above us!"

As the shout came to the back row, Dwarf Shaman was already digging through his bag of catalysts. "Another one? Well, comin' right up!"

"A hole? Whaddaya want with a hole?" Spearman shouted as he worked his weapon to hold back the encroaching tide of enraged goblins. His body was covered in small cuts, evidence that he was not invincible. Even with several experienced adventurers on the front row, numbers would eventually win out. Small pains or small fatigues, piled atop one another, still amounted to death when the moment came.

"I have a plan," Goblin Slayer said shortly and slammed the sharpened edge of his shield into a goblin's forehead. Seeing that the creature still refused to breathe his last, Goblin Slayer took the freshly stolen hatchet and pretended he was chopping wood.

There was a satisfying *splorch*, and brains went flying all over the walls of the cave.

"But first, I want to frighten them deeper into the cavern."

"Casting Fear and Tunnel at the same time is going to be a little much even for me!"

"Milord Goblin Slayer, they need simply be sent deeper in, yes?"

Dwarf Shaman was standing on his bag of catalysts in order to reach the ceiling, on which he was inscribing a sigil. Lizard Priest had moved up to cover him; now he bared his fangs fearsomely.

The moment had come for him to let his spiritual prowess, which he had conserved until this exact point, show forth.

Lizard Priest brought his palms together in a strange gesture and took in a breath, filling his lungs with air. He looked like a dragon preparing to use a breath weapon.

"Bao Long, honored ancestor, Cretaceous ruler, I borrow now the terror of thee!"

The moment he finished chanting, Dragon's Roar burst through the tunnel. The noise that Lizard Priest breathed out of his jaws shook the very air.

The goblins, hearing a great and terrible dragon right there in the tunnel, felt their courage shrink.

Goblins are never that brave to begin with. They are at their most violent only when in a superior position or when taking revenge.

And when afraid, they have no concept of an orderly retreat.

"GORRRBB! GBROOB!!"

"GROB! GGROB!!"

Squawking and dropping their weapons this way and that, they began to dash away. Witch cast Light to pursue their fleeing forms.

Lizard Priest snorted at the pathetic spectacle. "They will soon be back," he warned. "Even a dragon's power cannot last forever."

"I don't care," Goblin Slayer replied, but all the same he kept his low, guarded stance and stared into the distance.

High Elf Archer, beginning to look tired, patted him on the shoulder. "Orcbolg, are you planning to use another scroll?"

"I had only the one."

"...That doesn't make me feel better at all."

Goblin Slayer nodded as he watched Dwarf Shaman continue to work a pattern into the dirt.

"There is a lake above us."

§

The boy's shout, amplified by magic, echoed through the air and off the trees of the forest.

It was just a very loud voice. Hardly remarkable for something supposedly produced by words that could alter the very logic of the world.

His professors at the Academy would never have let him hear the end of it—but he wasn't at the Academy now.

It may have lacked the physical threat of Fireball, but his great voice was overpowering. Most important of all, the area of effect was far larger than Fireball's. Goblins who were immediately nearby fell unconscious, while others froze in surprise, and still others forgot everything else and started running.

"GOOROB?!"

"GROOB?! GRRO?!"

The boy gripped his staff, biting his lip so hard that blood dribbled from it, and stared fixedly at the goblins' backs.

He had wanted to kill them.

Such selfish creatures they were. Violent and murderous. Yet, now they ran. And he was letting them.

It wasn't enough.

There was his older sister to think of. The adventurers they had killed. The acolyte he and his party had rescued.

Then there was the humiliation they had all been subjected to. The hopelessness. The sadness. The anger. All the things that burned inside him.

To let all those things come bubbling forth—what a pleasure that would be! How wonderful!

Yes, but…

"We're getting out of here!"

It was Priestess's shout that brought the boy back to himself. She held aloft her staff, which still shone with Holy Light, and used it to gesture in the direction they should go.

"Head straight out of the woods and make for town!"

"You got it!" Rookie Warrior shouted back. He buried a blade in the throat of the unconscious goblin beside him then started forward. "Here we go. Getting home is our top priority! Follow me!"

"Let him lead the way! I'll keep an eye on this group—you watch our rear!"

"Sure thing!" Rhea Fighter replied to Apprentice Cleric. In spite of all that fighting, she didn't appear fatigued. Was that a rhea trait, or was it just her?

Rhea Fighter passed by the boy as she headed for the back. "Nice work. That was really something." She could only smile at him in passing, but it was heartfelt.

After a moment, the boy nodded. "…Thanks."

As the party surrounded the adventurers and began running, the boy stole a glance back over his shoulder.

The spell he had used was not intended to kill, just to give them an opening to escape.

It was true: his goal in this instance had not been to kill goblins.

It had been to help others. To get them out of there and safely back to town.

How satisfying it would have been had he been able to slaughter all the goblins.

But—yes, but.

I'm no Goblin Slayer.

The boy broke off from the battleground and faced forward, running with the others.

He didn't look back again.

§

The goblins had come like a tide, and now they were swept away by one.

The lake water that came spewing through the ceiling turned into a mudslide, pouring into the goblin tunnel.

Unfortunately for them, the nest was on a downward slope. The party of adventurers had scrambled uphill a bit, and it was enough to keep them safe, but as for the goblins who had fled back into the tunnel…

"GORRRBB?!"

"GBBOR?! GOBBG?!"

The goblins bobbed to the surface of the flood then sank again, drowning in the muddy water. It was an awful spectacle.

"I guess this feels good, as far as it goes," Spearman said, smacking a drowning goblin in the head with the butt of his spear and watching it sink once more. "But we can't pursue them like this. What if they just attack again when the water goes down?"

"When Tunnel runs out, cast some kind of ice spell." Goblin Slayer issued his next instruction to Witch, whose expression was ambiguous. "The ice will expand when it freezes, destroying this passageway. They won't be able to use it anymore."

"Good. I, under…stand."

"We will have to search aboveground for the nest and destroy it."

Goblin Slayer had already been making some mental calculations. The goblins had stolen only construction tools, no food. The earlier quest had been much the same: they had merely kidnapped prisoners to help them pass the time.

All this meant that the heart of their operation could not be too far away.

What had the goblins thought when they saw the building under construction and the adventurers gathering there? He had no way to know.

"…I think I'll let you guys handle that. Me, I'm beat." Spearman grasped his weapon wearily then sat down at the side of the tunnel. "Next time you wanna double-date…I hope it's something other than goblins."

"I understand."

On reflection, none of them had rested for several hours. Everyone had been fighting through the night. They were all eager to sleep like logs.

High Elf Archer, physically the weakest of these six Silver-ranked adventurers, found her ears drooping. "I'm so tired…"

"Don't treat the earth like that," Dwarf Shaman scolded her as she leaned against a wall. "He just said we still have to find and destroy the nest."

High Elf Archer pursed her lips. "Yeah, I know, but…!"

She wasn't really that upset. She wiped her mud-stained cheeks and muttered, "This is why I hate goblin quests."

Most adventurers probably would have agreed with her.

The water burbled and coughed as it rose up and down. Was that the sound of goblins dying or just the flood rushing along?

"I'm quite impressed that you knew we were beneath this lake," Lizard Priest said calmly as he watched the waters. "Has milord Goblin Slayer been to this area before?"

"Yes," Goblin Slayer said dispassionately as he watched the monsters drown. "Long ago… Very long ago."

Many goblins died that day, as did many adventurers.

But the adventurers won.

The training grounds were defended.

Yet, even so, there seemed to be just as many goblins in the world as before.

INTERLUDE

Of the Hero Who Went There and Back Again

"Hyaaahhh!"

There was one tremendous shout.

Next was an explosion woven of the light of the sun, and then the ultimate weapon, the holy blade, slashed through the space between dimensions.

The nameless evil spirits caught up in the force of it were sundered at the minutest level imaginable.

This gave new meaning to the word *Disintegrate.*

With neither corpse nor soul left behind, they would not trouble the physical world again.

The hero let the momentum of the slash carry her into a four-dimensional somersault, and she jumped out of the rent in space.

"We're here…!!"

She landed in a field that seemed vaguely familiar.

A breeze blew gently under an azure sky. The sun was bright, the clouds were white. The place smelled pleasantly of early summer.

"Sheesh… That took long enough."

"…It just means interdimensional travel is something you have to take your time with."

One by one, stalwart party members emerged from the Plane of Annihilation back to the real world.

"Man, that was tough. I'm spent." The hero gave a big stretch then squinted up at a sun she had not seen in far too long.

Going to the place between planes of existence to deal with Hecatoncheir, then coming back here, had been quite the adventure.

It would have been simple enough—yes, simple enough to come straight home, had they so desired.

But there had been so many enemies there as to make them question whether the physical world functioned differently in that realm. So many people suffering abuse and torture.

As the knights who traversed the storms of the three thousand realms, this was something they could not overlook.

If there was something they could do to help, then they must give their all to do it. This was a principle she always clung to.

"But it was fun, huh?"

"I'm not sure *fun* is the word I would choose for it," Sword Master said with a grin, giving her a playful smack on the head.

"Eeyowch!" she exclaimed, clutching her head but also giggling.

"...In any event, I worry about this world. We must ascertain the situation as soon as possible," Sage said with a thin smile. The hero nodded her assent.

Well, with or without them, the evil cult would work in the shadows and monsters would run rampant. That was just the way of the world.

One simply could not do everything alone.

"I bet the king's got problems, too. What say we pop by the castle?"

"Perhaps, but first we need to determine where we are. Somewhere along the western frontier, I think..."

At that, the hero looked away. In the distance, she could see a new village being built.

Boys and girls not so different in age from her worked and laughed together, sweat pouring down their brows.

She had never experienced anything like that herself.

She suddenly had a thought. What would her life have been like if she had been a normal village girl, or a typical adventurer?

It wouldn't all be straightforward success. She would fail sometimes, too. Perhaps even die.

'Course, I coulda been turned into interdimensional dust on this trip...

She would gather with her friends at the bar, go on journeys and adventures, experience joy and sadness as she saved her wages each day.

Maybe fate or chance would have brought her some incredible encounter.

The fantasy made her pulse pick up. But then she smiled and shook her head.

But if there's something only I can do, then I'd better be the one to do it.

"Welp, better ask at that village, then! Excuuuuse meee!!"

No sooner had she spoken than the hero ran off, waving for attention.

Her party members—her precious, precious friends—were left to chuckle, say "There she goes again," and follow after her.

This much was true: she had encounters and adventures as well. In that, they were all the same.

No difference among them. That, at least, brought the hero contentment.

The young person who noticed her coming wiped the sweat from their face as they looked up.

On that face was, of course, a smile.

"Welcome! This is the adventurers' training ground!"

CHAPTER 7

ONWARD TO ADVENTURE

"There! Excellent work!"

The sound of Guild Girl stamping the paper echoed around the room. She smiled brightly and straightened the paper up, signaling the end of the interview.

Phew! Priestess's little chest sank as she let out a well-earned breath.

Yes, she and Guild Girl knew each other, but it would have been almost impossible not to be nervous about one's promotion interview. Especially not with Inspector, the servant of the Supreme God, using the Sense Lie miracle the entire time…

"Good job," Inspector said. "Don't worry, you're fine. I know you weren't lying about anything."

"Y-yes, thanks. But it still makes my heart pound…"

"I think if it didn't, you might not even have a pulse!" Inspector responded, waving away Priestess's concern.

Beside her, Guild Girl relaxed her pasted-on smile and chuckled. "There are two things you should be a little afraid of if you want to survive in this world: enemy monsters and your bosses."

It was best to be nervous and then to go ahead and act. One who behaved rashly, without knowing what they were dealing with, was foolish. Or anyway, so *he* had said.

"The only thing you had to get through was the solo performance. Hang on a second, please." Guild Girl took a brand-new metal tag from a box. She took a quill pen and began to write on the blank face in flowing letters.

Name, age, class, skills, and so on…

An exact copy of Priestess's Adventure Sheet, the proof of who she was.

One year.

It had been one year since she had gone on that first goblin-slaying quest, fallen into danger, and been rescued by that person.

She had made friends that she cherished, fought an ogre in some old ruins.

She had run through a field in the dark of night to set an ambush for a goblin lord who had come with his army.

In the sewers beneath the water town, there had been the horrific blow from that goblin champion.

Then the battle with the eyeball creature in the innermost chamber, and the rematch with the champion, in which a bold stroke had saved their lives.

She had put on the vestments for the autumn festival and danced a prayer to the gods.

And immediately after that, she had faced a dark elf in combat.

Come winter, they had turned north, fighting the goblins who had been attacking a village there from their fortress.

There she had met Noble Fencer, slain the goblin paladin, and greeted the new year with *him*.

And then… And then…

"…"

Priestess closed her eyes, the details of each memory, each event, each experience flashing through her mind.

All of it had happened after her promotion from Porcelain, the sign of a newly minted adventurer, to Obsidian.

And yet…

"Right…"

Even now, being promoted for a second time, it still didn't quite feel real to her.

Had she really reached the eighth rank?

Was she really strong enough for that?

She wouldn't say it had all been a mistake, but she feared that her true colors might come out sooner rather than later…

"You'll be fine," Guild Girl said, as if she could read Priestess's thoughts. Priestess realized she had been unconsciously clenching her fist. Guild Girl was still focusing on the tag, writing quickly with an experienced hand. "The evaluation suits your demonstrated abilities. Not that it's any guarantee of how things will go in the future."

The quill fluttered furiously as Guild Girl wrote, and then she breathed on the tag. Finally, she carefully put her tools away and picked up the tag politely, with both hands.

"You have skills, and people speak well of you. Even if it's all one big fluke, that would at least mean you're lucky, huh?"

Then she held out the level tag: a small piece of steel, the eighth rank. It was attached to a fine chain that could be hung about the neck. Priestess took it reverently.

"I guess…you're right."

The tag seemed too light for confidence.

Priestess held back her golden hair with one hand as she put on the necklace. Then she tucked it gently under her vestments and placed a hand to her chest.

"I don't know yet… But I'm going to do everything I can to find out."

"Yes! That's the spirit!"

Priestess nodded at Guild Girl's encouragement.

She didn't know yet whether she really had the ability. But she did have people who believed in her.

And that would be enough for now—she was sure of it.

§

Just one step beyond the Guild door revealed sunlight streaming through the blue sky that was almost blinding. The richness of the rays showed that spring was ending and summer was starting in earnest. Priestess squinted against the bright sky.

Now then, what to do?

She probably ought to go to the Temple and make a report, but…

That was when her eyes met those of an elf girl sitting on the curb.

The elf's ears twitched in surprise; she stepped off the curb onto the walkway and stretched like a cat.

"Hey, you. All done? How'd it go?"

"Good. I got promoted this time."

Priestess pulled up the chain around her neck to show off the new level tag. It glinted in the sunlight. High Elf Archer looked very pleased.

"Well, good for you. This is, what, the eighth rank? You're a real priestess now." She took Priestess's hand and shook it vigorously, looking as happy as if it were she herself who had been promoted.

Priestess's head almost spun, but the elf's wiggling ears made her laugh.

"Yes. But—"

High Elf Archer leaned forward, detecting a shadow in Priestess's manner.

"What's up? Not happy about it?"

"Oh no, it's not that..." Priestess waved a hand to dismiss the notion. That wasn't it at all. "It's just... Those goblins, I..."

I let them get away.

That night, she had taken action to save the young adventurers from the danger that took hold of them.

It had been similar to a goblin-slaying quest, but not quite the same.

She knew what would come next. She had been taught about it, seen it for herself...

"Listen here."

"Eep?!!"

High Elf Archer broke into Priestess's gloomy ruminations by grabbing her by the nose.

"You're not Orcbolg, okay? So don't worry about it."

"Right..." Priestess pressed a hand to her stinging nose, her eyes reflexively tearing up. She focused on High Elf Archer.

The elf snorted and stuck out her modest chest then declared confidently, "He's a bit of a *weirdo* anyway!"

A weirdo, I tell ya, she repeated to herself, spinning her finger in a circle in the air.

"For example, you know why goblins don't use fire? He says it's because 'they haven't yet discovered fire as a military tactic'!"

And there were lots of other examples, too.

Fire, poison gas. Destroying ruins, digging holes, flooding places. *Yeesh!*

High Elf Archer was practically livid. *Honestly! I swear, Orcbolg isn't right in the head!*

Anyway…

"You can't compare yourself to someone who thinks like that all the time," she said. "Everyone thinks different things, in different ways. That's what makes the world an interesting place."

You're you, he's him. That's why we can have adventures.

In High Elf Archer's eyes, the world was exceedingly simple.

Priestess found herself gaping at the archer. A gentle breeze came through, and the elf's long ears wiggled slightly.

I see…

Over the past year, Priestess had tried in her own way to follow along with Goblin Slayer and the others. And now, she had been promoted.

It wasn't because she had killed the goblins. It was because she had managed to help the adventurers escape.

That was what people appreciated and valued.

Well, that works for me, then.

She felt something in her heart fall into place.

I'm sure I'll keep working with him.

And that's okay.

A gust of wind caught her hair, and she held it back with one hand.

Something about the sight prompted High Elf Archer to exclaim, "Right!" and nod sharply. "This calls for a celebration! Let me get you some lunch. What do you like?"

"Oh, uh, are you sure? Um, well then…"

What should she do? What should she choose? That decision by itself was enough to make her heart jump.

Maybe…since High Elf Archer was offering…maybe she'd pick something just a little bit fancy. The gods wouldn't mind, would they?

"Hey, what about Orcbolg?"

"Oh, that's right," Priestess said. Her smile, like a blossoming flower, communicated something that others wouldn't understand. "He treated me last year… So I think he'll pass today."

§

At the town entrance—just outside the gate next to the Guild, down the street a ways, an unlikely pair walked along purposefully.

One wore a cheap-looking steel helmet and grimy leather armor: Goblin Slayer.

The other was a red-haired boy, dressed in a robe and carrying a staff.

The boy had luggage slung over his shoulder; it was plain to see he was ready to travel.

"I think I'm gonna see a little more of the world, build up my skills."

"I see," Goblin Slayer replied, nodding just a little. "Are you not going back to the Sorcerers' Academy?"

"Er… No… I wanna get even with the bastards who mocked my sister, I really do. But…" The red-haired boy scratched his cheek gently then shrugged. His shoulders looked light, as if they were free of some burden. "I kinda think they'd go on making fun of her no matter what I did. So…it's okay."

"…"

"Let 'em laugh. For as long as they live, if they want."

"Indeed."

Goblin Slayer's helmet moved emotionlessly. The boy stopped and looked up at him.

That helmet was filthy. And it made it impossible to tell what expression the face inside was wearing.

This man was kind of disturbing, pathetic, totally obsessed, and killed nothing but goblins. He hardly seemed to qualify as a real adventurer.

"Look, I still don't really like you."

"I see."

Even when confronted so directly, his answer remained dispassionate, and the boy smiled in spite of himself. One could be stubborn, or get annoyed, or act self-important. But this man never got angry.

So what did that make the red-haired boy? A child rebelling against an adult?

"But I've been thinking about lots of other things, too."

Like what comes after this.

Like what came before this.

About my older sister.

About all you guys, and all the help you gave me.

My own failures.

And my own successes.

Plus…what I want to be.

"I couldn't stand to do what you do, so I'm gonna do something else. I—"

Yes, *I.*

The boy took in a breath, stuck out his chest, and announced proudly, "I'm gonna become Dragon Slayer!"

His remark would have made even a child laugh out loud. It was such a cheap dream, an all too common one. The sort of mundane fantasy that everyone, whether or not they seriously thought of becoming an adventurer, had entertained at one time or another. *Hunt dragons. Kill the strongest wyrm in the land.*

But Goblin Slayer, of course, nodded and replied, "I see."

"Then I'm going with you!" a bright voice interjected from nearby. Someone new jumped up next to them, her movements light and fluid.

She was wearing light armor that allowed for good mobility, along with a sword and shield. A rhea girl, ready to travel herself.

The inconspicuous entrance was a rhea specialty, and indeed, the red-haired boy stared, agog at her sudden appearance.

"Wh-who said you could come with me?!"

"One Porcelain-ranked spell caster all by himself? You wouldn't last five minutes!"

"…Says the other Porcelain-ranked warrior. The *girl* Porcelain-ranked warrior."

"Exactly. It's dangerous out there!"

"I told you, I'm traveling all on my own!"

"What luck! So am I."

When he made a point, she rebutted. When she talked around him, he made a different point. But rare is the person who can out-talk a rhea.

"Argh! Man, this is why I hate rheas…" The boy pulled at his hair in frustration.

That was when something happened that caused them both to stop in their tracks.

He and she both looked at the third member of their group as if they couldn't believe what was going on.

It was ever so faint and ever so slight, but they were sure they'd heard it…

"_____"

The softest muffled sound of laughter.

It creaked a bit, like an old door that hadn't been opened in years.

But Goblin Slayer was laughing.

He was actually laughing out loud.

"If you meet a rhea who goes by 'Burglar,' mention my name." *If that old curmudgeon even remembers the boy he once looked after…* "He may give you a little bit of help."

That caused the boy to scratch his cheek again. "I'll tell him, if I remember." He laughed; his expression was like a sharp sword kept carefully in its sheath.

Sigh. Okay, fine. A companion for the road and compassion for the world, *as they say.* The boy nodded at the rhea girl.

"Well, let's go, then… Together."

"Okay!" The girl nodded, beaming. Her face was bright, a flower turning toward the sun. "See ya next time, Goblin Slayer!"

"Yes."

The boy and the girl—no, the adventurers—waved as they walked happily away.

As they went down the road, luggage on their backs, they elbowed each other and laughed and chatted.

It wasn't, Goblin Slayer suspected, exactly because they were friends.

It had to do with what was beginning. Friendship, or trust, or perhaps something else. For better or for worse.

Goblin Slayer didn't know whether his words would be of help to them. He had no certainty. After all, he knew that cantankerous old rhea all too well.

But there was no such thing as too much help on a journey. Such was the way of things.

Goblin Slayer squinted slightly beneath his helmet then turned slowly on his heel before striding off at his usual bold pace.

This would not change what he did next.

Tomorrow, presumably, he would kill goblins.

And the day after that. And the day after that.

Every day.

His rest, his training, his purchases of equipment, were all in the service of killing goblins.

Why? Because he was Goblin Slayer.

"All done?"

He had stopped in the road, near the fork that led to the farm.

There was his old friend, lounging among the dappled shadows of a grove of young trees.

"Yes," he answered, and she bounced up from the root she was resting on to line up beside him.

Let's go home together. She didn't have to say it for them both to understand.

She set off eagerly, and he followed at a more measured pace. Careful neither to overtake her nor to fall behind.

"It seems they are going on a journey together."

"Oh yeah?"

"Yes."

"...I heard the lake dried up."

"Yes," he said. Then he thought for a moment before eventually adding, "...I'm sorry."

"...Mm."

That was as far as their discussion of the incident went.

She didn't say anything, nor did he.

Nothing about the fact that the training grounds had been built on the bones of their village nor that the area was becoming quite lively.

Not a word about how he had annihilated the goblins who had attacked those training grounds.

Not about how the ground was soft now, after he had emptied an entire lake into a tunnel beneath it.

Nor how it would now be difficult to build around that lake.

They didn't mention any of it—not a word.

The sky was blue, the trees' leaves bursting into a vibrant green. The wind rustled through the grass, and the sun was hot enough to make them sweat.

That road ran back to town, but they took the fork that would lead them to the farm.

It was too short a distance to communicate all that they thought yet too long for their hearts not to hear each other.

"Hey..." she said suddenly, pattering up in front of Goblin Slayer. Her hands were joined behind her, and she spun around. "You seem kind of...happy."

"...Hrm," he grunted deep in his throat. He hadn't considered it. "I do?"

"I can tell. You better believe it."

"I see..."

She chuckled triumphantly and puffed out her generous chest. "I understand you. I always do."

She sounded rather proud. But she looked like she was having fun, just as they always had since the days when they dashed around that open field together.

"Something good happen?" she asked.

"...Yes," Goblin Slayer responded, nodding. Then he looked back.

The road stretched ever on and on under the blue sky, and far down along it, he could just make out two figures, growing smaller in the distance.

Perhaps someday—be it tomorrow, next year, a decade from now, a century—there would be talk of a red-haired wizard dragon buster.

Maybe the deeds of those two dragon slayers would become tomorrow's legends.

It was so easy to call it impossible, a childish dream.

But what if?

If, someday, they truly did it, then that—

"That would be a very good thing."

"*Oh yeah?*" Cow Girl murmured, smiling, and then the two of them set off walking together along the road home.

Afterword

Hullo, Kumo Kagyu here!

So what did you think? Did you all enjoy *Goblin Slayer*, Vol. 6? It was a story in which goblins appeared, so Priestess tried hard to do something about them.

I really feel I put my all into writing it, so I hope you enjoyed it.

"An evil-woman executive, a killer for hire, a spy with a dark past, and a mountain ruler. What do you expect a high-schooler to do?!"

"Shoot your bow, Only-Good-at-Shooting-Arrows-Man!"

Incidentally, the dancing girl I mentioned in the last volume has achieved stardom as a performer of the Ultra-Purgatory Dance.

O Love of mine! You truly put the *-tory* in *Purgatory*! With your magic increasing her dancing skills fourfold, she can end at a mythological level!

...She was just supposed to be an ordinary fighter, but it turns out life follows art. Onward!

I also wish a long and prosperous life to Only-Good-at-Shooting-Arrows-Man.

As proof that you never know what's going to happen in life, we've made it to *Goblin Slayer*, Vol. 6.

I could never have come this far without the help of everyone around me. You have my heartfelt gratitude.

Noboru Kannatuki-sensei, thank you for always providing such superb illustrations and character designs. Rhea Fighter looks exactly the way I imagined her: super cute!

Kosuke Kurose-sensei, I love reading your manga version each month. I think this book should be coming out about the time you're reaching the climactic battle from Volume 1. Yah! Take that! Finish him!

To all my readers, and those who have supported me from my web days onward, you always have my thanks.

To the admins of the summary sites, I'm constantly indebted to you. Thank you, really.

To all my gaming buddies and the other creatives in my life, thanks for always making time for me…

To everyone on the editing team, my publishers and PR people, the distributors, and the translators (!), thank you so much!

I still can't really believe that my work has crossed the seas and is being enjoyed by people abroad.

Seriously, I'm pretty sure that any minute now, I'll wake up and find myself in bed.

The plan for next time: goblins appear in the elves' homeland and must be exterminated.

I'll continue to pour my heart into my writing, so I hope you'll keep on reading.